CARA'S PROTECTOR

Personal Protection Specialists

Guardian Hostage Rescue Specialists: Guardian
Protectors

ELLIE MASTERS

MASTER OF ROMANTIC SUSPENSE

JEM Publishing

Editor: Erin Toland

Proofreader: Roxane Leblanc

Published in the United States of America

JEM Publishing

This is a work of fiction. While reference might be made to actual historical events or existing locations, the names, characters, businesses, places, and incidents are either the product of the author's imagination or are used fictitiously, and any resemblance to actual persons, living or dead, business establishments, events, or locales is entirely coincidental.

ISBN: 978-1-952625-73-2

Dedication

This book is dedicated to my one and only—my amazing and wonderful husband.

Without your care and support, my writing would not have made it this far.

You pushed me when I needed to be pushed.

You supported me when I felt discouraged.

You believed in me when I didn't believe in myself.

If it weren't for you, this book never would have come to life.

Also by Ellie Masters

The LIGHTER SIDE

Ellie Masters is the lighter side of the Jet & Ellie Masters writing duo! You will find Contemporary Romance, Military Romance, Romantic Suspense, Billionaire Romance, and Rock Star Romance in Ellie's Works.

YOU CAN FIND ELLIE'S BOOKS HERE:

ELLIEMASTERS.COM/BOOKS

Military Romance

Guardian Hostage Rescue Specialists

Rescuing Melissa

(Get a FREE copy of Rescuing Melissa

when you join Ellie's Newsletter)

Alpha Team

Rescuing Zoe

Rescuing Moira

Rescuing Eve

Rescuing Lily

Rescuing Jinx

Rescuing Maria

Bravo Team

Rescuing Angie

Rescuing Isabelle

Rescuing Carmen

Rescuing Rosalie

Rescuing Kaye

Cara's Protector

Rescuing Barbi

Military Romance

Guardian Personal Protection Specialists

Sybil's Protector

Lyra's Protector

The One I Want Series

(Small Town, Military Heroes)

By Jet & Ellie Masters

EACH BOOK IN THIS SERIES CAN BE READ AS A STANDALONE AND IS ABOUT A DIFFERENT COUPLE WITH AN HEA.

Saving Abby

Saving Ariel

Saving Brie

Saving Cate

Saving Dani

Saving Jen

Rockstar Romance

The Angel Fire Rock Romance Series

EACH BOOK IN THIS SERIES CAN BE READ AS A STANDALONE AND IS ABOUT A DIFFERENT COUPLE WITH AN HEA. IT IS RECOMMENDED THEY ARE READ IN ORDER.

Ashes to New (prequel)

Heart's Insanity (book 1)

Heart's Desire (book 2)

Heart's Collide (book 3)

Hearts Divided (book 4)

Hearts Entwined (book5)

Forest's FALL (book 6)

Hearts The Last Beat (book7)

Contemporary Romance

Firestorm

(Kristy Bromberg's Everyday Heroes World)

Billionaire Romance

Billionaire Boys Club

Hawke

Richard

Brody

Contemporary Romance

Cocky Captain

(Vi Keeland & Penelope Ward's Cocky Hero World)

Romantic Suspense

each book is a standalone novel.

The Starling

~AND~

Science Fiction

Ellie Masters writing as L.A. Warren

Vendel Rising: a Science Fiction Serialized Novel

To My Readers

This book is a work of fiction. It does not exist in the real world and should not be construed as reality. As in most romantic fiction, I've taken liberties. I've compressed the romance into a sliver of time. I've allowed these characters to develop strong bonds of trust over a matter of days.

This does not happen in real life where you, my amazing readers, live. Take more time in your romance and learn who you're giving a piece of your heart to. I urge you to move with caution. Always protect yourself.

ONE

Cara

For the second time in my life, I walk away from everything I know and venture into the unknown.

After a harrowing escape, and enduring several agonizing hours wedged into a cramped middle seat in the back of economy, I find myself in another unfamiliar place, without a name, and utterly clueless about what comes next.

The moment I disembark the plane, the pandemonium of San Francisco's bustling airport amplifies my already frazzled nerves.

I close my eyes, regulate my breathing, and steel myself to face what comes next.

I'm here.

I'm alive.

That's all that matters.

It's time to start life number three—maybe this time, I really will disappear from enemies who want me dead. I scan the crowd, looking for my newest protector.

The airport teems with the hustle and bustle of hundreds of lives, if not thousands. People dart around me in all directions. Public announcements blare over the public address system, people shout, kids wail, tired parents attempt to navigate the chaos without losing a bag, a child, or a spouse. Occasionally, a runner sprints by, frantic to make their connecting flights. Harried gate agents strive to keep the crowd in check while placating disgruntled passengers with unwavering smiles.

The sheer energy of the place is overwhelming. My constant companion, anxiety, spikes my heart rate, tightens my chest, and turns my palms into a sweaty mess.

After the Witness Protection Program failed to safeguard my new identity, another organization took over my protection. Although I'm not sure what to think about the Guardian Hostage Rescue Specialists, they're the ones who stepped up to protect me. It's a daunting name, but I'm neither a hostage, nor do I need rescuing. What I require is protection from men who want me dead.

One man in particular: Artemus Gonzales, a wealthy Nicaraguan businessman involved in human trafficking.

I'd ask if these people are qualified, but my last handler gave me specific instructions in case things went south. With his dying breath, he gave me a number and instructed me to call Guardian HRS.

Which I did.

Chase.

I look for a man holding a sign at the gate with the name Chase written on it. Not at baggage claim. The voice on the end of the line was clear about that. My personal protection specialist will meet me at my gate and take it from there. I scan the crowd, seeking the stranger whose sole job is to keep me alive until I testify.

What happens after that?

Does the FBI's protection of its witnesses end after they put away the bad guys? Do I get to return to my old life? Do I continue in limbo with a fake name and fake life?

A multitude of people throng the gate area, preparing to board the next flight. I think that's going to be a problem until I glimpse an opening in the crowd. Not quite open, but filled by two formidable, intimidating men. Their military bearing is unmistakable and people unconsciously create an empty zone around the men.

To my surprise, one of them holds up a placard with CHASE scribbled over it.

I approach cautiously. No one should know that name except for the man sent to protect me. There aren't supposed to be two men.

What do I do?

I take a deep breath and move forward, attempting to project as much confidence as possible, even though my heart pounds and my palms slick with sweat. The men sense my unease, telling me I'm horrible at feigning confidence when I'm anxious. One of them steps forward with a reassuring smile on his face.

"Name's Rafe. This is Hayes." The man has a gruff, but friendly voice. "We have a third, Alec, scouting the crowd."

"Um, where's Chase?" This isn't what was supposed to happen, but I'm stuck now.

"Do you have a laptop? Cellphone? Any electronics in that bag?" The man does not answer me. Instead, he points to my purse.

I nod.

"If you could hand them to Hayes, please?" The command in his voice compels me to surrender my belongings without questioning why.

"A traffic accident delayed your Protector. Guardian HRS asked us to provide security and take you to him"

I exhale a sigh, relieved that I'm in the right place, even though I'm not with the right men. "How do I know you're..."

"...who we say we are?" Rafe cocks an eyebrow.

"Yes."

"You shouldn't." He reaches into his pants pocket and pulls out a phone. "Do you remember the hotline number you called?"

"I do." I'll never forget it.

"Call it now. Confirm they cleared Bravo team to escort you to Chase." He hands me his phone while the man beside him—Hayes, I think—holds my purse and scans the crowd.

Quickly, I dial the number. A woman picks up on the other end.

"Hello, this is..."

"I'll stop you there. No names, please. From the phone you're using, I assume you're with Rafe."

"Um…"

"Your Protector is stuck behind a wreck. Bravo was sent to fill the gap and take you to him. There should be two other men there: Hayes and Alec. A fourth is the driver and will pick you up at the curb. His name is Zeb."

Stunned by how smooth the person on the other line is, I stare at the phone, then glance up at Rafe. Everything he said matches up, but I need more reassurance. There's one name Rafe didn't mention.

"What's the name of your driver?" I grip the phone and hold my breath.

"She's a smart one." Hayes grins and holds my purse in front of his chest.

"Agreed." Rafe turns toward me. "Zeb is the fourth in our party. Smart checking that out." He extends his hand, requesting his phone back.

"Now what?"

"Do you have luggage to claim?" Hayes asks.

"Hank said no luggage. Nothing they could track."

"Excellent. And your electronics are in your purse?" Hayes continues to interrogate me.

"Yes."

"That's a beautiful watch. May I see it, please?"

An odd request. I surrender my watch and furrow my brow as Hayes takes a closer look. "It was my grandmother's. It's nothing special and barely keeps time. It has to be manually wound every day."

"No electronics." He hands it to Rafe, who completes a similar inspection before handing me back the watch. "Completely analog."

"If you'll follow me." Rafe signals for me to accompany him and I step in beside him. Hayes stands a little behind us, still holding my purse.

When we arrive at an intersection of terminals, Rafe halts in front of one of those exorbitant boutique shops that charge an arm and a leg, as well as your firstborn, for their wares. The clothing is aesthetically pleasing, but not my style.

"This looks good." Rafe glances at me. "Forgive me for asking, but what size do you wear?"

"Excuse me?"

"What size?" He gestures to the store.

"Um, I don't think we have time to shop, and I certainly can't afford that."

"We have the time. Chase is still stuck. Furthermore, this is on Guardian HRS's tab." Rafe crosses his arms over his muscular chest and stares me down.

"What Rafe means to say, and is totally blowing," Hayes interjects, "is everything you're wearing needs to go."

"Go?"

"Correct."

"Why?"

"Because we don't know how your identity was compromised. Everything you brought with you stays here."

"What do you mean by *stays here*?"

"Did I stutter?" Hayes gives me a stern look and takes a step back when I reach for my bag.

"I'm not leaving my things here."

"This is nonnegotiable," Rafe jumps in, trying to soothe me. "It's for your protection."

"Everything?" I glance at my grandmother's watch. It's the only thing I have left of my real life.

"The watch can stay. We're worried about trackers and bugs. We don't have time for an exhaustive search of your things. Anything you need will be provided, and anything identifying the woman who walked off that plane will be destroyed. Your new life started the moment we met. Now, we have time to buy a change of clothes, but we don't have time to argue about it."

"Fine, but not here." I scan the row of shops. "Over there. That store."

One of those general all-purpose stores, it sells everything from newspapers, to bottled water, to San Francisco themed apparel.

"That one? Are you sure?" Rafe looks at me like I've gone crazy.

"Positive." I take back a tiny modicum of control and march toward the store. Rafe and Hayes trail behind me.

I continue to scan the crowd, but so far, I haven't made out the third man.

It takes all of three minutes to find a matching hoodie, T-shirt, and leggings. I glance at my Coach purse I adore and how Hayes clutches it possessively. I hastily grab a cheap purse, lip balm, and other necessities. I walk out with a traveler's dream kit of comfy clothes, traveling essentials, two books, a neck pillow, new purse, and snacks for the road. Rafe covers the expenses, and together with Hayes, they escort me to a public restroom.

"Not that it needs saying, but put everything you're wearing back in the bag after you change. We'll take care of it from there."

I eye my Coach bag with longing, but I've been through too much to resist their efforts to protect me. I could object, but that's not my nature. Instead, I head into the women's bathroom, switch outfits, check my appearance in the mirror, and brace myself for whatever comes next.

Upon exiting the restroom, Hayes no longer holds my belongings.

"Where's my…" I don't complete my sentence since they were clear about not leaving the airport with anything I had on or carried into it.

My anxiety intensifies, and I've never felt more lost and adrift.

As we thread our way through the mass of people, Rafe and Hayes shield me from the crowd, but that uneasy, panicky sensation grows.

I loathe crowds. Crowds hide threats. Anything can happen inside a crowd.

My breaths turn progressively shorter and shallower as we board a packed tram. I must appear confused because Rafe leans in and whispers into my ear.

"We're shifting to another terminal and meeting our driver at arrivals, in case your flight was tracked."

I nod shakily and clutch the metal pole in front of me as the tram follows its endless loop of the busy airport. We disembark three stops later and head toward the exit. It's peak travel time, and I don't know whether it's fear, apprehension, or both, but there are more people, more noise, and just more of everything.

Rafe moves at a steady clip, and it's a struggle to keep up with him. With each step, the crowd seems to push back harder than before. Fear takes over, and panic rises within me.

"Take deep breaths." Hayes grasps my elbow and pulls me close. "We're almost there."

But I can't take deep breaths. It's as if my body has forgotten how to breathe.

"What's wrong?" Rafe looks at me.

"Panic attack." Hayes tugs me to his side, doing what he can to shield me from the mob of people all around us.

"Miss, we're almost there." Rafe steps closer, forming an impenetrable wall around me as the faces in the crowd blur into a mass of hostile eyes and cruel intentions. The air crackles with tension, and a desperate urge to run fills me with dread.

About to break free of my guardians, Hayes's grip on my arm tightens. "Almost there." He tries to inject confidence into his tone, but all I hear is a droning hum. "Step up the pace."

Rafe's pace quickens, and I scurry to keep up. They keep me close as we exit the airport, where there's a vehicle waiting for us at the curb. On high alert, they scan the area as I slide into the middle of the back seat. That's when I finally see the third man. I think Rafe said his name was Alec.

The men climb in, and the driver, Zeb, eases us into the flow of airport traffic.

"En route." Zeb's comment isn't for me, or the others, but to someone on the phone.

"You notice anything out of the ordinary…" The voice on the other end sounds strained.

"Tom, this ain't my first fucking rodeo." Zeb's irritation shows in his abrupt response. "I know what to do. Your job is to take care of any kinks along the way. How far out are we from Chase?"

"He's past the traffic accident and making good time. I've located a place for you to make the exchange," Tom replies, rebuffed by Zeb, who looks at me through the rearview mirror.

"Nice to meet you, Miss…" He waits for me to supply a name, but I don't know what new name I'll take. Safe in the car, the weight of my circumstances settles on my shoulders. This is not how my life was supposed to go.

It may be rude, but I'm tired and my nerves are fried from the events which led me here. The driver appears to understand because he doesn't press me for an answer.

The rush of traffic outside the car window streams by as we transition from city streets to the freeway.

Nearly twenty minutes later, Zeb breaks the silence. His view shifts between his side mirror and the rearview mirror.

"Check out the tan sedan." He elbows the man beside him, Alec, getting his attention. "Five cars back. It's made our last four turns."

"How long?" Alec uses the passenger side mirror to check out the suspicious car.

"Been a few minutes," Zeb says.

"Agree. Looks suspicious."

A knot of fear bunches in my gut. A tail? How did Artemus Gonzales's men find me? Hank Stafford's last words ring through my head. *There's a leak.* With his lifeblood bleeding out while I held him in my arms, my former handler and protector, gave me the number to a Guardian HRS hotline.

Artemus Gonzales is a filthy-rich, middle-aged political power monger in Nicaragua. He's more than a wealthy businessman. He's connected to powerful men, like the President and the Minister of the Interior of Nicaragua. He's also heavily vested in the cartels, but I didn't think he had the resources to track me down this quickly.

How did he do it?

"Hold on," the driver calls out a warning.

The others brace as we veer off the freeway. Sandwiched between Rafe and Hayes, I barely move. Zeb takes an off-ramp, slamming me against Rafe as we zoom around the cloverleaf at speeds far over the posted speed limit.

We take the first off-ramp, pass under the freeway, and take the next on-ramp heading north, directly opposite the direction of our previous travel. I think we're headed back the way we came, but Zeb continues to the next off-ramp, and then the next. We take all four off-ramps at high speed and wind up back on the freeway, headed along our previous direction of travel.

"Did they follow?" Zeb scans the rearview mirror.

"Don't see them." Alec stares at the passenger mirror, looking back.

"If they're in front of us, that's where they'll stay. Meanwhile, might I suggest changing our current rendezvous with Chase?" Zeb calls whoever he was speaking to earlier and reports what happened.

I blow out a breath and close my eyes. The rapid beating of my heart slows with yet another narrow escape. I wish I could say I was getting accustomed to living life in constant fear, but there's no getting used to this.

After a few miles, we take another off-ramp and arrive at a small, unassuming hotel off the beaten path.

We pull around to the side and park next to a black, tricked-out Jeep with a lift, a wench on the bumper, and a carrier strapped to the top. A mountain of a man, easily over six and a half feet tall, climbs out of the vehicle. With broad shoulders, tree trunk legs, wavy brown hair, and a face chiseled out of granite, the man is both beautifully stunning and uniquely terrifying.

The black T-shirt he wears struggles to contain all his muscles, and well-worn blue jeans draw my eyes where they shouldn't go. His black, steel-toed boots scream *Don't mess with me*, and he looks mean enough to kick ass without breaking a sweat. He surveys the deserted parking lot before heading toward our vehicle.

"You have her?" His deep, modulated voice sends chills down my spine.

"We do." Zeb doesn't exit the vehicle.

He opens the door to the back seat. Rafe climbs out, and the man extends his hand, speaking quietly to me. "It's nice to meet you. Name's Chase, Chase Lawson."

His touch sears my skin, sending an electrical charge zinging up my arm. Every cell in my body screams to run away, yet I find myself inexplicably drawn to this man. He's intimidating and fierce, but dangerous to me for reasons that have nothing to do with protecting me.

TWO

Chase

MY CHARGE—HER NEW NAME WILL BE CARA—CLIMBS OUT OF THE back seat, trembling and uncertain. I take in every detail and gulp. The woman's stunning—a perfect blend of innocence and strength. Deep pools of spectacular sea green stare at me with fear and that same flicker of attraction I get from women all the time.

Unlike them, however, she snuffs out that tiny spark, turning her expression cold, distant, and detached.

My inner voice screams at me to keep things professional, but the urge to pull her into my arms, run my hands through her golden hair, and kiss her rosebud lips—if only for a moment—is impossible to deny.

But I am a professional.

I clear my throat and step back, giving her space to breathe and me room to clear my head.

I turn to the men of Bravo team and lift a hand. "Thanks for the assist."

"Any time, man." Zeb returns my wave. "Welcome to the team."

He shifts the vehicle into reverse, and he and his teammates leave me with my very first client as an official Personal Protection

Specialist working for the Guardian Hostage Rescue Specialists, or Guardian HRS for short.

I scan our surroundings. Always vigilant for potential threats, Zeb did a great job shaking anyone who might have followed. For the moment, she's free of any danger that might have followed her here.

I open up the passenger door before turning back toward Cara. Making a conscious effort, I keep my expression serious, but my voice as kind and gentle as I can. "I have one nonnegotiable rule. Follow it and I promise to keep you safe. Break it and I cannot guarantee your safety."

"What's the rule?" She gulps.

"My job is to protect you until you're called to testify. No matter what happens or where we go, you follow my instructions without question. Without hesitation. Got it?"

She nods before quickly climbing in and buckling up. A twinge of alpha-male protectiveness surges through me. I give one last glance around before jumping in and cranking over the engine and driving off.

We travel in silence for a while; time I need to examine my overwhelming reaction to my client and decide if that attraction is going to be a liability. When interviewing for a position as a Personal Protection Specialist with Guardian HRS, they wanted to take me on as a Guardian instead of a Protector, but I'm a solo operator.

Nearly all the Guardians come from a military special ops background. Most are former SEALs or Delta group operators. I come from Army Special Forces; Scout sniper. My skill set is unique, and while very similar to the training of the SEALs, there are notable differences. The most important being that I trained to work in isolation from my team; aka...alone.

Which makes me a poor fit for a Guardian team, but perfect as a Protector.

She sits in the passenger seat, eyes wide, body tense, fingers twisting in her lap—completely overwhelmed. I glance at her, trying to decipher her expression, but whatever thoughts whirl around behind those beautiful sea-green eyes remain a mystery.

Finally, I break the silence.

"How are you holding up?" The desire to reach across and place my hand on her leg overwhelms me, but I rein in that urge and remind myself I'm a professional. She and I just met. I'm not here to provide emotional support.

Keep your hands off the client and your dick in your pants.

My inner rule follower is a bastard, but always right, even if I rarely heed its advice.

"I…" She glances out the window and purses her lips, thinking hard about how to answer what should normally be a straightforward question. "I'm okay."

"Are you?"

Her jaw clenches, and her eyelids flick with irritation. Note to self: don't challenge her and stop with the flippant comebacks.

"Sorry. I was trying to break the ice. From the way you're twisting your fingers, I'm worried you might twist one off and bleed all over my Jeep."

"Twist one off?" She spins toward me, eyes wide with shock. The punchline of my joke falls a beat too late before she realizes it was a joke. A sheepish grin appears on her face, and she shakes her head. "Sorry."

I can almost hear the tiny voice in her head chuckling at her for misinterpreting me. A flush of embarrassment rises on her cheeks. I'd love to hear what her inner voice is saying. Instead, I do my best to cut through the tension.

Clearing my throat, I attempt to lighten the mood. "Not everyone gets my sense of humor. Didn't mean to offend."

"There's no need to apologize." She shrugs and looks away, still tense and uneasy. "It was funny, but…"

"You didn't laugh." I make a joke of it.

"Probably because I'm anything but okay." Her smile vanishes and her expression turns serious. She averts her gaze, as if she can't bear looking at me. She takes a deep breath and rubs her palms against her pants.

"Want to talk about it?"

I debate reaching out to take her hand in mine. The poor thing needs a hug, but reflecting on the flash of heat searing my hand when we first met, I decide not touching her is the best course of action.

"Not really." She shakes her head and looks back at me with an apologetic expression on her face.

I don't blame her for not wanting to share. This woman's been through hell and back.

"Then how about we talk about the job?" This is my cue to change the topic and get to the nuts and bolts of the job.

"The job?" My question seems to confuse her. She tilts her head to the side.

"Keeping you alive," I reply with a smirk, smiling at her until she looks up and meets my gaze with a small smile of her own. "Your new identity."

"Oh, that."

"Yeah." My smile's a little larger, maybe a bit smug. In trying to relieve the tension and inject humor into our conversation, I stumble. "Your new name is Cara Jade." I reach out to shake her hand. "And I'm Chase, but you already knew that." I give a brief rundown on the new identity. Nothing detailed. This isn't witness protection. She won't be living a normal life, going to work, or meeting new people every day. It's just enough to answer the basics.

"I'm exceptionally bad at remembering to say thank you." She doesn't take my hand. Instead, her fingers go back to twisting. I don't think she's aware she's doing it. "So when I forget, just know how incredibly thankful I am to you for helping me."

"It's my job. No thanks needed."

"It's no ordinary job and comes with significant risk. So, *thank you*." She notices her fingers and crosses her arms as she responds. Her voice is full of admiration and respect.

"Thanks accepted. Now how about we talk specifics?"

"Specifics?" Skepticism fills her tone and matches perfectly with the way she raises one eyebrow.

I've never been able to do that. On her, it's sexy as hell.

"How we go about keeping you safe." Normally, I'd maintain eye contact during this part of the conversation, emphasizing the importance of what I'm about to say, but I can't do that and pay attention to the road at the same time.

"Oh, sorry. What is your plan?"

"Simple is safest in my mind." I let that sink in.

"Part of the keeping it simple mindset?" She peeks up at me from the corner of her eye. Her long lashes flutter, making her look hot as sin, and stir a rather unprofessional reaction in me.

And by *me*, I mean my dick.

"I'm definitely a believer in Keeping it Simple Shithead." I can't help but smirk.

Her eyes widen at my language, then narrow as she takes in a breath. "It's stupid." She averts her gaze to the floor, perhaps feeling embarrassed for correcting me?

"Excuse me?" I call her out, intrigued by everything about her.

"It's stupid, not shithead." She speaks quietly and slowly meets my gaze, cheeks flushed with embarrassment at what she said, but she's strong in her conviction to stand by her words. "It's *Keep It Simple Stupid*."

"Oh, sweet thing, there's one thing you must know about me before we go any further." My voice drops, turning huskier than I intend.

"What's that?" She's curious and I love that.

"My parents were Merchant Marines. Met and married on a cargo ship. *Motherfucker* may very well have been my first word. *Shithead* was likely a very close second. Does swearing offend you? Because I sprinkle that shit liberally when I talk."

I call victory when a smile finally reveals itself, turning the stunning woman beside me into something truly beautiful. Then I groan and bite my lower lip. Why couldn't my first client be a fat, middle-aged bastard instead of this amazing creature?

She leans back, and for the first time, stops the tense finger-twisting thing. It's nice to see her relax.

"As for keeping you safe, I have a couple of ideas."

"What does that mean?" She nibbles on her bottom lip and cocks an eyebrow.

"That I have ideas? Didn't think that would be confusing." I smile ever so slightly, although my expression remains serious.

"Don't you have a safe house set up? I thought…"

"Whatever you thought about personal protection, throw it out the window. Guardian HRS protection services are not like those of the FBI's WITSEC program. There's no safe house where you hide out until the trial. I do things differently." I drum my thumbs on the steering wheel.

"Then how…" Her voice trails off, uncertain and hesitant.

"I'm pulling you off the grid." I watch her reaction, gauging her response. What's she going to think when I tell her?

"Huh?" Her eyes widen in confusion.

"Trust me." My expression softens with compassion and sincerity.

"I have no option but to trust you, but I don't understand." She swallows hard, resigned to her fate, and takes a deep breath. Instead of looking at me, however, she turns away to stare out the window.

"Before I explain…" I pause before continuing, wondering if I'm able to guess accurately. "Do you consider yourself an outdoor girl, or a city girl?"

Her face tightens, and her eyes narrow with indignation, making me regret my choice in words. This one's sensitive.

"I am a woman, not a girl." Her tone turns cold. She clearly takes offense.

"Didn't mean any offense." I try to diffuse the moment.

"None taken." But her tone is terse. Her shoulders push back.

"Seems like some was taken," I mutter under my breath and square my shoulders in defense.

"I don't like it when men call women girls." Her gaze turns icy. "It's demeaning."

"Demeaning?" My brows furrow as I process what she says.

"Yes. Demeaning." Tone firm, she digs in for a fight.

Fire lights up inside of me, taking offense to her taking offense.

"I'd like to see you say that to my mom's face." I grit my teeth and tell myself to calm down. "She spent her entire career in the Merchant Marines, where there were a hundred men to every woman. She was quite happy to call herself a girl, and had girlfriends, not woman-friends. Girl's nights out instead of women's nights out."

I pause briefly to collect myself and continue in a calmer voice. "Asking if you're a city girl or an outdoor girl is no different from saying you or y'all, or using the word guys for both boys and girls." I clear my throat pointedly, before adding on, "Sorry, for men and women."

"Dang, you're sensitive." She gapes, but remains indignant. If possible, more so than before.

I stare her down stonily as my posture turns rigid and defensive. "For you calling me out on the words I use? You bet." There's an edge to my voice and I don't care one bit if it's sharp or not. "If you can be offended because I say girls instead women, then I can be offended when you try to categorize me as a chauvinist."

"That's not what I…" Once again, her voice trails off as she takes note of the challenge in my piercing stare.

I have a feeling this is a conversation, given the current social climate, she thought she'd win, but I'm not the kind of guy who rolls over and takes it. My mom didn't raise me that way.

"You sure about that?" I cock an eyebrow, not letting this go. Doesn't matter if she thinks I'm an asshole or not. My job remains the same, but I take offense to the assumptions she makes about me before getting to know what kind of person I am. What my values are. Or how much respect I have for both men and women, no matter their race, religion, or their social status. My parents taught their son right, and I don't appreciate being stereotyped.

"You're making a mountain out of a molehill. I would just prefer if you didn't call me a little girl."

"Never called you a *little* girl." The corner of my mouth twitches as I grind out the words. "But I sure as shit have certain thoughts about you now."

"And what's that supposed to mean?" She tenses, but there's an underlying challenge in her voice.

I clench the steering wheel, and my jaw tightens. It's a struggle to keep my anger in check, and to keep the reply poised on the tip of my tongue from cutting deep. I dig deep and take a slow, intentional breath before containing my anger enough to respond constructively.

"People are too fucking sensitive these days, taking offense where none is given or intended. I use the language I grew up with, swearing, cussing, and all the rest. I'm offended by your unwillingness to allow me to express myself the way I see fit."

Her jaw drops open for a moment before she snaps it shut.

"Damn." She narrows her eyes in disbelief. "You're one righteous prick."

Okay, my words were far from constructive. I glare at her and curse the palpable tension clotting the air.

"Now, why did ya' have to take it there, princess?" My lips curl into a smirk as I return her pointed look.

"*Don't* call me princess." Her lips twist in contempt, eyes blazing in anger. But props to her for meeting my gaze and staring me down. This girl has spit and fire.

I keep my voice low, but determined. "Don't call me a prick." Low and determined sounds more like a growl, but I'm in too deep to back out now. "You started with the name calling, and if you do that, then you can be damn sure I'll finish it. Now, if you're done being *offended* by my language, and resorting to calling me a righteous prick, I'd like to talk about how the fuck I'm going to keep you alive."

Momentarily taken aback by the force of my words, the fight in her eyes slowly diminishes. She stares at me for a long moment, sitting in stunned silence, before mumbling something unintelligible.

"You're-you're…" Her voice is barely above a whisper.

"I'm what?" I raise an eyebrow and wait to see what she says next.

Her eyes darken, and she clenches her jaw before responding. "You're the most infuriating man I've ever met." She looks directly at me, eyes blazing, pupils dilated.

Holy fuck, but is she turned on? I don't know about her, but this heated discussion makes my blood burn and rouses a desperate hunger.

I pause a moment before turning to her with a serious expression on my face. My words are slow and deliberate. "Don't poke the bear." I mean my words as a warning, but not in the way she may appreciate.

This woman ignites something inside of me, something primal and fierce. Something I need to treat with great respect.

This woman may very well cost me my job.

The corner of her mouth twitches as she responds with caution. "And what does that mean?"

"Only that I'm sick and tired of apologizing for what and who I am." My voice takes on a tone of resignation. "I'm so fucking tired of people judging and blaming instead of working the problem."

"What does that mean?"

"I grew up in a home where my mother was busting balls from day one in a male-dominated career field." As I recount my mother's story of courage to succeed in a male-dominated world, pride swells in my chest. "That woman raised me, never needing to teach me how not to be a sexist prick because she showed me women were no different than men. My father left his job to take care of me, because it was in our family's best interest for my mother to continue in hers."

"I only meant…"

"You said what you meant." My voice fills with conviction. "When it comes to women, you can do whatever the hell you want, and no woman needs a man's permission to do it. I'm the exact opposite of the sexist prick or chauvinist asshole you want to make me. I'm your number one advocate, yet you stereotype, judge, and call me out for something I'm not."

"But…"

"No." I don't let her finish. I'm too wound up and on a roll. I should probably stop before I put my foot in my mouth, but I've got too much momentum built up to stop now. "You turned me into an enemy you can rage against for injustices of the past, and I take offense to that. You had no problem calling me a sexist prick, but if I dared to call you a raving bitch, this would be an entirely different conversation."

She listens intently as I rage. Toward the end, a spark of admiration shines in her eyes, but I'm too upset to let go of my anger just yet.

This is totally not how I wanted our first meeting to go. I'm here to protect her. Not to argue with her. To do that, I must gain her trust. We've blown that totally out of the water with this stupid-as-shit argument.

I turn my attention to the road and let silence fill the space between us while I let my anger simmer. It's going to be a very long night.

Hell, it's going to be torture.

I'm pissed, angry, enraged, and totally and completely turned the fuck on by the most infuriating woman I've ever met.

THREE

Cara

I LOOK UP FROM MY HANDS, WHICH I CAN'T KEEP FROM FIDDLING with, to meet Chase's gaze. He stares straight ahead, attention focused on the road. The miles pass, and the silence between us deepens until I can't stand it any longer.

"I didn't mean to start an argument or imply any of those things. I really am thankful for what you're doing, and I didn't mean to start things off on the wrong foot. I'm sorry I called you a prick."

He takes a beat, almost as if stunned by my apology. "It's me who needs to apologize. In today's climate, it's hard not to be defensive. Things are changing for the better, but I hate when people label me as part of something I have no part in. All I want is to make the world a better place. It's my fault for taking offense."

"My entire life is upside down. I'm scared to death, and I took that out on you. I'm sorry, and I won't let it happen again."

"How about we start over?" He glances at me and there's a softening of his expression. "A clean slate?"

"I would like that."

"Well, Cara—welcome to your new life." His voice is low and steady, far better controlled than mine.

"I could use a new life. Mine's a nightmare."

"I'm sorry about that, but I hope you understand how valuable your testimony will be."

"That's what *they* keep saying." I use air quotes to punctuate my point. "My testimony will put Artemus Gonzales away for good."

"But…" He pauses, waiting for me to fill in the gap.

"But if I'm supposed to be safe in WITSEC, how do they keep finding me?"

"That's a legitimate question, but not one we need to solve."

"Well, if not Guardian HRS, then who?"

"I'm here to protect you and ensure you make it to the trial. I'm not here to uncover some plot within WITSEC to silence you for good."

"I'm sorry." I lean my head against the headrest. "Mitzy said there was a problem with the U.S. Marshals. A leak in their WITSEC protocols."

"Of that, I'm certain. All I mean is that it's not my job to plug that leak. You're my priority."

"And I'm grateful for that. I didn't mean to spend our first few moments arguing. I really am sorry about that."

"Consider it water under the bridge."

"Does that mean you forgive me?"

"It means I'm done discussing it."

"Oh."

"As for what comes next, we need to go over Guardian HRS protocols and what you can expect as my client."

"Mitzy already went over that with me."

"She gave you the basics. I'm here to explain how that manifests in the here and now."

"I'm listening."

"The key to disappearing from the world is to literally disappear. There are several ways to do that, some more risky than others."

"What does that mean? *Literally disappear?*"

"Within the U.S. Marshals WITSEC program, they create a new identity for you and set you up in a new life, usually something far different from what you know."

"That's what they told me."

"But there are problems with that."

"Evidently." I can't argue with that. "They moved me twice. Artemus kept sending hitmen to… Well, you know."

"Which means they have a leak in their department. That's something they're dealing with and why you're with us now."

"I get that."

"We have two options when it comes to keeping you safe. The first is to do what the U.S. Marshals did to begin with. Set up a safe house and hide you from the rest of the world."

"That didn't work."

"Yes, and I'm sorry for your loss. I heard your handler didn't make it."

"Hank didn't deserve to die like that."

"Is he the one who mentioned Guardian HRS?"

"He is—I mean he did."

"And did you share that with anyone?"

"No. He was very clear about not sharing anything. When he died…" I choke up and it's a struggle to continue. "When he died, it hit me how close I came to—well, to not making it out alive."

"That's good. If that's the truth, there should be no one who knows where you are."

"I suppose."

"What's that mean?"

"The Guardians who met me at the airport."

"What about them?"

"They had me toss my purse, my phone, and even my clothes."

"Standard protocol."

"They claimed they could track those things. But how is that possible?"

"You'd be surprised what they can and can't track. It's a good thing they followed protocol. You're now what we call naïve."

"I'm not naïve." I bristle at the comment.

"That's not what that means." He pauses, then continues. "All it means is there's nothing on your person that can be tracked. Did you divest yourself of everything?"

"I did."

"Underwear?"

"Excuse me?"

"Bra and panties? Are you still wearing the ones you flew in with?"

"I don't see how that matters?"

"It matters because people can insert trackers anywhere." He pulls over to the side of the road.

"What are you doing?"

"Stopping."

"I get that, but why?"

"You haven't answered my question, and I'm not driving another inch until you do."

"What do you mean?"

"Panties and bra? Are they the same ones you wore when you flew into San Francisco?"

"I don't see how that's any of your business?"

"My business is literally to keep you alive. Answer my question, and I'll remind you of my one and only rule."

"I don't remember what that is."

"You do as I say, when I say, and with absolutely no hesitation. I don't have the time to carry on a long, complicated discourse about how trackers can be embedded in your bra, or your panties, or how those who want you dead may, or may not be, tracking us right now. If they are... If that's the case, you really don't want to live. Now, answer the goddamn question."

"I..." It never occurred to me to strip out of my bra and panties when the Guardians picked me up, and I'm not entirely sure Chase is telling the truth.

Surely, this is overkill?

"Don't." His tone is sharp and cuts like a knife.

"Don't, what?"

"Don't try to reason your way out of this. Answer the fucking question, or exit the vehicle."

"Exit the vehicle? We're in the middle of nowhere." We've been driving forever, leaving the busy city behind, and are somewhere in the foothills of the Sierra Nevada mountain range.

I think.

"If you refuse to do what I ask to keep you safe, then I'm not putting my neck on the line. Answer the damn question." The rigid set of his lips tells me everything I need to know. This is nonnegotiable as far as he's concerned, which leaves me with very few options.

"I don't even remember what the question was."

"Panties and bra? Does that ring a bell?"

"You don't have to be an ass." I roll my eyes, irritated at his directness and embarrassed I made him repeat himself. "They bought me clothes, and I put those on."

"Panties and bra? I'm losing patience fast."

"Fine." I rear back, offended by his persistence regarding my unmentionables. "I'm still wearing the same pair."

"Get out." He shifts the gear into park.

"Excuse me?"

"Get out now."

"But…" I look at him, confused and more than a little scared.

"Get out of the fucking Jeep. Strip out of your bra and panties. Shit, I can't believe…" He pounds on the steering wheel. "I know Bravo team mentioned this. There's no way they didn't."

"They might have said something." I look at Chase in shock. "But it's not like they sell bras and panties in the airport. What was I to do?"

"Toss them like you were told." He gives me a look like I'm an idiot.

"How was I to know?"

"Get out of the fucking Jeep. Strip down. Give me your bra and panties. You realize they can track you right now?"

"I'm sorry."

"Doesn't matter. What does matter is you're not stripping down." He points to the side of the road. "Get out now."

"You're really kicking me out?"

"Unless you want to shimmy out of those in here? I figured you might want some privacy, but by all means, you do you. Meanwhile, I'll try to figure out what we do next."

"I don't get why this is such a big deal." I open the passenger door and step out of the Jeep. A part of me fears Chase will drive off and leave me stranded on the side of the road. Another part wants exactly that. We're completely, and totally, incompatible, and I don't like how rigid he is with these damn rules.

Muttering under my breath, I do exactly what he says—following his one and only rule to the letter—and strip out of my panties and relieve myself of my bra.

"What do I do with these?" If he's going to make me go commando, I'm not against making him as uncomfortable as possible. I wave my lace panties and bra at him, but Chase doesn't react.

The man is like a machine: single-minded and mission-focused. He's exactly the kind of man who can keep me safe, which makes him exactly the kind of man I hate.

Domineering.

Insufferable.

Infuriating.

Intolerable.

Obnoxious.

"What we do is dispose of them."

"Like leave them here?"

"And litter?" He gives me a look like that's the most insensitive thing any human has ever said to another.

"I thought that's what you said?"

"I'm not leaving trash lying around. We dispose of those properly at the next stop, in a trash can."

"Geez, overly sensitive?"

"Because I like to keep the planet clean?"

"It's not that big of a deal."

"Leave only footprints." He waits for me to buckle in before heading down the dark, deserted highway.

"Is that your mantra?"

"It is, and it should be everyone's. Our job is to leave this place better than we found it."

"It's just a pair of panties and a bra. Totally natural and

biodegradable. You act as if leaving them behind is a crime against nature."

"Isn't it?"

"If you say so." There's no winning this argument. Chase and I simply don't see eye to eye.

At the next exit, I toss my undergarments into the trash and walk around feeling self-conscious in my commando state of dress. Chase purchases a case of water, several boxes of oatmeal, and a smattering of nuts and granola. With his don't soil the earth tirade, I figure he's a bit of a granola head until he adds three bags of lemon drops to the mix.

I eye his selections with interest but keep my mouth shut. His orders when we pulled up were to relieve myself and keep my mouth shut. I'm following his damn rule to the letter, and there's no way I'm going to give him any reason to say I didn't follow his stupid rule.

With a full tank of gas, we head into the night, following a dark and deserted highway. All the while, I try to make sense of what brought me to this—driving into the dark with a man I don't know.

When I was twelve, this was definitely not how I saw my life. When I was fifteen, my aspirations never included this. At twenty-one, I made a few sketchy decisions, but not once did I see this in my future.

After an hour of silence, I can't stand it anymore.

"Can we turn on the radio?"

"No." Chase's reply is clipped and curt.

"Why not?"

"I don't listen to music while I drive."

"Why not?"

"Because I don't."

"But doesn't it make you sleepy? Staring into the darkness with nothing to occupy your mind?"

"My mind is plenty occupied." His gaze cuts to me and I swear it dips down to my breasts.

"What if I want to listen to music?"

"He who drives is in charge."

"Well then, can I drive?" Knowing full-well what his answer will be.

"No."

"Are you always this cranky?"

"Cranky?"

"Yes. You're hard to get along with."

"Because I'm not willing to sing *Kumbaya?*"

"Because you're completely inflexible." It may be my imagination, but I swear the corner of his mouth lifts in a smirk.

Is he having fun with me? I lean forward and flick on the radio, then grimace as the radio blares out a country ballad, but it's better than Chase's terse replies. It's as if he actively discourages conversation.

I take that as an insult, and I'm a delight to be around.

To my surprise, he doesn't turn off the music. Instead, we travel for the next two hours in complete silence, except for the music, and begin our climb into the mountains. We make one more pit stop for a bathroom break and refueling before we're back on the road and back to not speaking to each other.

We hit Lake Tahoe and keep driving down the other side of the mountains until it's well past midnight. My eyes drift closed, and I hit REM sleep right when we suddenly veer off the road and careen into the desert. If I didn't know better, I'd think he did it on purpose.

FOUR

Cara

CHASE MANEUVERS THE JEEP OFF THE HIGHWAY AND ONTO A DIRT road. I grip the side of my seat as the Jeep bounces along, jostling me around until it feels as if my fillings are going to bounce right out of my teeth.

"What the hell are you doing?" I grip the armrest as the rough ground tries to bounce me out of my seat.

"Ah, Sleeping Beauty is awake."

"Of course I'm awake. What are you doing?"

"Finding a place to spend the night."

"Out here?"

"That's the plan."

"Why not a hotel?"

"Why do you think?" His tone's dismissive as if the answer's obvious.

"Why don't you answer my question?"

There's a grin tugging at the corners of his lips, but he doesn't answer. Bastard's having fun with me.

"You know what? I don't care." Frustrated to hell, I've had enough. "Call whoever you need to call. Say whatever you need to say, but we're done. I want a new Protector."

"Ah, princess, I'm all you've got."

"You're a fucking tool."

"Looks like I'm not the only one with a colorful vocabulary."

I try not to let my irritation show, but that's hard. Especially when I don't know where we're going. Chase remains stubbornly quiet and my questions go unanswered for the next hour. The silence goes on so long that I forget whether I'm not talking to him, or he's not talking to me. I grind my teeth and bounce around in the Jeep.

Since he's not talking, I turn my attention to the dirt road and the land beyond. We're on the other side of the mountains and wind through a seemingly endless landscape of rocky hills and scrub brush. The terrain changes from hard-packed dirt to sand, and then to rocky terrain as we climb up and then down a series of small hills that appear to shrink in size the further we head into the wilderness.

The Jeep lurches and bumps and I'm thrown around in the seat for the nth time. I bite back a curse as I try to keep from bruising my shoulder. Despite the dry terrain, something about the landscape feels alive—there's an energy here that's both comforting and a little daunting.

It feels like hours pass before we finally reach our destination—a hill with a somewhat flat top. Chase smiles as he parks, looking out over the horizon with awe.

"This is the place." He shuts off the engine, looking pleased with himself.

I look out on a world of the deepest black. Not a light in sight. No houses. No towns. Nothing to indicate human activity. He sits for a minute, tapping on his phone. The radio silence between us continues until I can't stand it anymore.

"Where are we?" I twist in my seat and look out at nothing but blackness. Well, that's not entirely true. There are shades to the night, darker shadows against lighter grays and the stars. A gasp escapes me as I take in the multitude of stars shining overhead.

"BLM land." He grips his cellphone and opens his door.

"BLM? What's that?" All I come up with is Black Lives Matter, but I'm certain that's not what he means.

"Bureau of Land Management." He provides no further details.

"Can I get a little more than that?"

"BLM land is federal land. To be preserved for future generations. Most BLM land is in the West. You can think of it like a Natural Park without the Park designation. It's basically open-use land for the public."

"Never heard of such a thing."

"That right there tells me you grew up in the East."

"How's that?"

"Because if you're from Alaska, Arizona, California, Colorado, Idaho, Montana, Nevada, New Mexico, Utah, Washington, and Wyoming..." He ticks off each state with his fingers. "You would know about public land. That's the kind of thing that's going to make you stand out."

"What does that mean?"

"The geographic differences and assumed knowledge that shape our experiences."

"Because I don't know what BLM means?"

"Tell me the truth. Did you think I was talking about Black Lives Matter, or public land, when you heard BLM?"

"I..." There's no reason to lie. He already knows I'm not from around here. "Well, it's not like it's a big deal. How much land can it be if no one knows about it?"

He raises an eyebrow, lips pursing. "It's a big deal when you realize the BLM manages one in every ten acres of land in the United States."

"No way. That's not true." I can't hide my disbelief and challenge what he says. My brow furrows with skepticism as I shake my head.

"Look it up." Nonchalant, his tone tells me I'm wrong. He gives a pointed look, gesturing to my pocket as if I have a phone tucked away in there.

"I'd love to," I bite my lip with irritation, "but my phone and all of my belongings are in a trashcan back at the airport."

He crosses his arms again. "And good thing too. Bravo team was definitely spot on about that." He studies me with an intense expression, then crooks a grin.

"Exactly what are the chances anyone's actually following us?"

"You're the one whose cover in WITSEC was blown. You tell me." He crosses his arms over his chest in a show of conviction. Then he nods toward the door. "Might as well hop on out. Camp won't set itself."

My mouth gapes. After driving into the middle of nowhere, it's not as if I expect five-star accommodations, but I know nothing about setting up a camp or pitching a tent. Maybe I'm a bit of a princess when it comes to that. Honestly, none of this is what I expected when Guardian HRS took over my protection detail.

I figured it would be the same as WITSEC, with a safe house and round-the-clock security. Instead of that, there's only Chase, and we're in the middle of nowhere with no backup and no support. I grit my teeth, because I can already hear his smart reply, but can't stop myself from asking the obvious.

"We're really camping out here?"

"Definitely." He gives a curt nod.

"Why?"

The hard lines of his face soften as he looks away for a moment. When I'm about to come back with a sharp comment about ignoring me, he turns back to meet my gaze with his mouth set into a hard line.

"You tell me?"

"If I knew, I wouldn't have asked you. Can you please stop answering all my questions with questions I don't know the answers to?" I swallow my irritation and do my best to be a team player. "I'm out of my element. Can you give me a break?"

"We're not staying at a hotel because your image can be traced through the surveillance cameras, if you've got the right gear. Until we know how your information was leaked, our best bet is to stay away from anywhere where your face can be traced. Out here, no one can sneak up on us. If they do, I'll see them coming from miles away."

"How? It's pitch black out here."

The corner of his mouth crooks up in a grin, and he cocks his head. "Come on, you're smarter than that. First off, no one in their right mind travels out here at night without lights. We'll see them."

"But what about during the day?" There's no way I'm mentioning anything about headlights at night. That was a stupid miss on my part, but I've got him with this question.

"Luv, this is dry, arid ground. No one moves without a plume of dust following them."

"Oh." My brows tug together.

"Don't be so hard on yourself. If you're not familiar with a place, you're not familiar."

"This feels a bit like overkill." I open the passenger door and hop out of the Jeep. "Are Guardian Protectors always this OCD about everything?"

"Anything involved in keeping you breathing is a priority for me. And while I'm not OCD, attention to detail is critical in this line of work. Don't worry about being out here for long. This is temporary, as I've only got enough water for a few days."

"We're going to be here a few days?" Apprehension bubbles in my stomach. I'm not an outdoor girl.

"Yes, if anyone is out there looking for you, they're going to have a hard time when you've dropped off the map." His lips twitch with a hint of a smile. "We stay in the desert for a few days, and then we move on."

"And where will that be?"

"Don't know."

"How can you not know?"

"If I don't know where we're going, no one else can know."

"Somewhere in there, that might actually make sense."

"It does. Trust me." He gives me a look that sends a chill up my spine before turning away.

"You say that a lot."

"There's a reason for that." He gives me a look, then walks around the front of the Jeep. "Welcome to your new home. No fire tonight. No fires any night."

I glance around and nod. Unless he brought something to burn, there's nothing out here big enough to feed a fire. It's sand and rock, as far as the eye can see, with a bit of scrub brush mixed in with cacti.

Chase wanders to the edge of the overlook, scanning the distance.

I make my own way to the edge, watching my step as I go. It's dark, darker than I've ever seen, but that doesn't mean there's no light. I vaguely make out the features of the rocks and do a fair job of not tripping over my feet.

I take the win.

When I get to the edge of the—bluff? Overlook? Hill? I'm really not sure what to call this place, my breath catches as I take in the desert far below. The land goes on for miles and miles. I've never been in such an open place before.

When my gaze finally makes it to the horizon, the mountains are a darker, jagged black cut out against the sky. Then I turn my attention to the millions and millions of stars overhead.

"It's beautiful, isn't it?"

Absorbed in what I'm seeing, I don't hear Chase approach and can only gape at the wonder in the heavens.

"I've never seen stars like this. There are so many." I tilt my head back, spellbound by the beauty overhead.

"You're in luck tonight."

"Why is that?"

"It's a new moon, which means its light won't overpower the stars. You can see the Milky Way and all the constellations."

"The only constellation I know is the Big Dipper, and we rarely saw it where I grew up."

"Well, tonight is the perfect night to stargaze. If you're lucky, we'll see a meteoroid shower. You can wish upon a falling star, but if not, it's perfect for viewing the Space Station. It'll be overhead shortly."

"Wow." I spin in a slow circle, taking in something I've been told about all my life, but never truly understood. "It's incredible."

"Definitely." Chase's comment is soft and gentle. Almost friendly.

When I look at him, however, he's not looking at the sky like me. Instead, he studies me, which makes me wonder if he directs his comment at the stars above—or me?

Coming hard on the heels of that thought, my stomach lurches and I swallow hard. I'm in the middle of nowhere, with a man I don't know, and we're all alone with no other humans within twenty miles or more.

"Do you want to stargaze for a bit, or are you tired enough to sleep?" He goes to the Jeep and opens up the back, unpacking supplies, while I gaze at the stars.

"Yes, and yes." I spin around and drag my attention from the stars to Chase. "If you tell me what to do, I can help set camp."

"Setting up camp is far easier than you'd think." He comes around to my side of the vehicle and reaches overhead to the roof.

With the flick of a few latches, the carrier opens up like a clamshell. He yanks on something and a ladder unfolds from the roof, reaching all the way to the ground. He climbs halfway up the ladder and unfolds a rooftop tent.

"Wow." I shake my head in surprise and a bit of awe at the engineering behind something like that. "That's really cool."

"And super convenient. No tent spikes to hammer into rock-hard ground and it keeps us off the ground and away from scorpions, snakes, and other critters."

"Did you say scorpions?"

"And snakes. Scorpions come out at night. Snakes are more daytime critters, soaking up heat from the sun."

"I'm officially grossed out, but how are we going to fit up there? It's awfully—tight?" I was going to say close but didn't want to go there.

"It's cozy. No doubt about that, but it's built for two people." Chase finishes setting up the tent, which takes all of two minutes, then he's back on the ground and headed to the back of the Jeep again. He pulls out two sleep sacks. They're too thin to be called sleeping bags.

"Here." He hands me the sleep sacks. "How about you take those up?"

"Okay." I eye the ladder with skepticism. It doesn't look sturdy, but it handled Chase's weight without a problem.

I climb the ladder and toss the sleep sacks into the tent. It looks even smaller from up here. To my surprise, the base is padded with some kind of closed cell foam that provides some cushioning. It's got a little bit of give, but we won't be living in the lap of luxury.

"Here you go." Chase lifts a small canvas bag and I take it from him.

A quick inspection reveals a couple of flashlights and some kind of headband with lights. I pull that out and look at it. What a cool idea.

"Before we call it a night, this is a good chance for a bathroom break. You're not going to want to climb down in the middle of the night."

"Aren't we past the middle of the night?"

"It's a bit late but let me show you where we're setting the latrine. Tomorrow, you'll get a crash course in high desert camping, but for now, we stick to the basics."

The basics, it seems, other than a latrine that's not much to speak about... Actually, I'm not speaking about the chest high boulder that provides the only privacy in sight for latrine activities. But other than the latrine and how to check for scorpions and snakes who are curled up for the night, I get a crash course on how to use a flashlight and why we're sleeping fully dressed.

Shoes go right by the stairs leading down, at the entrance of the tent, and the tent gets zipped closed for any bugs interested in a late-night snack. As for our accommodations, the inside of the rooftop tent is cramped, with barely enough room for two people.

The walls are nothing but a thin layer of canvas, and that foam padding is comfortable, but stiff. Chase hangs a flashlight on one of the few hooks, to be within easy reach, he says.

I feel every move he makes in the small space. Now that we're settling down, I regret the sharpness of my tongue and the arguments it created. This man doesn't know me, yet he's willing to risk his life to keep me safe.

"Can we keep the light on?" I settle into my sleep sack and try to give him more room.

"No. It's not worth burning through the batteries." He slides into his sack. "Is this your way of saying you're afraid of the dark?"

"Not afraid so much as I've never slept in a tent before, and never one perched on the top of a Jeep. I just thought…" I hate to ask for any concessions from this man.

"How about a chem light?"

"I don't know what that is."

He fishes something out of the canvas bag I placed up here earlier. There's a snap and a yellow glow fills the interior of the tent.

"How's that?" He ties it to a string hanging overhead.

"Better." I pull the fabric of my sleep sack up to my chin like a little girl and stare at the ceiling.

Chase settles down beside me. As much as I try not to touch him, that's simply impossible. I feel him all around me.

FIVE

Chase
_____

I TAKE A DEEP BREATH AND TRY TO FOCUS ON ANYTHING OTHER THAN
the woman beside me. The chem light casts an eerie, yellow hue on
the inside of the tent, making it feel like we're in our own little
world.

The warmth of Cara's body radiates outward, making me
acutely aware of how close our bodies are to each other. It's
impossible not to touch her inside this tent. It may be built for two,
but that's a very cozy two.

After the day we've had, and all the arguments, we're anything
but cozy.

The entire drive, all we did was argue, at least until I disengaged
and decided silence was a better option. I'm not sure if that was a
good idea because the vibe between us remains strained.

The cramped quarters definitely distract me. With her beside
me, my mind wanders where it shouldn't. Before long, all I can
think about is what it would feel like to have her hot body wrapped
around me. I take a deep breath, close my eyes, and try to focus on
the sounds around us rather than the beating of my heart. Or the
throbbing in my dick.

All I can think about is how close she is. How much I want to touch her. How my heart races as my imagination takes things to the next logical step, and that's where I rein things in.

This woman is more than I bargained for, and, for the hundredth time since we met, I wish she was a fat, middle-aged man instead of a stunning beauty. If I let myself get too close, there's no telling what might happen between us.

I see the way she looks at me. There's a definite sizzle in the air, sparks of attraction and lust, that can be deadly for us both. She draws me in, in a way I can't explain. I definitely feel protective, but that isn't a surprise.

I'm her Guardian Protector. It's my job to protect her.

The problem is this feels different. Something deeper is happening between us. Despite our rocky start, there's a sexual attraction brewing between us, and I don't know how to deal with that.

This isn't the time for distractions. I need to be focused on the job at hand, and not on the woman who makes that impossible. I try to push those thoughts from my mind and attempt to find sleep. Only sleep is impossible when everything Cara fills my senses.

There's definite tension swirling in the air between us. It's evident in the stiffness of her body as she lies beside me. It's in the hitching of her breath and the awkward silence.

I take another deep breath and try to push away my thoughts. Eventually, my breathing slows and my mind drifts away from thoughts of Cara. Almost asleep, she whispers something in the darkness. Something I don't think she intends for me to hear.

"Thank you." Soft and almost below my hearing threshold, her quiet *thank you* sets my heart pounding.

I debate turning toward her, but her breaths deepen as she slowly drifts off to sleep. Once I'm sure she's asleep, I shift to my side, trying to give her more room.

Which is a mistake. Cara shifts in her sleep, turning away from me, which should be a good thing. Except her body presses against mine, spooning with me.

Well, I wanted to know what it would feel like to hold her in my arms.

I curve my body around hers. Keeping my hands off her is harder than I think, but I manage not to initiate anything sexual. Spooning like a couple, instead of two strangers at each other's throats, I focus on slowing the beating of my heart and do my best to catch what sleep I can.

Tomorrow, we'll be back on the road, heading east, further into the Great Basin and eventually to the foothills of the Rocky Mountains. I have a destination in mind, but we're taking the slow road. A road where I can see for miles until I'm absolutely sure no one is following us.

Instead of focusing on the woman in my arms, I go over our route in my head and drift into the comfort of a dreamless sleep as I plan our next steps.

In the morning, my eyes slowly open, and the first thing I feel is Cara nestled against me and her soft body tucked tight against mine. She looks so peaceful, so beautiful, that I can't help but watch her sleep for a few moments before I move.

The woman is stunning. Her thick eyelashes fan out over her sculpted cheekbones, and the soft light of the morning sun casts a golden glow over her features. I could lie here all day and spend hours watching her breathe, but I have to move. I can't afford for her to wake up with my arm draped over her hip, or feeling my morning wood poking her in the ass.

The sun is just beginning to peek over the horizon, which tells me it's time to get up and start our day. Careful not to wake her, I extricate myself from her body and slip from the tent. She mumbles something in her sleep but doesn't wake as I stand outside the tent and take in the view before us.

The high desert of northern Nevada stretches out in rainbow hues and a sea of rolling hills and stunning mesas. The sky above us will turn a deep blue as the sun climbs higher. For now, however, it's beautiful, with shades of lavender peeking over the horizon. Greens and yellows will follow before the deep, stunning blue of day takes over and sweeps the sky.

This sight is enough to take my breath away. I grew up in the outdoors and know these lands well, but no matter how many times

I see the sunrise, it never fails to amaze me. With one last look around, scanning the distance for any signs of someone headed our way, I set to whipping up a field breakfast of biscuits, sausage, and gravy.

The Jeep is my pride and joy. After years of off-roading, and adding in the customizations, it allows me to slip off the grid for as long as I like. Opening the back door, I pull out a table and snap the two legs that hold it in place. The back of the Jeep supports the other edge. A Coleman stove sits on top of the table, fed by a propane tank secured in the back of the Jeep. I fill a kettle with water for hot cocoa and mix batter for biscuits.

A small fridge keeps perishables fresh. It feeds off a solar battery with a backup attached to the Jeep's engine. I remove a pack of sausages and set it down on the prep area, then hear Cara stirring inside the tent.

"It's a gorgeous morning, and I've got hot cocoa," I call out to her. First, to let her know where I am, and second, to orient her to her surroundings.

She emerges with a tentative smile that grows brighter when she catches sight of my spread. "And he cooks." She scoots to the edge of the tent, then slowly spins around to climb down the ladder.

"I do my best." I take a sip of hot cocoa and lift the tin cup. "Do you like hot chocolate? Apologies if you're a coffee drinker, but that's the one thing I don't have."

"Actually, I'm not a fan of coffee. Great smell, but…"

"…horrible taste." Her cheeks flush when I finish her sentence. For the first time, we're in sync instead of at each other's throats.

"Exactly." She takes a few steps from the Jeep to stretch. "This view is amazing."

"It is, isn't it?" She didn't answer about the hot cocoa, but I pour her a cup and take the steaming beverage to her. She turns at my approach and her frown turns into a smile. "Thank you."

I stand beside her, maybe a bit closer than I would with a stranger, but after holding her in my arms through the night, I figure we're past the stranger part of our relationship.

She takes a sip and her eyes close when the flavor hits. "Mmm… this is good."

"Glad you like it."

"I've never been a hot chocolate drinker before, either. This is good. It's different."

"It's nothing special." Which is a total lie. I'm a hot chocolate connoisseur.

"Well, it smells fantastic and tastes amazing."

I like this—this easy back and forth. It's way better than our tense conversations from the night before.

"What's for breakfast, and what can I do to help?"

Thrilled she's willing to help, I give her the rundown on breakfast. "We're having sausage, biscuits, and gravy. One of my favorites. The biscuits are rising, the gravy is simmering, and the sausages are almost ready to put on the grill. So you can wander around, if you like, but don't go too far. Also, mind where you step. The snakes are rousing."

She wanders over to the Jeep to check out my setup. "Wow, this is impressive."

I spend the next few minutes showing off the customizations I've made to the Jeep, then set to finishing breakfast.

Cara excuses herself and heads to our designated latrine while I plate our breakfast. Pulling out two folding chairs, I set up near the edge of the outlook toward the desert for our morning view. Cara joins me a few minutes later, and I hand her a plate.

"I don't know your preference for salt, so I kept it light." I hold up a small salt and pepper shaker. "Please add to taste."

She takes a bite of biscuit and gravy, then closes her eyes. "Wow. This is really good."

"I've had a lot of practice."

"From the tent on top of the Jeep, to the customizations in the back, I have a feeling you do this a lot?"

"There's nothing I love better than the outdoors. There's just something about it that makes my heart sing."

"I like that."

"What?"

"Makes your *heart sing*. It says so much in so few words."

"Really?"

"Yeah, or maybe it was the way your expression changed."

"I suppose." I really didn't mean much more than what I said.

"I've never been an outdoors kind of girl. I grew up where the only nature was in the city parks. The only time I ventured outdoors was to get from one place to the next. All of this is new to me, and if I'm being honest, it would be terrifying if not for you."

"You find this terrifying?"

"Yeah." I scan the distant mountains and the expanse of nothingness before it. "It makes me feel small and way out of my element."

"I can see how that could be, but there's not much to it."

"Maybe for you." She gestures to the desert. "I'd be dead in a day. I don't know the first thing about surviving something like that."

"Fortunately, you have me, and we have a lot of time. I can teach you pretty much everything you need to know about basic survival skills. If you're interested."

"I am."

"Great. Consider this a crash course."

"Please don't expect too much. I'm a horrible student, and I ask a lot of questions."

"I'm a fabulous instructor, but how about we break camp and get back on the road? And I promise to answer your questions." I hold out an olive branch, curious if she'll take it.

"Thanks, and I'll try not to ask too many dumb questions, but I do have one."

"What's that?"

"Where are we going?"

"Deeper into the desert." I can't help but laugh at her expression.

"I should've guessed, but then what?"

"Like I said last night, I don't have a firm plan. Right now, we're simply letting time pass. As long as no one's on our ass, we can take all the time in the world to putz around out here."

"I never thought…" Her words trail off, and she bites her lip.

"Thought, what?"

"That I would ever be in a place like this. This is totally not how I saw my life going." Without explaining further, she carries her plate back to the Jeep, where she pauses and looks back at me. "How do we clean the dishes?"

"For now, scrape the residue over there." I point at a bush some feet away. "Until we're out of the desert, I ration the water and we use cleaning wipes to wipe off the dishes."

"Cleaning wipes?"

"Yes, disinfecting wipes. They're great for hundreds of things." I join her back at the Jeep and show her what I mean. "Our biggest threat out here is water. For now, we're strictly rationed, but we'll break out the biodegradable soap when we come across water."

"If you say so." She takes a wipe and studiously cleans her plate. "Same for the skillet?"

"For that, I just wipe out any particulates and stow it."

"With the grease?"

"With the grease."

"But what about bacteria?"

"I always heat the pan to kill any bacteria before adding food. It's no different from the way you might clean a grill at home. Heat, in this case, is our friend."

"Oh." She scrapes out the pan while I clean out the kettle.

"It's also why I boil the water before we drink it. The water buffalo in the Jeep is good for drinking, but after adding the hot cocoa to the kettle, I always boil the water inside it before drinking. Same reason as the grease. Don't want to drink any bad bacteria. The one thing you don't want out here is the runs because you didn't clean your cooking gear."

"And already, I am learning new things." She stows her plate and takes another look at the customizations of the Jeep. I leave her to it, enjoying the easy flow of our conversation. She's quite pleasant when she's like this.

Curious.

Lingering beneath all of that, however, she's under significant strain.

I clear my throat and break the silence. "So, how did you end up in WITSEC anyway?"

She takes a deep breath. I can tell she's debating whether to tell me, but she eventually speaks. "It's complicated."

"We have time."

She looks away and keeps her gaze on the horizon. "I witnessed a murder, but there's more to it. Not only did I see who killed my father, I know who's responsible for putting out the hit on him, and there's more."

"I'm sorry for your loss." Such a corny phrase, but obligatory when someone loses someone close to them. "I have no words. To watch a parent be murdered in front of you..."

"My father is—*was* a complicated man living a double life. He was my everything. My hero, but then I saw something I shouldn't have seen, and my entire world fell apart. That's why I'm in WITSEC. To keep me safe until I can testify, not only against the man who murdered my father, but the man who sold..." Her voice cracks and she turns away, hiding her face.

My gut twists because, while I don't know the specifics of her case, I know what comes next. It's in the set of her jaw, the slump of her shoulders, and in the shame filling her face.

"Sold, what?" Although I know that's the wrong question. It's not *what*, but *who*.

Cara sniffs and swipes at her eyes. It takes a few moments, but then she tells me more.

"Women." Her voice catches. "My father was involved in human trafficking."

"He kidnapped and sold women?"

"He connected the buyers to the men who kidnapped and sold women. He's the one who made the introductions and facilitated the transactions. I thought you knew about that?"

"I don't."

"You don't?" Her brows pinch in confusion. "Then how..."

"How can I protect you?"

"Yes. I just assumed…"

"I don't need to know the specifics of your case or what you'll testify to in court to protect you. That kind of information isn't necessary to my job. With that said, however, knowing who wants you dead, and what resources they have at their disposal, can provide insight into what threats we may encounter."

"I just figured you knew all the gory details." She shrugs but continues staring off into the distance.

"I didn't, and I really am sorry about your father. You suffered two great losses."

"I don't know about that. After I found out what he was doing… My father isn't who I thought he was. He's a horrible human being. *Was* a horrible man."

"You lost the hero you thought he was. Discovering those truths about your father changed your opinion of him forever. You're allowed to mourn the loss of your hero and losing your father. No one can take that from you. Despite what he did, he was still your father, and it's okay to mourn his death."

"Thank you." She places her fingers to her temples and tries to wipe more of her tears without me noticing, but I notice every little thing about the woman in front of me.

I'm so moved by her story that I can't help but reach out and give her shoulder a gentle squeeze. My heart pounds at the contact, and I pull away before I do something I might regret.

"I'm very sorry for your loss," I say it softly and hope she hears what I have to say. She didn't do the things her father did and doesn't deserve to carry the burden of his crimes.

"Thank you."

With that, we break camp and begin her introduction to living off the grid outdoors. I show her how to close the clamshell of our tent and stow the ladder. Then I show her how the table fits under a shelf I created inside the Jeep. We go over the water buffalo and propane tanks. Then we're ready to move on.

"Are you ready?" I shut the back of the Jeep and wait.

"As I'll ever be." She looks unsure, but less uncomfortable.

Cara's bright. She soaks up information like it's candy, which gives me an idea.

"Great." I gesture toward the driver's side. "You're driving."

"I'm, what?" Eyes round, she doesn't believe me, but I jump into the passenger seat and gesture once more for her to take the wheel. Today's lesson will cover the basics of how to drive off-road.

SIX

Cara
_____

CHASE SQUINTS AT ME FROM THE PASSENGER SIDE OF THE JEEP. "Come on, let's get started."

I eye the unfamiliar Jeep with uncertainty and then stare at the driver's seat like it's one of the poisonous snakes he's warned me about.

"You really don't want me to drive." I back away, holding my hands up.

"Yes, I do, and today, you are." He points at the steering wheel. "Give it a go."

"Are you sure?"

"It's easy, and I'll coach you every step of the way. You'll need to be comfortable driving and best to learn where the ground is mostly flat."

"Meaning there will be areas that aren't."

"Exactly."

"I think you should drive."

"What if something happens to me?"

"Is something going to happen to you?"

"No, but better you learn now, where I can teach you, than when I can't." He winks at me, which makes me smile. It does other things too. Like, makes my heart race. Butterflies dance in my belly, and heat burns in my cheeks.

"Okay." I don't like this, but how hard could it be? I know how to drive. This is exactly the same, except for the bumps and lack of pavement.

While the Jeep's suspension can take a beating, it's not so forgiving of bumps. The ride's far from smooth. I maneuver the Jeep back down the road we took up to the top of the hill last night, nervously navigating the ruts. Chase gives me a few pointers, nothing I couldn't figure out on my own, and tells me to go faster.

"Is that a good idea?" I ask in a small voice.

"You'll be fine."

"There are a lot of bumps in the road. Won't the Jeep…? Isn't it bad for the suspension?"

"It's built for far worse than this, and you'll be surprised how a little speed can even out the bumps. Go ahead and try it." He gestures to the hard-packed ground all around us.

As for being off-road, we're still on a dirt road. We're not technically traveling overland, where there are no roads.

"What are those signs for?" I point at a post ahead of us with a series of letters and numbers on it.

"That's the name of the road we're on. There are maps that show you all the BLM roads and forestry roads. For off-road enthusiasts, it's great to know where you are."

"And you're an enthusiast?"

"Guilty as charged." He leans back with a grin.

"How long have you been doing this?"

"Twelve?"

"Twelve? Twelve years?"

"My father taught me how to drive and shoot the moment I was big enough to hold a gun, and big enough to reach the brake pedal."

"Twelve?"

"Yeah."

"Wow."

As we drive, I become more comfortable with the Jeep and its capabilities. The bumps and ruts in the road no longer feel like obstacles to overcome, but things to move over. I enjoy the thrill of being in control and am eager for a bit more of a challenge.

After a while, we come to a clearing with a breathtaking view of the surrounding area. I stop the Jeep, and we climb out.

"What an incredible view." He stands beside me, close enough for the backs of our hands to brush against each other. He doesn't move away, and neither do I. Despite our rocky beginning, we're becoming more comfortable with each other.

"Ready for something a bit more challenging?" He nudges my shoulder and winks at me. It's a test, one he knows I'll pass.

"Yes." I can't keep the eagerness from my voice.

"First, let me show you the basics behind map reading, in case…" His voice trails off, but I know what he means.

I just hope it's not what I fear.

"In case you're incapacitated?" There's only one thing I won't be able to handle: if the same thing happens to Chase as what happened with Hank.

"Exactly." There's a smirk on his face, a bit of lightheartedness in his tone.

"By what, exactly? What would incapacitate you that wouldn't incapacitate me?"

"Snake bite? Scorpion sting? Twisted ankle."

"Twisted ankle?" I can't help but laugh. "A twisted ankle will not take out a Navy SEAL."

"Not a SEAL."

"I thought all Guardians were SEALs?"

"Most Guardians are Navy SEALs, but not all. Guardian HRS draws from all branches of the military special ops community. I'm a Scout Sniper in the Army Rangers. Not a frogman."

"Frogman?"

"It's what SEALs call themselves."

"Oh, I didn't know. Scout Sniper? That sounds impressive and a bit ominous."

"Does it bother you knowing I'm trained to kill?"

"I assumed that was part of it, but sniper? It brings certain images to mind. Is it anything like what they show in the movies?"

"Yes, and no."

"How?"

"For one thing, snipers are not hotheads like they show in the movies. We're solo operators who need to be able to work on our own and be independent from command. You know, make sound decisions in the heat of things? Hotheads can't be trusted."

"Oh, I always thought you worked with a team."

"Yes, and no." He grins at the repetition of his previous answer. "It's a solitary job. I was with a team, but often separated from them to accomplish my mission. Now, how about Map Reading 101?"

"You're really on a mission to teach me all the things."

"Knowledge is power, and we have the luxury of time. I've got all the time to teach you, and the more you know, the more independent you will be. I'm all about self-reliance and self-sufficiency."

"Okay, I'm game. Where's the map?"

Chase pulls out a folder of laminated papers and gestures for me to join him at the hood of the Jeep. With the sun climbing, I wipe the perspiration from my brow and blow out my breath. The heat builds and I feel it draining me.

"This top one is an overview of the pages beneath it. See how it's divided into a grid?"

"Yes."

"Each grid is associated with one of the pages underneath, which are all drawn in higher resolution." He's eager to teach and shows me the basics of figuring out north and south and how to find those on the map. Most of what he says is obvious, like paying attention to the distance scale in the lower right corner. He's patient and doesn't ridicule my questions, no matter how basic they seem.

We stand shoulder to shoulder, which makes it impossible not to brush against each other. At first, it's an accidental touch, but as he leans over the map, stretching to show me something, or when I do the same, those accidental brushes of skin against skin turn much less accidental.

There's an easiness that flows between us, and a new tension builds. Not one of anger, but the law of nature: the attraction between male and female.

I nibble on my lower lip as he leans close to show me how the squiggles on the map reveal topographical features, like how steep a particular area might be.

"And these are the designators for each road." He points to the letters and numbers. "The signposts we passed?"

"Yes. I remember." I tug at my shirt, feeling the heat. I'm eager to get back in the Jeep where the wind cools me off. Chase's Jeep may be impressive, but it doesn't have air conditioning.

"You're doing great with driving. So here's your first test." He flips to the page with the map showing where we're located. "Do you remember where we are?"

There's been so much flipping of pages. My mind swims with all the information he's thrown at me. I blow out a breath and wipe at the sweat on my brow.

"I'm not sure." It's the truth. I'm embarrassed to admit it because I'm usually an excellent learner.

"No problem." Instead of showing me, he picks up the notebook and walks a few feet from the Jeep. "Start with what you see around us."

It's another test, and I'm determined to try my best.

"Um, flat all around?"

"Is that true?" He points to the hill we're on and the others beyond it that are higher than the one we're on. "Look at the landscape, then look at the map." He hands me the map and I take it from him. "Orientate yourself first."

"Okay." I look down at the map and the cardinal directions, then glance at the sky. There's not much around us to determine direction, but I know where the sun rose and where it is now. Using that, I orient east on the map to east where I stand.

"Don't forget the topographical marks. They're there to help you."

I stare at the map and all the squiggly lines make my eyes cross, but then I see it. In front of me, the land flows out from the mountains, getting flatter and flatter. To the west, the hills grow in size.

Chase watches me as I piece everything together.

"This shows a river or a stream bed back that-a-way." I point back in the direction we came. "But there was no stream."

"It's a dry riverbed and seasonal."

"Huh?"

"In the summer, it's devoid of water. In the spring, it flows with the snowmelt from the mountains."

"If that's the case." I stroll back to the Jeep and place the map on the hood. Tracing out what I remember about the stream, and looking at the hills, I take my best guess. "What about here?" I point to where I think we are.

He leans over my shoulder, checking my work, which brings the scruff of his beard close to my cheek. If I move, that scruff will scrape against my cheek, so I stand exceptionally still. The heat between us intensifies, but so far, neither of us acts on it. It's more of a casual thing, heating up to something more than casual interest.

"Great job, but you're ten miles off." He places his finger next to mine, and for a moment we touch. That touch sends tiny electrical pulses racing up my arm, but then he drags his finger away from mine, ten miles south of where I thought we were.

Still hovering over me, his chiseled chest rubs against my shoulder blades. The air crackles and pops with electricity as I'm hyperaware of his presence. His breaths, every slow inhale, almost a whisper, supercharges the air between us.

"Do you see where you went wrong?" He keeps talking as if standing this close to me is completely normal.

His voice is softer than before, more husky, more intimate. I try not to focus on the way his breath tickles my ear, or how my heart races as I struggle to maintain my composure. I stare intently at the map while he explains my mistake. I bite my tongue and close my eyes, attempting to regain control over my treacherous body.

"Don't worry, princess." His words drip with something deeply seductive and carry an intensity that makes my heart flutter. "You'll get the hang of it. That was a hard one."

He takes a step back, and for a moment, I feel cold without him there. My breath steadies now that I have time to think, but when I turn around and look up into his eyes, our gazes linger for longer than they should, while all around us the air sparks with a flurry of electricity.

My head swirls from my attraction to a man I barely know. The intensity of the emotions confuses me and I silently vow to remain detached and aloof around him. But something inside of me is different now.

In a flash of awareness, I realize his *princess* had a sweet tone rather than the harsh, derogatory sound from the night before. A spark ignites deep within me, a desire—a wish—for maybe something more. This time, I'm the one who takes a step back, only there's nowhere to go with him standing so close. I duck around him and clear my throat before daring to speak.

"So—what now?"

He cocks his head, studying me, and I turn away beneath that scrutiny. For the very first time, he makes me nervous. Heat fills my cheeks and I curse how easily I blush. I face away from him and pretend like an intense wave of desire didn't just flash through me.

"We challenge your newfound skills." He sounds proud of himself for offering this challenge, and there's amusement lingering in the edges of his voice. "I want you to fully trust your abilities."

"It's just a bunch of dirt and rocks. I think I've got it." My words come out sharper and louder than I intend. Talk about overcompensating.

His feet scuff the ground as he approaches. Then he places the palm of his hand against the small of my back. It's meant to be comforting, but I flinch at the contact. Undeterred, he rests his chin on the top of my head and whispers in the wind while I pray he can't feel the pounding of my heart.

"Not necessarily. You've mastered the basics, but let's try some rougher terrain."

I take a deep breath and press a fist over my belly. Trying to remain cold and aloof, I stare at the harsh landscape and try to block out everything about Chase.

I focus on the hot wind, the heat of the sun baking the ground, and the tiny sounds of the scrub brush swaying in the wind. I try not to think about how good he smells. Or how his chiseled body turns me on. I try not to think about how the air between us sizzles and pops, or how that electrical charge tunnels through my nerves when he touches me.

I try all of that and fail miserably.

"I think I've had enough for today. It's getting hot, and it's giving me a headache. Can you drive?" I run the back of my hand over my temple, surprised there isn't more sweat.

Overhead, the sun bakes the ground. Its heat is relentless, and with no shade, impossible to escape. At least the Jeep provides some respite. It shades us, and when moving, the wind helps to cool me down. Regardless, it's oppressive and saps my strength.

"Sure. I can't promise anything, but we can try to get out of the direct sun. There's a river an hour or so away."

"I thought they were all dried up?" We had this conversation. *I think*. My brain's foggy.

"Most are, but there are some that flow year-round." He reaches down and takes my hand in his. The moment he touches me, I can't help the tiny gasp escaping my lips.

Chase says nothing. Maybe he feels nothing, and all of this is in my head? He leads me back into the Jeep, and we're off again.

After another hour, the bumping and jarring ride gives me a real headache. The trail he takes us on is much narrower than the dirt road we had been driving on before. The Jeep bounces along as he navigates ruts made by previous drivers and over rocks hidden in the dry soil.

The terrain becomes more uneven with each twist and turn, yet Chase appears completely at ease, like it's nothing. Maybe it is for him. He definitely guides us through tight spaces effortlessly. I marvel at his skill as he navigates through terrain that I consider impassable, but he has experience I lack.

After about another hour of driving, I'm beyond worn out. I don't know why it is, but this kind of travel exhausts me. We finally arrive at a clearing with a few large boulders, a couple of twisted trees that provide a small bit of shade—and there's a small riverbed with actual water flowing through it.

"Ready for a break?" He looks at me, brows pinched in concern.

"Definitely."

"You need to drink more water. Heat exhaustion is nothing to shake a stick at."

"I've been drinking."

During the drive, he's been methodical in measuring out water. He calls it keeping up with hydration goals. I call it too much to drink, but then I haven't peed since this morning.

"You're losing more water than normal because of the dry air and sweat. Which means you need more water than you'd otherwise think. I'm doubling your ration. When was the last time you peed?"

"This morning."

"Damn. This is my mistake. Come on. Out of the Jeep."

"Why?" He parked under the shade of the scraggly trees and it feels ten times cooler in the shade.

"What's my one rule?"

"Do as you say." It's impossible not to roll my eyes.

"Without question." His voice is stern.

"Without question." With that, I clamber down from the Jeep, surprised by how light-headed I feel. My head spins and my forehead is hot and devoid of sweat. "I don't feel so great."

To me, my words sound slurred, like I'm drunk or something. In my foggy state, Chase jumps into action, grabbing a bottle of water.

"Let's get you under some shade."

"Yeah, that sounds..." I take a few sips, but my legs buckle underneath me.

Chase catches me before I hit the ground, scooping me into his arms as he curses and runs me over to the small river. I think he's going to stop there, maybe wet his shirt and put it around my head, but he wades straight into the knee-high water and sits down in the stream bed, holding my limp body while my mind drifts into delirium.

The chilly water, however, revives me, washing away my fatigue, and clearing my mind. In its wake, it leaves behind a dreamy emptiness as he holds me close. There's nothing sexy about it, but it feels deeper, like we share some connection.

I don't know how long I drift in and out, dreaming, but not dreaming, but I finally have a chance to really look at him and see a different man: a compassionate man with a heart of gold.

A man I'm developing feelings for when I should stay far away.

"Why are you holding me?" Still confused, my words slur and spots dance in my eyes.

"You need to drink more water." His tone turns gruff and full of hard edges. "You're suffering from heat exhaustion. Hell, it may have been heat stroke."

I don't understand why he sounds so angry. His fingers rub along my arm, a soothing sensation I allow myself the pleasure of drifting in for a while. The gentleness of his touch heightens my senses, but I'm too sleepy to enjoy it. My hand lifts of its own volition to cup the side of his face and my fingers dance over days-old stubble.

"Don't." His entire body tenses as my fingers explore the seam of his lips. He grabs my wrist and yanks my arm down. "For God's sake, don't tempt me."

All of a sudden, we're moving. He lifts me in his arms and carries me to the rocky riverbank. There, he sets me down and walks away with a curse.

SEVEN

Chase

I RUN AWAY FROM THE RIVER, BOOTS POUNDING AGAINST THE ground, leaving Cara safely by the riverbank. There's no stopping until I'm on the other side of the Jeep, putting as much distance between her and my addled mind as I can. I need a barrier between us—figuratively and literally—but not so far that I can't monitor her condition.

She's exposed, vulnerable, and deserves careful observation, but I can't do that standing beside her. Or holding her in my arms. Or feeling the delicate press of her fingers against my lips.

I can't do any of that and keep things professional between us.

I can't allow myself to get too close, and yet I can't seem to keep my distance. A wave of conflicting emotions overwhelms me; the need to stay and protect her wars with my desire to explore the undeniable attraction between us.

What I need is to keep my distance and listen to that voice in my head screaming at me to keep our relationship strictly professional.

It shouldn't be this hard.

She makes me feel things that go far beyond my professional obligation to protect her. There was real fear when I thought I might lose her, and from a stupid oversight on my part.

I lean against the Jeep and tip my head back against the metal frame. With the Jeep a physical barrier between us, I watch her in the mirror, keeping an eye on her from a distance.

She rests on the ground, unmoving. Her eyes remain closed and her arms fold in on her chest, right where I put them. Her face remains ruddy, flushed with heat, and smudged with dirt. It's hard not to stare when the sun kisses her skin with a golden glow, highlighting her luscious curves. I pull my attention back from staring at her and focus on what's important.

Things a professional would notice.

Her breathing is deep and regular. Her chest rises and falls in a steady rhythm. I itch to touch her but know better than to tempt myself. Best to watch from a distance.

A safe distance—literally and figuratively.

I lean my forearms against the Jeep and lay my head on my hands as my muscles tense. It does nothing to keep me from thinking about her in ways I shouldn't. Frustrated, I rake my hands through my hair, feeling helpless. This is a battle I'm doomed to lose.

The sun beats down on me, and I take a moment to appreciate the silence of the desert. I listen as the river flows by, its gentle gurgle calming my nerves. With it being several hours past noon, the heat of the day fades. That kicks up a warm breeze that rustles through the scrub and brush.

I close my eyes and take several deep breaths in an attempt to silence my racing mind. It doesn't help—my thoughts keep returning to Cara lying on the ground next to the river. She's safe for now, but if anything happens to her, it's my fault.

I'm so busy thinking about her, I nearly miss it when she stirs. She rubs her eyes blearily, trying to make sense of her surroundings. Her cheeks remain flush from the heat, and I feel guilty for not watching her more closely throughout the day.

For not protecting her.

My gut twists in knots as my feelings for Cara grow stronger still, despite all that has happened today—and despite all that could happen if I don't keep myself in check.

My growing attraction toward her is officially a liability.

I thought I could control how I felt. My head tells me it's not fair to let things progress for either of us. After the trial, I'll be out of her life and onto the next assignment while she attempts to rebuild a new life.

I need to be distant. Inaccessible. Purely professional from here on out.

If I don't, I'll only wind up hurting her, and there's no way in hell I'm adding any negativity to her life. The poor thing's dealing with enough shit as it is.

My fingers rub at the back of my neck, and I glance up at the sky. Shade is difficult to find in this land. I kick myself for not thinking through her physical limitations and how that would affect her ability to withstand the heat. I'm used to the desert heat. I know how to hydrate, how to monitor my body and stay ahead of the curve.

"Fuck." I kick the tire and grit my teeth. Then her soft moan reaches my ears. "Cara?"

I rush to her side and feel her forehead. Still hot, but no longer dry. She's sweating again. Which is good. We're only dealing with heat exhaustion instead of heat stroke. That can be deadly.

I scoop Cara up into my arms, cradling her against my chest, and carry her back into the water. She weighs nothing in my arms. She's soft where I'm hard. Delicate where I'm strong. But that doesn't mean she's weak. Far from it. She's an amazing woman who's stronger than she knows.

Once I reach the edge of the water, I gently lie her down so that only her head is out of the water. Her face remains flushed from the heat, so I shift my body to shade her face. Cradling her head in my lap, I brush the wet strands of hair from her face. I allow myself to relax now that she's recovering. Her core temperature is still elevated, but the coolness of the water will take care of that.

She looks so fragile. So delicate. Her eyes remain closed, but she breathes easily. That, too, is an improvement.

I keep a close eye on her as she rests in my lap. Her core

temperature needs to return to normal, without heading in the opposite direction.

After a few minutes, she stirs.

My heart swells with emotion as I keep vigil until she regains consciousness. Her mind is foggy due to heat exhaustion, and I doubt she'll remember the way she tenderly cupped my cheek, or the sensual way she traced my lips with her fingertips.

My pulse pounds with the shock *that* was. Talk about instant erection. Talk about totally inappropriate. Talk about how falling for your client violates everything I know.

I hate how much my body craves this woman.

We seem to be having a disagreement about what is right and proper. *We?* I laugh. That's me and my dick chatting away. Eager fucker needs to stand the fuck down.

Fortunately, we're past the worst heat of the day. The sun will set soon and the evening will bring cooler temperatures, and I have a new problem. One I don't know how to handle.

Cara's clothes are completely soaked and gritty from the bits of sand in the river. She has nothing else to wear, but I need her stripped out of her clothes if they're going to dry before we bed down for the night and the temperatures drop.

Our argument from last night fills my head—Mine and Cara's. Not me and my dick—although me and my dick had a conversation about her last night as well. Regardless, I remind myself what she's not wearing under her clothes.

Yet another thing I didn't think through. I should've asked about her clothing size and provided a few days of clothing. Or I could've at least bought her another shirt at the gas station.

Movement draws my attention to her face. Her eyelids flutter and her brow pinches in confusion. She lifts a hand to her forehead, then jumps when water splashes in her face. Her eyes pop open and she gazes up at me in confusion.

"Where am I? What are you doing?" She looks left and right, then struggles to sit.

"Whoa, take it slow." I place my hands on her shoulders,

holding her in the water. "You passed out from heat exhaustion. You're going to be dizzy if you move too fast." I wait to see if she hears me before continuing. "Do you understand?"

Her gaze shifts back and forth between my eyes before she slowly nods in understanding.

"How do you feel?" I keep my voice soft, trying to soothe her.

She manages a weak smile as she murmurs in confusion. "What's going on? Why are you holding me?"

Her confusion is no surprise, and a testament to how cloudy her thinking is right now, she doesn't think to ask why she's in a river. I'm patient and repeat myself as she slowly comes to and can process what I'm trying to say.

"You suffered from heat exhaustion. I had to get your core temperature down as quickly as I could. That's why you're in the river. Are you still hot? Feeling cold?" Somehow, my desire to put literal and figurative distance between us translated into holding her head in my lap. I'm so fucked.

"I feel strung out. Like the worst hangover of my life." Her words are less slurred, easier to understand. I'll take the improvement.

"That's the headache from the heat exhaustion." I shift so that I can help her to the sitting position. "Here, let me help."

With my help, I guide her to a sitting position. She's able to spin her legs around and sit somewhat steadily in the water.

It comes up to my hips but is at her waist. She looks at the water in confusion, trying to piece things together. As she does, her hands slowly scull the water while she stares, perplexed.

It feels like I'm watching her slowly piece together the information her body's telling her.

Despite the heat of the desert, this water is from snowmelt in the mountains, which means it's cool and refreshing, but not safe to drink. I pull out a water bottle and hand it to her.

"You need to drink, but go slow. Start with a sip."

"Why?"

"Because your stomach will reject it if you drink too fast. Take a sip. Wait a minute, then take two. Keep on with that repetition until the bottle's empty."

She takes a sip and her eyes close as the refreshing liquid hydrates her body. I was able to reduce her body temperature with the river water but could do nothing about her hydration status. She remains dangerously dehydrated.

"Feeling more steady?"

"A little." She takes two more sips, gulps really, but I don't correct her. She's trying to listen to me. It's her body that demands more.

"We need to get you out of those clothes."

"Why?" Her response is a beat behind. She takes another sip, chugging more water than before.

"Slow down on the water, princess. Trust me."

Those two words seem to hit just right. She pulls the bottle from her mouth and stares up at me, head cocked to the side, as her brain struggles to connect her thoughts.

"My clothes?"

"If they don't dry before night, you'll be even more uncomfortable."

In an odd contrast, evaporative heat loss can be extreme enough to cause the opposite of heat exhaustion. It can lead to hypothermia, even in the desert. More so because the temperatures in the desert plummet at night. It might push a hundred and ten degrees right now, but I won't be surprised if we hit the high forties tonight.

I need her in warm, dry clothes before we bed down, because if she's naked, there's no way I'll be able to keep my hands to myself. My restraint only goes so far.

"Okay, but…" Uncertainty fills her expression. "What do I…" She's too embarrassed to ask. Or maybe she's still struggling to process thoughts.

I curse myself all the more for not thinking things through. When I got the call for this protection detail, I figured a week in the desert would be long enough to ensure no one pursued her. I also knew Bravo team would divest her of all her things. It's standard operating protocol. If the wreck hadn't delayed me, I would've done the same. So why the fuck didn't I provide her with something else to wear?

Because I'm an idiot, and that lack of foresight is the kind of shit that will get her killed. All the more reason why I need to rein in any attraction I may have for Cara and remind myself why I'm here.

I'm Cara's Guardian Protector. That's where it begins and where it ends.

"I have a shirt you can wear. It should be big enough that it'll hang to your knees. It's not ideal, but the best I have." I try to shut off the part of my brain that insists on telling me she'll be completely naked under my shirt.

My shirt.

My scent.

My girl.

A possessive growl builds in the back of my throat. It's animalistic, primal, and sounds like a caveman.

Dear Lord, get me through this day.

She tries to stand but remains dangerously unsteady on her feet. I stride toward her, but she stops me with an outstretched hand.

"No. I can do it." It should be a simple thing, but her legs don't seem to want to cooperate and her feet keep slipping out from under her.

She tries to stand but loses her balance and falls back into the water, landing on her ass with an ungainly splash. Poor thing looks bedraggled and pathetic. She thrashes in the water, trying to steady herself, but that only makes things worse.

"Come on. Let me help." No longer able to watch her struggle, I offer a hand.

Cara reluctantly takes my hand. She's tentative and unsure, but I help her to her feet. Surprisingly, she manages a weak smile and meets my gaze, where we both trip and stumble as emotion twists with the latent attraction swirling between us.

My heart thunders in my chest as I look into her eyes. Part of me wishes this moment would last forever. The other part knows how dangerous such thoughts can be. My job is to protect her and keep her safe. It's not the time for silly fantasies or romantic notions. It's time to face the truth and accept the cold, hard practicality of the situation.

Which brings us face to face, and chest to chest. Or rather, chest to breast. We stand there for a few moments—me offering support with my arms wrapped around her waist. She leans into me and I hold her in my arms, cursing the desire flowing through my veins.

My arms reflexively tighten around her before I control myself and take a step back. It takes every ounce of strength left within me to break the contact between us.

But I do. I try to separate because if I don't, things will get much worse and far more complicated. She looks up at me, eyes wide and confused, as if she's trying to process what's happening too. We stand in each other's arms, two strangers who don't belong with each other.

I force myself to take a step back, but her legs buckle, which leaves me holding her in my arms until she stops weaving on her feet.

Don't look down. Don't even think about it.

But my gaze drops to her cleavage and the way the wet cotton of her shirt molds over the gentle swell of her breasts. My hand cups her tiny waist, and everywhere her body presses against me, my skin heats and my arousal grows.

I feel like a volcano ready to erupt, and it takes everything I've got not to kiss her senseless, but my sensibility kicks in. This is neither the time nor the place. Instead of kissing her, I take a deep breath and focus on the task at hand—getting Cara into dry clothes with as little fuss as possible.

This should be easy.

Not.

I bite my tongue and carry on yet another conversation with my dick, as a guilty flush creeps up my neck. She notices the sudden stiffness in my posture.

"What's wrong?"

"Nothing." I clear my throat awkwardly and try to explain without making things too problematical. "It's just... I didn't think about what you're *not* wearing under your clothes, and you're too unsteady to undress yourself."

EIGHT

Cara

_____

TOO UNSTEADY TO UNDRESS MYSELF?

I'm a disaster waiting to happen.

"What do we do?" My words are slow and slurred. Thinking is harder than it should be. It's as if my thoughts swim through molasses before they reach my mouth where I can spit them out.

The world spins. My vision swims. Blurry and indistinct, I shut my eyes and try to steady myself. Chase's strong hand steadies me and brings me back to the present.

"Do you trust me?" Unlike me, Chase's voice is steady and sure.

Again, it takes half a beat before his words work their way from my ears to my brain. I blink, not sure I understand, but there's one thing I know beyond any doubt.

I trust Chase.

I trust him with my life.

But do I trust him to strip me out of my clothes?

Now that's an entirely different question.

"Yes." My answer is a whisper.

I want to trust him, but I'm afraid I'll only embarrass myself if I try to remove my clothes on my own. None of my extremities appear to work the way they should.

"I'm just going to help." His voice soothes my nerves, and his hands steady me.

I close my eyes and breathe deep. He turns me around, facing away from him, resting his hands on my shoulders. My breath hitches as his hands glide down to the hem of my shirt, raising goose bumps in their wake. The wet fabric of my shirt sticks to my chest, drags against my skin, and makes my nipples tingle as the fabric brushes over them.

"I'm going to remove your shirt, then help you into one of mine. Keeping you as covered as I can."

"Okay." My body shakes as he walks me over to the Jeep.

"Hold on to steady yourself."

"Okay." Apparently, my vocabulary is comprised of one word.

I take a deep breath and exhale slowly, trying to calm the riot of sensations that threaten to overwhelm me. It's just clothing, and he faces me away from him. I trust Chase not to take a peek. I trust him to be a gentleman, but there's a stirring deep within me, something that wants something far different.

I hold my breath as he grips the bottom of my shirt and slowly works it up my body. Heat-baked air hits my breasts, and they tighten with the stimulus. My cheeks heat, and I'm certain they glow bright red. He guides each of my arms through their respective sleeves, then pulls the soaked fabric over my head. More goose bumps break out over my entire body as the arid air hits my skin.

He leans over me, pressing his chest against my back, then pulls away. This time, he repeats everything in reverse. He guides my head through the collar of one of his shirts and pulls my wet hair through. Then he helps me thread one arm, and then the other, through the sleeves.

The richness of his scent envelopes me, and I can't help but pull in a deep lungful of air, wanting to fill every crook and crevice within me with his scent.

"Doing okay?"

I bite my lower lip and nod. It's the only thing I'm capable of with the way I'm hyperaware of his presence.

"Time for your jeans."

My breath hitches as he kneels behind me. I can only imagine how this looks from afar. Him kneeling with his face inches from my ass. I jump as he grasps one of my ankles, then chide myself for being jumpy.

"Sorry about your shoes. They're soaked."

"It's okay."

"When you collapsed, I didn't think everything through."

"It's fine." Other than repeating myself, I'm not sure what to say. At some point, very soon, Chase is going to strip me out of my pants, leaving me completely bare beneath his shirt.

He unties my shoes and slips first one foot, and then the other, free. To my surprise, I stand on a small mat. When did he put that there?

I don't remember.

My thoughts remain sluggish, but I appreciate not having to stand on the ground.

Then his hands are on me again, moving under the shirt—his shirt—reaching for the button of my jeans with shaking fingers.

He expertly unclasps the button before sliding the denim down over the flare of my hips. His touch is liquid fire against the chill of my skin.

I want more, despite being too dazed to understand what's happening between us.

If anything is happening at all?

This crazy attraction could be all in my head.

He slides my jeans down my legs, and I'm left in nothing but his shirt. I should feel exposed, even vulnerable, but I feel safe—a strange sensation considering the intensity of our situation. It's as if there's some kind of tether that binds us, despite the fact we only just met.

Chase stands and gazes at me for a long moment before nodding to himself and turning away.

Turning away?

He leaves me there, standing by myself, confused and wondering if I didn't imagine the flash of attraction increasing between us.

But he's closed off and distant.

Without a word, he goes about setting up camp for the night, while I stand confused and unsure. My shoes are a soggy mess and there's no way I'm walking around in bare feet. I'm too afraid of scorpions, or snakes, attacking me in self-defense. So instead of helping Chase, I open the door to the Jeep and crawl into the passenger seat.

There, I lean back and blow out a breath while looking out over the desert landscape. The sun is on its way toward the horizon. In an hour or two, the orange and pink hues of sunset will herald the end of another day. There are no clouds in the sky. Not a single puff or streak of white.

It's the most beautiful sight, and I watch it completely alone while Chase gathers firewood outside. I doze, too, falling in and out of fitful dreams. Most of them some variation of Chase's amazing touch, but then his velvety-smooth voice rouses me.

"How are you doing in there?" He comes to the passenger side window with a bottle in his hand. "Have you had anything to drink?"

I want to say *Yes*. My need to please him nearly brings the lie to my lips, but more than needing to please Chase, I want to be honest.

"Sorry." I give a little shake of my head, then glance down at my clasped hands in my lap. "I was dozing."

"Drink up, princess. You're still dehydrated. Let's get some water into you." He offers me the bottle and cants his head to the side, concerned but not forcing the issue.

"Thanks." I take the water bottle from him and twist off the cap. He doesn't leave until I dutifully take a drink.

Satisfied I'm on the mend, he sets another bottle on the dash, a not-so-gentle reminder to drink more, which I do. I suck down the first bottle, then sip at the second until it's empty.

An hour passes. He brings me more to drink. Then another hour passes. The sun continues its descent from its highest point in the sky, and as it nears the horizon, the temperature drops.

Feeling steadier than before, stronger and more coherent, I slide out of my seat and balance on the hard ground. It's hard-packed dirt, baked for centuries under an unforgiving sun. Heat radiates up from the ground, warming my feet. I glance at the camp Chase sets up for us. Despite what he said last night, it looks like we'll have a fire tonight. He gathered river rock and formed a fire ring. Inside that, dried wood forms a stack in the center.

A quick glance around the area, and I find where he set my clothes to dry. I walk over on tender feet, minding pebbles and rock as best I can, and check on the progress of my clothes.

Still damp, like my shoes. I leave my clothes, but pull on my shoes, minus the socks. They're going to take longer to dry, but I need to walk.

"How are you feeling?" Chase returns with more wood for the fire. When he looks at me, his entire face lights up.

"Better. Thank you."

"Want me to put out a chair for you?"

"That would be nice. Can you set it by the water?"

With the sun inching toward the horizon, it's comfortably warm, instead of oppressively hot. Chase deposits the wood next to the fire ring, then heads to the Jeep to grab one of the folding chairs.

"I thought you said we couldn't have any fires?" I twist to look at the fire ring.

"I figured you earned one tonight. Something cozy. I thought we'd cook dogs over the fire."

"Dogs?"

"Hot dogs." He looks at me like I have a screw loose.

No loose screws, just a muddled mind.

"But what about it lighting a beacon?"

"There's no sign of anyone following us. Unless you don't want one? I can cook on the grill?"

"No. A fire would be fun. I feel horrible. I feel like I should be helping."

"Thanks, but I don't want you to exert yourself."

"I'm not as hot as before."

"It's still hotter than it feels. I'd rather you regained your strength and continue hydrating."

"I feel like I've swallowed a river."

"Have you peed?"

"Excuse me?"

"Simple question, but let me explain why. Until you pee, you're still dangerously dehydrated. Your one and only job is to drink water, rest, recuperate, and pee. We're in no rush to do anything."

"My one job is to pee?" I place a hand on my hip, not sure I hear that right. "That's what you're telling me? To pee?"

"Pee and watch your clothes dry." He glances at my shoes. "And try not to walk around too much in those until they dry. Don't need to add blisters to the rest."

"Understood." I click my heels together and give a little salute. "Message received."

"You're a goof." He shakes his head while I grin. "If that's your version of standing at attention, we've got work to do."

"I really feel like I should do something to help out. Can't you give me one job?"

"I already did. Drink water and pee. Then we'll talk."

"So glamorous."

"Such is the life of a princess." Chase winks, and I lose my mind.

How does something so simple make my heart race and butterflies flutter in my stomach?

When this man winks, he's the most handsome man in the world. His eyes sparkle when he winks. Mix that with the gentleness of his smile and that five o'clock shadow that makes him look rugged, along with handsome, and he's my kryptonite.

His full, sculpted lips tempt me in a way I wish they didn't, and that deep, velvety voice does things that make me want forbidden things.

"And here I thought I was the goof." I can't help but respond, loving the easy banter between us.

"Well, I'm almost done foraging. Firewood is few and far between out here, but I think I've got enough for an hour or two. Sit. Relax. Regain your strength." Chase sets my chair next to the tiny river.

His gaze keeps dipping down toward my breasts, where it lingers longer than socially appropriate. It's almost comical watching him snap his gaze back to my eyes, only to have it dip again. He's definitely thinking about my boobs.

The man tries. I give him props for that. Secretly, I don't mind. I want more than his eyes on my breasts. I want his hands and mouth on me.

A rush of desire flows through me, powerful enough to make me stop in my tracks. I have to deflect. I have to do anything to keep him from suspecting the direction of my thoughts.

"Wish I had something to read." I blow out a breath and turn my attention to the water flowing down the stream.

There's something about water and the way it sparkles and shimmers in the sunlight that brings a sense of calm to the most troubled mind. The water's crystal clear, rushing over a sandy gravel bottom. I could sit here and watch the water flow by all day long.

I position the chair at the water's edge and remove my shoes. When I dip my toes in the cool water, tiny ripples form around my feet. The little river smells different than the campsite, where it's musty and dry. The air tastes sweeter. Smells clean and crisp. It entices my soul to let go of any stress it carries and tells my heart to take a chance it otherwise wouldn't.

I push to my feet to stand, letting the water swirl around my ankles. It's cold, not warm like I would expect. From the way the sun beats down on the ground, it's a wonder the water doesn't steam. I gather Chase's shirt around my legs, careful not to get it wet, and stick my hand in the water, enjoying its cool caress. When I press my fingers to my lips, curious about how the water tastes, Chase calls out.

"Don't drink the water. It looks clean but can make you sick."

"I wasn't going to…" I stop myself because I was totally going to try a taste.

"I brought you something." He holds up a tablet.

"What's that?" I wade back to the bank, careful not to splash too much.

"An e-reader packed full of books. You said you wished you had something to read."

"Wow. Thank you." This man is not what I expect. Beneath his tough exterior, he's incredibly thoughtful.

"Well, there's everything from science fiction to romance" He carries a small towel in his other hand.

"Um, thanks." I take the tablet from him and scan the contents of the library. "Are these all your books?" Chase continues to surprise me.

"My tastes are eclectic."

"Thanks. I'm sure I'll find something."

"Awesome, but can I ask you to move back to the Jeep?"

"Why?" What a weird request.

"Because I'm hot and sweaty, and this is a perfect time to take advantage of free water." He points to the stream. "You can stay, but fair warning…" There goes that devastatingly handsome wink again. "I'm stripping all the way down. Just thought I'd warn you, and figured you'd be more comfortable over there, unless you want to watch?" There goes another of those playful winks that make my stomach flutter and my heart race.

"Um, okay."

Before I move, Chase strips out of his shirt. His ripped muscles ripple beneath golden skin. They tighten and flex as my gaze moves down his back, heart pounding and mouth agape. For a moment, I forget to breathe, but then I square off my shoulders. If he's going to strip in front of me, I'm going to enjoy the view.

The real question is why am I reluctant to strip down and join him?

The way his muscles move under his skin mesmerizes me, and I continue to stare as he kicks off his shoes and strips out of his pants. He faces away from me. I think it's on purpose, teasing me with this striptease.

It almost feels like a challenge—like how far will I let him go before running back to the Jeep?

Well, I'm not that shy and selfishly enjoy every flex of muscle as he kicks off his pants. His jeans join his shirt on the sandy ground while I continue to stare at Chase in nothing but boxer briefs. When he walks into the water, he glances over his shoulder and grins with a knowing smile.

"You might want to shut that."

"Excuse me?"

"Your gaping mouth. Like what you see?"

"Nice briefs." My reply catches him off-guard. Guess he didn't expect that.

"Thanks." The corner of his mouth lifts in a smirk, and his eyes latch onto mine as he grabs the waistband of the briefs and slowly drags them down over the sculpted perfection of his ass. "Do you want to join me?" His voice turns husky, darker and edgier than before.

I snap my mouth closed, not expecting that invitation, and realize I'm not nearly as brave as I think. With a grip on the tablet, I sever our connection and turn around.

"I'll just be... Um, I'm just going to sit over there." I practically run back to camp, heart pounding, desire stirring, second-guessing my choices.

When I dare to turn around, Chase faces away from me. The water only comes up to his knees, which means I see the entirety of his broad back and tight ass. He glances over his shoulder and catches me staring at him.

This time, he's the one to give a cheeky salute, but then he bends down to cup water in his hands. When he does, it's impossible not to see other parts of his anatomy, which makes me clench my thighs against a sudden pulsating ache.

Unable to tear my gaze away, I continue to watch as he lathers his body in soap. When it comes time to rinse, he goes to his knees, where it's easier to scoop water over his head and shoulders.

The man is absolutely stunning.

While Chase and I are in this together, his job as my Guardian Protector creates an effective barrier between us when it comes to giving in to our desires. He clearly offered an invitation, but it's up to me to act on it. As much as I want to, something holds me back.

I turn away and try to focus on anything other than the naked man washing not more than a few yards from me. After what feels like forever, Chase finally emerges from the water. I think nothing of it as I twist in my seat, expecting to see a smile on his face and maybe catch another of his heart-throb winks.

But my eyes widen in shock as he saunters toward me, shirtless, no pants, and dripping wet. His wet hair drips onto his shoulders, and those drops of water trail down his chest, drawing my eye as they head further south.

He holds the small towel over his groin but makes no effort to hide what's behind it. He stops right in front of me, eyes intense and searching. That gaze is so powerful; it feels as if he can see right through me.

"The water feels amazing. You may not remember from before, but if you want to freshen up, I promise not to peek, but if you need help scrubbing your back, or washing your hair, I've got a spare hand and plenty of time."

Now, if that's not a blatant proposition?

Talk about an escalation.

The question is, what am I going to do about it?

"Umm…" I close the tablet and place it in my lap. "I don't know…"

Do it!

I stand and drop the tablet in my chair. I take a step back and shake my head for even considering giving in to temptation.

"This is wrong." My gaze drifts to the towel he holds over his groin. "We shouldn't…" I stammer as he gives me a knowing look. My stomach ties itself up in knots as I fight the desire to give in.

I mean, what's the worst that can happen? We're two adults.

Two consenting adults.

And we're going to be spending a lot of time together. Why not enjoy it? Why not live in the moment? I've never done that before.

In fact, the only thing I've done these past six months is run away. It would be a nice change of pace to run toward something.

"There are lots of things we shouldn't do, princess. Let's take a pause." His gaze lingers on my lips, like he's thinking about kissing me. "But I'm not going to pretend there's nothing happening here. I feel you in here." He thumps his chest. "But if you want to keep things professional, we keep things professional. The ball's in your court, but while you're deciding what to do, know that I've spent all day desperately trying not to look at you, and doing my best not to imagine what you look like under my shirt. I've failed miserably on both accounts."

"Chase…" I take a step back, mortified, but strangely turned on. "I just don't know. We can't…"

"You're absolutely right. We shouldn't do this at all." Instead of turning away, he takes a step toward me.

The words I need to say vanish as I place my palm against his chest. The solid *thump-thump* of his heartbeat does strange things to me. I press him back, knowing I'll regret this.

"I want…" I lick my lips and swallow the lump in the back of my throat. "I'm not going to lie and say I haven't thought the same things, but I can't do this."

"Then we don't." Nonplussed, he heads to the back of the Jeep. I keep my back to him as he rummages through his things and gets dressed. The wind kicks up as the sun kisses the horizon. Day is done, and night is fast on its heels, leaving me to wonder about tonight.

About sharing that rooftop tent with Chase.

NINE

Chase

OKAY, I FUCKED THAT UP. I GAVE IN, LOST SIGHT OF THE BIGGER picture, and pushed where I knew I shouldn't. I did everything I've ever said I wouldn't do, and now I get to dance around the fact I didn't blatantly come on to her.

To Cara.

And bombed big time.

Shit, I knew better, and now things are a whole hell of a lot more awkward.

At the back of the Jeep, I put on a clean pair of jeans, a faded T-shirt, and glance at myself in the tiny mirror I screwed into the plywood frame of a makeshift closet. My hand goes to the scruff on my face. I should've taken time in the river to shave, but I was too fucking full of myself, putting on a show for Cara, trying to get her to jump this way or that.

She chose *that*.

Wounded pride aside, I can fix this. I'm a pro at that kind of shit.

Digging through my gear, I pull out two metal roasting tongs, then grab condiments and hot dogs from the fridge. Marching back to the campfire, I set everything down on a rock I placed next to the fire earlier. Cara's up, standing next to our tiny river, staring out at the horizon.

It's a beautiful sight. Both the sunset and the woman enjoying it. I take a knee and light the fire. The scraps of wood I foraged are brittle and dry, perfect kindling to light a blaze, but poor performers when it comes to staying power. I'll be lucky if the fire stays lit past sundown.

Cara looks over her shoulder, watching me set up. I ignore her, which means I'm acutely aware of every move she makes, but grit my teeth and pretend she doesn't exist.

"Can I help?"

I startle at her approach. She takes off her shoes and sets them at the rim of the fire. Smart girl. She knows the best way to get them to dry.

"Drag your chair over. If you could grab mine?" I don't specify what I want her to do with it. It's kind of implied. I'll be walking a very thin line between coddling her and assuming she knows what to do.

Maybe that's what I should focus on? Teaching her how to survive out here on her own. With a nod to myself, I figure it's best to put all the simmering heat between us to the side and focus on keeping her alive.

Yeah, I can do that.

Which means no cuddling in the Jeep while we sleep. Tonight, we lay under the stars with several feet of separation between us.

Cara returns with not just my chair, but the kettle for boiling water.

"I didn't know if you wanted hot cocoa," she says, "or if we wanted to fill up our water reserves while we're next to the river?"

Holy fuck, she's an intuitive person. Yes, that's my plan. I was going to wait until the morning, but why not start boiling water now?

"How about you fill the kettle at the river? We'll boil it while we cook our dogs."

"Hot dogs." She glances at the package of wieners and grins.

"My father never let me eat them. Said they were full of—well, things I didn't want to eat."

"I don't know about that. He may be right, but hot dogs are fucking amazing when cooked over an open flame. Please tell me you'll eat a hot dog because our rations are limited."

"I love hot dogs. Always have, but never got them at home. I had to wait until I had a sleepover at a friend's house and would ask if we could have hot dogs instead of pizza."

"Ah, now pizza is one of my all-time favorite foods. Just not very trail friendly." With that, there's an awkward pause in our conversation while our gazes collide and twist with the chemistry brewing between us.

The very air sparks with energy, and yet I bombed big time.

Cara must sense my unease because she lifts the kettle and points to the river. "I'm just going to…"

Without another word, she spins around and marches toward the river while I admire the way my overly large T-shirt hugs her curves. It comes mid-thigh and suggests much about her tight, toned body.

Down boy.

My dick isn't on board with not pursuing the mutual attraction swirling between me and Cara. It wants more, and it wants it now. It's a struggle to beat back my natural instincts, but I do. By the time Cara returns, I'm back to being fully in control.

"Um, how do we heat it?" She eyes the fire, thinking it through.

"See that flat stone there?" I've got a good blaze going. The fire's going to chew through the dry wood voraciously, but I have enough to boil water.

"Yes?"

"We want to set it inside the fire ring, next to the flames."

"Just toss it in?" She approaches the fire cautiously and eyes it with trepidation.

"Well, not toss." I extend my hand. "Give it here. I'll show you."

She hands me the rock, and I set it inside the outer ring of stones, then place the kettle on top of it.

"The flames will heat it from the one side, but once we see steam, it's almost done."

"Almost?"

"I like to get a good rolling boil before I pull it off. Long enough to kill any parasites or bacteria that could be in the river." I point upstream, toward the mountains. "You never know who or what animal pooped in the water."

"Eww."

"See why I didn't want you to drink it?"

"Well, now, every time I look at it, I'm going to envision an animal pooping in the water."

"And that will keep you alive." I settle back on my heels, relieved that we're able to put the previous tense energy and awkwardness of my failed attempt to seduce her behind us.

This feels better. It's relaxed and comfortable. Not that the latent sexual energy isn't still simmering between us, but it's manageable now.

On the back burner as it was.

"Chase, about earlier…" She nibbles on her lower lip and her brows pinch together.

"You don't have to…" I cringe because the only thing worse than failing miserably is having to talk about it.

"No, just give me a second to get my thoughts out. I'll feel better if I can say what I want to say."

"Okay." This is where I should apologize for coming on too strong.

For baiting her.

Because that's exactly what I did. I pushed until she pushed back, desperate to see how far I could take things. It was a total dick move and I'm embarrassed by the whole thing.

"First off—" she takes a deep breath, "I told you I'm terrible at saying thank you. So, if there's anything you take away from this, know that I truly am thankful. When we first met, I wasn't at my best. I was tired, cranky, strung out, and terrified. I came off kind of bitchy, and I want to apologize for that."

"You don't have to apologize…"

"Just let me get this off my chest." She holds up a hand, stopping me.

"Sorry." I gesture for her to continue. "Go on."

"I'm terrified." She takes a deep breath and places her palm over her belly as if to steady herself. "I've never been more terrified in my life. When Hank was shot, everything hit me all at once. I didn't appreciate how much these people wanted me dead. You and I definitely rubbed each other the wrong way our first night together. I accept my fault in that. Which made what came next even harder." She swallows and looks away from me.

I give her the space to collect her thoughts as the silence stretches between us. After a few long minutes, she takes another breath and stares into the fire.

"But then, after we spent more time together, after you took the time to teach me how to drive, and explain why we couldn't have a fire, I saw another side of you. You're an attractive man, way out of my league…"

"I'm not…"

"Let me finish." Her eyes cut to me with irritation.

"Sorry."

"This—" she makes a vague gesture encompassing me, the Jeep, and the desert all around us, "—this is a dream. It's not real."

I disagree with that. The desert is a fickle mistress, ready to kill at the slightest provocation, but I bite my tongue and let Cara finish.

Everything about this is exceptionally real.

"And the fact we share some kind of chemistry just makes that dream seem more unreal. As if this is what I could have… If I wanted it." She finally drags her attention from the flames to look me in the eye. "And I want it. I would love to have it. But mixing these things up seems like a mistake. I don't want to rush into something that's never going to work out because I lost sight of the bigger picture." She bites her lower lip and breathes out, long and slow. "Does any of that make sense?"

"Princess…" I watch her expression closely, trying to gauge her reaction to that moniker. The lines of stress on her face soften, which gives me the green light to continue. "I agree with everything you said. We're out in the middle of nowhere, forced into close proximity. Spending that much time with someone either turns you into enemies from incompatibilities, or brings you together and heightens any attraction between you. But we have something else thrown into the mix. My job is to protect you, and I'm the one at fault for pushing boundaries or suggesting anything inappropriate. I'm sorry for that."

Her smile is soft and gracious. Cara closes her eyes and takes in a deep breath. Being this open and honest with another person doesn't come easily to her. I should be grateful she's comfortable enough around me to express herself honestly. It's a gift I won't squander.

"Thank you for understanding, and thank you for saving me from heat exhaustion."

"For someone who claims they don't remember to say thank you, you're definitely doing a bang-up job of it."

"Sorry. I do suck at it, but you've already gone above and beyond. I just didn't want to seem ungrateful, or have you think I didn't want…" She makes another vague gesture that's all too easy to decipher.

She wants me.

TEN

Chase

_____

"YOU KNOW WHAT?" I FIGURE IT'S TIME TO SWITCH GEARS AND END this conversation before it gets too deep.

"What?" Cara holds her hands in front of her, twisting her fingers. She does that when she's nervous.

"The sun is setting. The colors in the sky are vibrant and beautiful. Before long, the stars will be shining brighter than ever before. How about we cook our hot dogs, enjoy a meal, then camp out under the stars?"

"Like not in the tent?" She points to the Jeep where our tent remains folded inside its clamshell. "What about snakes and scorpions and other creepy crawlies?"

"I think we can risk it."

"You sure?"

"Absolutely."

"That sounds fun. I'd like that. I've never done any of this. It's as if I'm on a great adventure. I want to soak it all in." She sets up our chairs, then looks to me. "What's next?"

"Have you ever cooked over an open flame?"

"S'mores as a kid."

"Hot dogs are no different, and like S'mores, you get to decide *Flame On!* or *Flame Off.*"

"I prefer my *marshy-mellows* golden brown, not charred. I like my hot dogs just the opposite. Charred black. Makes them juicier."

"You're a woman after my own heart. It takes dedication and patience to roast the perfect *marshy-mellow,*" I repeat the weird way she said the word. "Did you mean to say it that way?"

"Oh, it's just a game my parents and I played. Made it seem like more fun." Talking about her parents kills the light in her eyes.

To witness the murder of a parent is a horrendous experience, rife with lifelong PTSD with horrific flashbacks. It seems Cara lost two things, which makes it all the worse. Not only did she lose a father, but she lost the hero she thought he was. Such a loss is unfathomable to me. My heart aches for her. I want to pull her into a hug and protect her from those memories. But I can't hug her, and I can't protect her. Instead, I try to keep things light.

"Well, I like it, and now I'm wishing we had some *marshy-mellows* to roast. Alas, I've only got hot dogs and oatmeal."

"Let's save the oatmeal for breakfast, pretty sure it won't cook very well on a stick." She crinkles her nose, making me laugh, and grabs the tongs I hold out for her.

Together, we spear our hot dogs and roast them over the fire. We sit in companionable silence for a time, turning our hot dogs, watching them sizzle and pop. The wood burns quickly, but I've got enough stored up to finish cooking our meal. If we were anywhere else, I'd build a raging fire and watch the flames dance and the embers glow.

But this works for several reasons. With the sun setting, light from the fire isn't easily seen, and by the time the sun disappears, the fire will be out, which means no one will see where we are. I haven't seen anyone traveling behind us, but that doesn't mean they're not out there.

For now, I enjoy being present in the moment, and as the sun sets, the first stars peek out of the sky. Beside me, Cara pulls her hot dog off the fire. Blows on it. Then take a bite.

With the way her pretty lips pucker when she blows, and how

those lips wrap around the hot dog, my mind goes all the way to the gutter. That forces me to shift and make a slight adjustment to my jeans.

Instant.

Fucking.

Hard-on.

"Mmm, that's good." Her little moan of satisfaction sends warmth tingling down my spine, where it coils in my balls and demands more.

I may have decided to keep things professional, but my dick isn't on board with that plan.

"You like it?" I smile at her and take my first bite.

There's nothing better than a hot dog grilled over a wood fire. The char on the outside makes the juicy flavors from within pop. It's enough to make me moan as well, but I don't.

I can't.

She catches me looking at her and smiles back. "You're really something."

"How's that?" I'm curious about what thoughts she carries in her head, especially if they're about me.

"A Guardian Protector with some really cool skills."

"Yeah, that's me. I've got tons of really cool skills." It's almost as if my dick hijacked my mouth, pouring out over-the-top innuendo. Fortunately, Cara doesn't seem to notice.

We sit comfortably as blended hues of purple and pink turn the horizon into a beautiful tapestry of light fading to black. The sky darkens overhead and ushers in the night.

After finishing my first hot dog, I roast a second while Cara stares up at the stars. Once my hot dog is charred, I kick out the fire, spreading the wood to let the flames die out. The embers will glow for quite some time but won't be visible from a distance like the flames. Out here in the desert, it's easy to be complacent about other people.

Easy to forget exactly how far one can see.

We settle back into our chairs next to each other, warmed by the embers and companionship alike.

"You told me you've never seen stars like this?" Overhead, the stars put on a show.

"Never."

"Can you pick out the Big Dipper?"

"That's the only one I can identify." She points to the sky and traces out the lines of the Big Dipper.

"Do you know how to find the North Star?"

"That, I don't know."

"The North Star, or Polaris, is easy to find on most clear nights. Just follow the two stars on the end of the Big Dipper's cup." I show her what I mean. "Those point to Polaris. Once you find the North Star, you've also found the tip of the handle of the Little Dipper. Some call it Ursa Minor, for little bear. The Big Dipper is Ursa Major, for big bear."

"That's cool."

"It is when I sit here and realize humanity has been staring at the same night sky for thousands of years. They connected the stars, forming patterns that reminded them of animals, people, gods, and things. Those became our modern-day constellations."

"That's really cool. Thousands of years ago, people saw the same thing we're looking at tonight."

"I've always thought so, and not only did they name the constellations, they used them to navigate by land and sea. It's why the North Star is so very important. Doesn't help you during the day, but you can set your direction at night and know which way you need to go in the morning. You said you only know the Big Dipper. It's only a part of Ursa Major. The handle of the Big Dipper is the Bear's tail."

I point out the rest of the constellation to her, loving the way it draws us close. Which isn't me putting the moves on her, but a necessity for her to see where I point. I hold out my hand, pointing to each star, while she leans over my shoulder, looking down my arm to where my finger points.

We spend the next hour exhausting my rich knowledge of the heavens when we're treated to a meteor shower.

"A shooting star!" Cara jumps in her seat and tugs on my sleeve.

"Look."

The meteor puts on a show with a trail of fire and sparks behind it. It's a big one, blazing across the sky for several seconds before burning out. Most last the blink of an eye, but we're treated to a true delight. It explodes in a million tiny sparks and the burned-out bits and pieces fade until they disappear completely.

"Did you make a wish?" I grab her hand, thrilled she got to see a truly rare event.

"I forgot." She scans the heavens, nibbling on her lower lip. "Is it too late?"

"I don't think there's a time limit."

"Well then, I just did." She nods, exaggerating the gesture, then looks at me with the brightest smile.

In my peripheral vision, another meteor lights up the sky.

"Look!" I can't help but shout, excited to be treated to not just one meteor, but another right on its heels. This one is smaller than the other, but blazes across the sky with greenish-blue fire.

"Wow." She grips my hand in excitement. "Do I get to make another wish?"

"Princess, you can make all the damn wishes you want."

"Look! There's more."

Indeed, there are more. Three lights streak across the sky.

"I think we're being treated to a light show."

"Are they dangerous?"

"No, the light you see is them burning up in the atmosphere. Those are small, but we have the best viewing conditions on the planet." I kick my ankle across my opposite knee, loving everything about tonight.

We're treated to an amazing display over the next hour. Then, as suddenly as it began, the meteor shower ends.

"Well, I guess the heavens are done. I'm going to pack up the Jeep and grab our blankets." One benefit of roasting hot dogs is cleaning up is a piece of cake. There are only the tongs to deal with and they're clean with one swipe of cloth.

I head back to the fire and toss down a ground cloth, then lay out our sleep sacks for the night.

"If you're done, I'm going to stow the chairs." I like to keep things tight, which means I keep a clean campsite; one I can vacate at a moment's notice without leaving trash behind. I'm a firm believer of leaving only footprints.

"I'll lay out our sleeping bags." Cara jumps in to help.

I don't correct her because there's no need. Soon, we'll need down sleeping bags, but we'll get there when we get there.

When I return to the dying fire, I take a pause. Cara lined up our sleep sacks side by side instead of setting them a few feet apart like I intended. Too late to fix that now.

I suppress a groan as I kick out the embers of the fire, douse them with water from the river, and bury the remains under dirt. Out here, sometimes all of that isn't enough. Coals from a hot fire can be persistent bastards.

"Isn't that a bit of overkill for putting out the fire?" Cara cocks her head, watching me intently.

"When I was young," I explain, "my parents and I started a fire in the woods. We followed all the proper safety steps. Doused with water. Covered in dirt. But in the morning, when I got up to restart the fire, I placed a fistful of pine needles over the remnants of our fire from the night before. I left for a moment to grab tinder to start the fire and came back to a wisp of smoke coming up from the pine needles. Evidently, there was enough heat in the buried coals, even after dousing them with water, to relight the fire."

"Really?"

"It's a lesson I've never forgotten. Always respect fire."

Cara and I bed down for the night—she in her sack, me in mine. We don't touch, but I feel her on a visceral level, and the urge not to turn to my side and take her into my arms is far more difficult than I could ever imagine. Instead of falling asleep, we curl in toward each other and talk about everything, anything, and nothing at all.

I could spend the rest of my life in this moment and be content, but one thing I've learned about this job is to never allow myself to be complacent. There are men hunting Cara, and it's only a matter of time before they find her.

ELEVEN

Cara

———

CHASE AND I STARE DEEPLY INTO EACH OTHER'S EYES AS WE GET ready for bed, but I'm not tired. I don't think I can fall asleep, not this close to Chase. Weirdly, being outside, with more room than the interior of the Jeep, feels more intimate.

More romantic.

And I'm dying to learn more about this amazing man.

"I'm really curious about your mother. She sounds like an amazing woman." I fold my hands over my belly, afraid that if I let them rest on the ground, I might accidentally reach out to touch him.

"She's incredible. Very no nonsense. Never put up with my shit."

"Do you have any siblings?"

"No. My parents couldn't have children. I'm adopted and an only child. I always wanted a sister, though."

I bite my lower lip, not sure what's appropriate to ask, or not ask. "How old were you when you were adopted?"

"I was a baby."

"A baby? What happened?" My voice trails off because this feels like intimate territory. There's sharing stories of our lives, and then there's diving in too deep.

This feels deep.

"My parents died in a car accident."

"Oh, I'm so sorry. That had to be horrific."

"I was adopted so young that my adoptive parents are all I've ever known. I don't have any memories of my parents or my older sister. In some ways, I think that's for the best."

"What do you mean?"

"There are no birth parents out there who gave me up because they didn't want me. I know mine loved me. Tragedy took them from me. Many adopted children spend their lives looking for their birth parents, needing answers as to why they were given up, only to be disappointed later. I don't have that."

"I can see how that might be rough." I stop for a second and replay what he said in my head. "You mentioned a sister. Was she adopted as well?"

"I'm not entirely sure."

"What does that mean?"

"I don't know if she survived. My parents only ever told me my birth parents died in the accident. They never mentioned my sister."

"If you were a baby when it happened, how did you find out about a sister?"

"There was one conversation when I was like ten or so. I got curious about where I came from and asked the usual questions. They mentioned it in passing."

"In passing? Did they know if she survived?"

"There's no record of it. No death certificate. My mother was always very open with me. They wanted a baby, like most adoptive parents, but weren't interested in an older child."

"How old was your sister when the accident happened?"

"About ten? Maybe twelve?" He sounds unsure.

"Have you ever wondered what happened to her?"

"This is going to sound terrible, and please don't judge me."

Don't judge? That's weird.

"Okay?"

"I want to believe she didn't survive."

"Didn't survive? You can't mean that. Why would you want that?"

"Because if she survived, she should've tried to find me."

"Maybe she tried and couldn't find you?" I press my lips together.

"Maybe." He shrugs. "I just thought if she wanted to find me, she would've. She's ten or twelve years older than me and had plenty of time to try. For me, it's easier to think she didn't survive."

"I'm sorry. I can't imagine what that must be like. Maybe there's a reason she didn't try to find you. Or maybe she tried and failed?"

"I don't know, and it doesn't really matter now. If she's alive, she's never been a part of my life, so it's not like I lost anything."

"I suppose." My heart breaks for him, and I'm not sure if I believe him. Not knowing must be like living with a bit of your heart ripped out. If it were me, I'd want to know.

"Besides, I've got the best parents in the world and a job I love. I think that's enough."

Enough?

Again, I don't believe him.

"When did you enlist in the Army?" I almost ask when he became a Navy SEAL, then remember he's an Army Scout Sniper. Different branch of service.

"When I turned eighteen."

"That's young."

"On my eighteenth birthday, my parents gave me a choice. I could follow my mother's career in the Merchant Marines, join the military, or go to college."

"And you chose the military?"

"Best decision I ever made. College wasn't for me. Although, I did eventually get my degree using the GI Bill." He rubs his sternum, as if in pain. "Once I joined, I no longer felt a need to find out if my sister survived. Call it selfish, foolish, arrogant, or whatever, but I had my parents, and the military is really one big family. Besides, it's too late now."

"Why?"

"Because, I don't want to go through the effort only to find out she survived and never bothered to look for me."

"What if she did?"

"Honestly, it's easier to focus on other things. I said my reasoning may not be the best, but I don't want to open myself up to that kind of heartache. Not when my life is good the way it is." He lets out a deep breath. "I told you it was bad. Please don't judge me too harshly."

"You have time now. It's not too late."

I promised not to judge, but if it were me, I'd want to know if I had a sibling out there. Not to mention, I would assume she'd want to know what happened to her baby brother. If there's one thing I can do for Chase, maybe it's this?

Can that be repayment for everything he's doing for me? Or will he see it as meddling where I shouldn't? Not knowing the answer, I shift topics and circle back to his degree.

"What did you get your degree in?"

"Criminal Science, if you can believe it."

"To be honest, I'm not surprised. I figure a lot of military wind up in law enforcement after they get out. Is that how you joined Guardian HRS?"

"Yes, and no. First, I looked into the FBI and CIA. They seemed more in line with the kinds of things I was doing as a sniper. Eventually, the FBI hired me."

"Why aren't you with the FBI now?"

"I was an FBI agent working in counter-terrorism, which is where I ran across Guardian HRS for the first time."

"How did you go from being an FBI agent to working with the Guardians?"

"One of their Guardian teams, Delta team, works closely with the FBI in difficult hostage negotiations. I worked with them on a hostage case, and they seemed a much better fit."

"Well, I'm glad you're here. Or rather, I wish you didn't have to be, and that I didn't need protection, but since I do, and you're here, I'm glad we met each other."

"Sounds ominous."

"Ominous? Why do you say that?"

"*Met each other?* Sounds like you've already moved on."

"That's not what I meant. I was just trying to say I'm glad we— I'm glad I had a chance to… Hell, I don't know what I'm trying to say."

"I'm glad you're here too." He reaches over and takes my hand in his. "It's a beautiful night beneath the stars, and late enough we should probably try to get some sleep." With those words, he releases my hand and shifts beside me, presumably to get more comfortable on the hard ground.

I remain on my back, staring up at the stars. It's a big surprise for me—a non-outdoorsy kind of gal—but I'm really enjoying being outdoors.

One thing that's odd is the temperature drop. No longer in oppressive triple digits, the temperature dropped the moment the sun set. It's almost chilly, but not so cold that sleeping outside is uncomfortable.

While Chase drifts off to sleep, I keep my eyes glued to the heavens, eager to see more shooting stars and make more wishes, but slumber eventually finds me and takes me into the land of dreams.

When I wake, it's to find myself tucked in the warmth of Chase's arms. His body curls around mine and his easy breathing tells me he's still asleep. The sun peeks over the horizon, painting another masterpiece in the heavens above.

I want to turn and look at him, but I don't want to rouse him too soon. Instead, I slowly extricate my way out of his arms. Once free, I stand and stretch, limbering up muscles tight and sore from sleeping on the ground. When I look down at him, sleep smooths out the hard lines of his face, turning him from handsome to absolutely stunning.

A strange feeling I can't quite explain overcomes me; a mixture of peace, comfort, and something indescribable.

I can't remember the last time I felt so safe. Funny that it would take running for my life to the place where our lives intersected.

A bird surprises me by chirping in one of the scruffy trees. It feels like forever since I've seen any sign of an animal since Chase took us off-road and deep into BLM land. I take a moment to soak in the beauty of the world around me; then I turn my attention to the virile man still asleep on the ground.

"Good morning, beautiful." He winks and I startle, nearly jumping out of my skin.

"I thought you were asleep." My heart races from fright.

"How could I sleep without you in my arms?"

"But you didn't move when I got up."

"It looked like you needed a moment, and I enjoyed watching you." He climbs to his feet and reaches for my hand. I move toward him, inexplicably drawn to this man. "How did you sleep?" He cocks his head to the side, gazing into my eyes.

"Fine, and you?"

"Never better. I prefer sleeping outside."

"I slept well, considering that is the first time I've slept outside on the ground."

"Really?"

"Yeah."

"Maybe we'll have to do it more often?" There's something about a smile on this man's face that makes me swoon. It makes me want other things as well, things I can't have.

"I'm still not convinced about sleeping on the dirt."

"Why's that?"

"You've got me worried about scorpions and snakes."

"Snakes aren't so bad if you leave them alone."

"But what if one crawls inside my sleeping bag?"

Chase chuckles and pulls me to him. My stomach flutters, and my knees grow weak. "They're not that active at night. Already found a warm rock to curl up with and very unlikely to leave the warmth of said rock to curl up with you. Remember, the sun spends all day baking the land. The rocks radiate that heat back into the environment at night. Curled under a rock is the perfect place to snooze if you're a snake or other creepy crawly."

"Oh."

My heart skips a beat when Chase's attention suddenly shifts from my face to something over my shoulder. His body stiffens, and his grip on me tightens as if preparing for battle.

"Shit." He hisses through gritted teeth.

"What's wrong?" I wrench away from him, turning to get a glimpse of what he's looking at.

On the distant horizon, a small wisp of dust twists into the sky. He said we would see lights at night and plumes of dust during the day if anyone traveled across the desert. That plume is too far to make out any details, but sudden terror slams into me. We're alone and exposed in this barren landscape.

If we can see them coming, won't they be able to track us leaving?

TWELVE

Cara

—————

"WE'VE GOT TO MOVE." CHASE'S VOICE IS URGENT AND LOW.

He releases me and starts packing up our gear with lightning speed. The urgency in his tone is a palpable thing, and his need to protect and keep me safe, transforms him into a single-minded machine.

I feel his objective—to protect me—reverberating through my bones.

"What is it?" I scan the horizon, but all I see are lazy trails of dust spiraling up into the air. "Who is it?"

"Don't know and don't care. Could be folks out having fun off-roading, or it could be someone sent to kill you." His voice is terse and grim. "Either way, we're not sticking around to find out. We need to go."

Another plume of dust appears in the distance, growing larger as it draws closer. Now I know why Chase needs us to move fast: whoever they are, they're headed right for us, and they're coming in fast.

Chase barks orders, and I jump to respond.

"Quick. Grab our things." He heads to the fire pit and kicks more dirt and gravel over the remnants of our fire from the night before.

Adrenaline pulses through my veins as I stuff our sleep sacks into the back of the Jeep.

Chase's eyes burn into me as he shouts. "In the Jeep. Now!" He races around to the driver's seat as I scramble to jump in.

"What's happening?" My voice is barely a whisper; I'm paralyzed by fear.

"We're leaving." His attention shifts to the cloud of dust in the distance. He starts the engine, and the Jeep roars to life. With a determined grip on the steering wheel, Chase slams his foot on the pedal and we surge forward, careening over the barren landscape.

My gaze drifts to the menacing plume in the distance, and I grip the seat tight, turning my knuckles white with fear.

Instead of keeping an eye on that plume of dust, Chase drives with an unwavering intensity. He smashes the pedal down hard, propelling the Jeep forward in a wild rush over the rough and uneven terrain. I bounce so high in my seat that my head bangs against the roof, and I grimace in pain.

Chase keeps one hand firmly on the steering wheel as he maneuvers us through and around cacti, rocks, sandy hills, and washed-out riverbeds. I cling to my seat as we jerk and bounce over the desert in a desperate attempt to escape our pursuers. He scans the horizon for any signs of movement or life, but all I see are endless miles of emptiness ahead of us.

My heart pounds as he drives at what I consider reckless speed. What if the Jeep breaks down? What if we're left stranded out here? I try not to think about who might be following us across this arid landscape. They could be harmless off-road enthusiasts enjoying a day off-road, but my gut churns and twists.

It knows the truth.

Whoever that is, they're after me.

And *they* want me dead.

How is Chase going to get us out of this?

Chase drives relentlessly, trying to gain distance. We climb up a steep hill, then swerve sharply down the other side. Tires skid over loose gravel as we fishtail down the steep incline. Washed-out gullies, areas impassable and thick with cacti, hinder our race across the desert. Chase faces a score of obstacles, which slow our pace, but the man is relentless.

He says nothing, but I feel the urgency that drives him. His need for caution outweighs his desire for speed, and I sense his frustration growing with every passing minute as we rush through narrow canyons and navigate around towering cacti until, at last, we reach an open expanse.

"Do you see them?" He glances through the rearview mirror, scanning behind us.

Sweat drips from my forehead and stings my eyes as I scan behind us. At first, I see nothing; an empty desert, arid land where nothing seems to live, let alone survive. Then I see movement behind us. A speck of black separating from the dust rising in the air. My gut twists because I see our pursuers.

Two black pickup trucks.

They're closer now.

Gaining.

"Yes. Two trucks."

"Shit." He steps on the gas, and we speed away faster over the rocky terrain, bouncing over the jarring ground. We weave in and out of gullies and down rocky streams devoid of water.

Far ahead of us, I see where Chase is taking us. There's a road —a paved highway. It's at least five miles away. Maybe ten. The Jeep roars forward with Chase urging us onward as he pushes past the limits of its power and speed. I'm afraid of breaking an axle or shredding the tires as we vault over berms and careen off rocks. We take sharp turns and veer around obstacles as Chase extends our lead.

I breathe out in relief as we close in on that highway, although what we're going to do when we get there is beyond me. The wind whistles by as we race toward safety, but then Chase suddenly steps on the brakes and we skid to a stop.

"What are you doing?" Fear grips my stomach and twists it into knots.

"Princess, I need you to get into the driver's seat."

"What?" I stare at him as he races to the back of the Jeep and pops open the back.

"Do it." His voice cuts hard, making me jump.

I scramble behind the wheel as Chase pulls out a long rifle and several sidearms. He crawls into the cramped space in the back, contorting his body around the customizations built into the Jeep.

The dust cloud grows, hanging heavy in the air with a deadly reminder of how close our pursuers are to catching up to us.

Chase lies on his belly, propping the barrel of the long rifle on what looks to be a burlap canvas sack. He loads his ammo and settles in while I shake in fear behind the wheel.

He takes aim at the lead vehicle.

A bright flash of light momentarily blinds me, but that's nothing compared to the sharp report of the rifle within the confined space of the Jeep. I cover my ears as pain rips into my eardrums.

But Chase makes the shot, blowing out the tires of the lead truck. It skids to a stop, and the second one slams into it from behind.

That'll teach them to drive so close to each other. Four men burst out of the first truck, arms and legs pumping hard as they dash for the second vehicle.

But Chase is ready.

He takes aim.

Fires.

The sharp, acrid smell of gunpowder fills the inside of the Jeep and stings my eyes. My nose crinkles from the sharpness of the smoke and I can't help but sneeze. When I'm done, the metallic tang of gunpowder settles thickly on my tongue.

Two of the men fall to the ground, their bodies limp and unmoving. The remaining men's adrenaline-fueled steps are clumsy and uncontrolled. They look back, faces twisted with fear as they struggle to make it to the relative safety of the other truck.

Only Chase's expert aim cuts them down as well.

"Now, princess," Chase's voice is low and commanding. "Drive."

My heart races as I grip the wheel and stomp on the accelerator, feeling the jerk as our vehicle lurches forward with a power I don't anticipate. The second vehicle extricates itself from the first, and resumes its pursuit, leaving four lifeless bodies on the ground behind us.

Four dead men.

My fingers claw the wheel in a death grip as the Jeep careens over the rugged terrain. While thankful for the lesson in off-road driving yesterday, I'm not prepared for this and am more likely to make us crash than reach the highway in front of us.

Chase twists from his position in the back, looking ahead.

"There. See that hill?"

"Yes?" I see the hill he points toward. A hill with no road leading up to it. It's nothing but a steep rocky grade going up for twenty feet or more. Steeper than anything I've driven so far.

"Get on top."

"But…" My hesitation causes him to curse under his breath.

"One rule, Princess. One damn rule."

Do as I say.

I jerk the wheel to the left, toward the steep bank and floor the Jeep. The Jeep tilts back, dangerously so, as its tires chew through the sand and rock, climbing upward while I pray we don't flip over backward and tumble down in a twisted mess of metal, but to my amazement, the Jeep crests the rise, and I slam on the brakes with a sigh of relief.

"Be ready." Chase looks back at me with one part pride and one part irritation.

I'm about to ask, "ready for what," when he leaps out of the Jeep. Swinging the back of the Jeep open, he props his weapon on the spare tire and takes aim at the truck hot in pursuit.

Watching him in action is an ethereal experience. The man is death with that rifle and his single-mindedness to kill makes me tremble.

While I watch, he takes aim, and it's as if the world slows down to a crawl. Like he did with the first vehicle, he takes out the lead tires, shooting both in rapid succession. This time, however, he doesn't wait for the men to exit the vehicle. He shoots the driver through the front window, then the passenger.

Chase turns to me.

"Do not move."

I hold up my hands, surrendering, although I don't know why. Perhaps it's because, for the first time since we met, I realize Chase is more than a Protector. He's a lethal killing machine with no remorse for those who meet the wrong end of his gun.

He drops to the ground. With the higher ground, he claims the advantage. After the way he barked his order at me, I don't dare move, but that doesn't mean I don't twist in my seat, completely transfixed.

Chase crawls to the edge of the cliff. There, he sets up his position and waits. A few seconds go by.

A minute passes.

I sit stone still, hands frozen in place and eyes glued to the man before me. The ticking of the clock is like a metronome counting down the seconds.

All I hear is the thudding of my heart and the blood racing past my ears. A minute stretches to five, and then ten. The smell of fear and anticipation hangs heavy in the air: a mix of sweat and gunpowder, and something else I can't place.

Time slows to a crawl. My anticipation builds and twists around my fear.

I'm about to open my mouth and ask what we're waiting for, when two sharp pops reverberate through the air and make my ears ring.

Suddenly, Chase is back. He stows his weapon, then hops into the passenger seat. I look at him, eyes wide and palms slick with sweat.

"What do we do now?"

"You keep driving." He pulls at his chin and scratches at the scruff on his face.

"What?" I nearly yelp in surprise.

"Keep driving, princess. Don't stop for anything."

"But… We're leaving dead men behind?"

"Don't." The sharpness of his tone takes me aback. "Stop questioning every damn thing. I don't have time to explain everything to you. Do what I say and do it without question. Without hesitation. Do you understand me?"

I pull back, chagrined, as he reminds me of our roles in the worst possible way. Chase is not some man to swoon over. He's here for one, and only one, purpose.

Keep me alive.

Anything beyond that is nothing more than a fantasy. What a way to put me in my place. Pain rips through my heart for foolishly believing things could be different between me and Chase.

Without any further prompting from him, I aim the Jeep for the steep incline and drive over the edge with my teeth gritted and my heart pounding. Somehow, I manage not to wreck us, which is a blessing. Without waiting for him to tell me which direction to go, I head toward the highway that's still several miles away.

I don't know what to do about the bodies, or the vehicles, but figure Chase will correct me if I'm not doing what he wants. From now on, I'm going to remember our respective roles.

I won't question a damn thing he says.

Not.

One.

Damn.

Thing.

As I head toward the highway, a little piece inside of me withers and dies. Eight men lost their lives today, and here I am pouting like a spoiled princess who got yelled at by a man.

This isn't who I am.

This isn't my life.

For the hundredth time, I curse my father. I curse him for what he did, and I curse him for turning me into a witness to his crime.

For the next several minutes, I say nothing. When I finally make it to the highway, I don't ask Chase which direction to go. If he wants to bark orders and tell me what to do, then he needs to bark those damn orders.

Until then, I'm doing whatever the hell I want and he can go fuck himself. I didn't deserve that dressing down, or the berating tone of his voice.

Once we reach the blacktop of the highway, I push the accelerator down and floor the Jeep. We race down the road, passing cars and trucks, until Chase places his hand on my thigh.

"Slow down. Where's the fire?"

I shove his hand off my knee, more forcefully than I intend, but he gets the message. Chase gives me a look, but says nothing. He folds his hands together and leaves them in his lap while I chide myself for letting my emotions get the better of me.

I foolishly allowed myself to think something special was happening between me and Chase, but he's made it clear my only role in this is blindly to obey his damn orders.

Intense situations bring about intense emotions. I don't know who said that, but they are very wise.

It's a reminder those intense emotions don't hold up once the pressure is gone.

Shame on me. I made a mistake.

I won't make another.

THIRTEEN

Chase

When I received this assignment, my intent was to take Cara and disappear into the vastness of BLM land. That intent depended on an assumption; that she was completely divested of anything that could track her.

If I'd been unsure about that, I would've handled things differently. Which begs the question: how did they find us?

That's a question I need to answer, because if I try to disappear with her again, they'll simply keep finding her.

The biggest pitfall to being a solo operator is I'm a one-man army. There's a limit to what I can do.

My best defense, the greatest protection I can offer Cara, is to prevent anyone from finding us in the first place. If that defense fails, then it's up to me to take out those who want her dead. Just like I did to the eight assholes who are currently getting fried to a crisp back in the desert.

What did I miss?

Bravo team separated her from all her possessions, along with her purse and cellphone. She kept her underwear on, despite being told to remove everything. I tossed her bra and panties immediately after discovering she still wore them. That was long before we turned off the road. She's not wearing, or carrying, anything from her previous life. She should be stripped clean, what I call naïve.

There should be *no* trace of her existence on this planet.

Zero.

My mind churns, looking for where I went wrong.

Cara takes a left turn onto the highway, heading north, which is perfect. She had a fifty-fifty chance and chose correctly. While she drives, I call in what happened to Command.

"Confirm identity." The monotone on the other end of the line sounds like a machine, but is really one of Mitzy's techies who mans the communications array.

I rattle off my information, confirming my identity, then add in the code for the severity of my situation. We're basically at *shit-hitting-the-proverbial-fan* on the scale of what makes up a shitstorm.

Eight bodies.

Eight bodies with my signature written all over them. That's going to leave a trail. Those bullets can be traced back to my gun and my phone carries a GPS tracker of everywhere I've been. That links me to Cara.

My goal was to cut Cara off from the world, not attach her to me in a way that can be positively tracked.

Fucking shit.

This is a shitstorm on steroids.

"Hey, Chase, hear you have a situation?" The baritone voice of none other than Forest Summers booms through the phone. This man, along with his sister, Skye Summers, founded the Guardians. Which turns this shitstorm into an ass-puckering event.

When the boss of your boss's boss is the first on the line? Yeah, I've royally fucked things up.

When I interviewed for my position, everyone mentioned the two founders of Guardian HRS, but mostly they speak about Forest Summers. I was told he tends to be very hands on when it comes to the operations of the company, but I never believed he'd be *this* hands on.

"If you consider leaving behind eight dead in the middle of the desert a situation, then I'd say I have a major shitstorm of a situation."

"Eight bodies?" Forest sounds impressed.

"Yeah. Two trucks. Four men a piece. I'm working protection on…"

"Cara." He completes my sentence for me, surprising me by using Cara's new identity.

I didn't think anyone but Mitzy's team knew that.

"Yes."

"Hang on." Indistinct sounds from the other end have me holding my breath, but then Forest returns. "I've got Sam and CJ on the line. Mitzy is here too."

All the top brass?

It's worse than I thought. I'm in deep shit and probably moments away from being fired.

"Chase, I hear you've gotten yourself into a bit of a mess." Sam's voice is as smooth as silk, but has an underlying hardness to it.

"Yes, sir. Two vehicles found us in the desert. I had no choice but to take them out. If I hadn't, they would have killed her."

"I've got eyes on it." The high-pitched voice of Mitzy, the technical lead of Guardian HRS, pipes up on the phone.

Eyes? What the fuck does she mean by *eyes?*

"We're getting images in now." There's a slight pause on the other end of the line, then she's back. "I see the bodies of one, two, three…" There's a pause on the line. Static crackles in my ear, then Mitzy's back. "You said eight?"

"Affirmative."

"Hmm…" She pauses on the other end and I can only imagine her mouth twisting over some discrepancy.

"What's that?" Sam's gruff voice demands an answer.

"*Our eyes in the sky* only see seven." The ways she places particular emphasis on *eyes in the sky* make me think she's referencing some particular tech.

I'm aware of *Smaug*, a high-altitude drone, created by Mitzy's technical team, and great for high-altitude surveillance. Its ability to discriminate objects on the ground is scary accurate, but *Smaug* needs to launch and needs to be directly over the area it's surveilling. This seems like something else.

"Definitely eight." I scratch my chin. "Is it possible one of them crawled under one of the vehicles?"

"Don't know. *Our eyes* can't see under the vehicles. But give me time." She pauses for a split second before continuing. "Although, if one of them crawled under one of the trucks to get out of the sun, we should be able to make out tracks on the ground."

"I don't leave the enemy living. If one of them is still alive…" I don't mean to sound defensive, but it's the truth. I'm an Army Scout Sniper. My bullets don't leave dead men walking.

"I've notified the authorities," CJ joins the call.

I imagine he's been quiet because he's been on the phone with my former employers. He confirms that a moment later as his lazy Texan drawl crawls through the line.

"The FBI is sending out a team to collect the bodies. You'll need to be interviewed at some point, but we'll handle that. Otherwise, continue on."

"Yes, sir." I run my fingers through my hair and tug at the strands.

Continue on? Guess I'm not fired yet.

"Any idea how they found you?" CJ asks the key question. The only one I don't have a solid answer for, but they found us somehow.

"Cara is clean. There's nothing she's carrying from her former life." Glancing at her tight grip on the wheel, a flash of silver catches my eye.

Fuck.

"Cara?" I lean over, looking at the watch.

"Yes." Tight-lipped, she keeps her eyes on the road.

"Where did you get that watch?"

"It's my grandmother's." Her lips press together, forming a hard line. "It's analog. The others said I could keep it."

Normally, that's the case. We don't worry about analog devices because they don't transmit damaging information, like our location.

"Shit." I run my hand down my face.

"What's that?" Sam's gruff voice sharpens.

"A watch. She still has her watch."

"Bravo never would've let her keep it," Mitzy jumps in, defending Bravo team.

"They looked at it." Cara raises her voice. "They said it was analog and could stay."

"Ditch the watch," Mitzy says. "I need my team to check it out. If there's a tracker in it, that answers the question of how those men found you. If not, we need to keep looking."

"Understood." This whole thing officially ranks as a shitstorm. "We can drop it, but we have another problem."

"Your Jeep." Mitzy's on the ball, reading my mind before I barely form my thoughts.

"Correct."

"Where are you headed?" Sam wrangles back control.

"Nowhere right now." I scrub my hand through my hair again. It's the truth. We're just driving to stay mobile. "North on…" I wait for a highway sign to appear and rattle off the number to my leadership team.

"You're going to have to ditch the Jeep."

"I know." My head hurts thinking about that. "Any chance to recover it?"

"Don't worry about that. We're not going crazy here." CJ huffs a laugh. "But we need to separate you from it. What are our options?" CJ's question isn't for me. It's for the others on the line.

"I'm checking possibilities." The sound of Mitzy's fingers flying over the keys somehow reassures me.

I may be a solo operator, but that doesn't mean I operate without support, and as far as support goes, Guardian HRS has that in spades.

"The best place to hide a tree is in a forest," Forest Summers quotes someone famous, but I don't have a clue who that might be, or what Forest means.

"What the hell?" Mitzy's high-pitched voice rises even higher. "What do trees have to do with anything?"

"Only that we find a good place to hide the Jeep. Chase ditches it someplace where we can pick it up. Then we figure out a way to hide Chase and Cara. We could always send them to the retreat."

The retreat? What the hell is he talking about?

"Ditching the Jeep is easy enough." I scratch at the scruff on my neck. Guardian HRS will retrieve it and search for trackers. "But we're in the middle of nowhere."

"Check storage lots with faulty security. The ones who don't renew their lease on surveillance." Forest's deep voice has an edge of control that somehow soothes me.

"Got it. That's smart." Mitzy's back on task. "I'm checking storage lots with security."

The idea of leaving my Jeep behind sickens me, but there's nothing to do about that now. We have to assume every detail about my Jeep is now in the hands of those who want Cara dead. They can use that to track our next move.

"As for hotels and transportation, I'll take care of that." No fucking way am I renting anything. My motto of leaving no trace behind works for a reason. I'm not about to abandon that now.

One survivor.

Fucker's going to cause me a lot of grief. I should've gone down and made sure none of them were breathing before we left, but I had to make a split-second decision.

"I've got the perfect solution to your Jeep." The *tap, tap, tapping* of Mitzy's fingers flying over the keys is a soothing sound.

"What's that?"

"Walmart parking lot." Her tone makes her sound smug.

"Excuse me?"

"They let people camp out in their parking lots. We park your Jeep in the parking lot. Send you and Cara inside to re-provision."

"And then what? Hoof it on foot?" No fucking way is that happening.

"Actually, that's not such a bad idea." Mitzy's smugness is now irritating instead of reassuring.

Still early in the morning, we're nowhere near hitting the highest temperature of the day. Nevertheless, it's already well over a hundred degrees outside.

"Need I remind you it's triple digits out here? We'd be dead within the hour." My words make Cara jump and the Jeep swerves onto the shoulder before she corrects herself.

Shit. I wish this conversation wasn't within earshot of Cara, but there's nothing to do about that now.

"Just hear me out." I almost see Mitzy holding up a hand, telling me to listen to what she has to say.

"It better be good because there's no way we're hiking along the road or overland in 120-degree heat." Which is exactly how hot it's going to be around noon.

"How about train tracks?" There it is again, a sense of smugness in Mitzy's tone.

"Are you fucking nuts? That's trespassing, and you know it. We'd be risking a felony. I'm not doing that."

"Considering you're in active service to the federal government keeping a witness alive, I don't think that matters. I was just throwing that out there to see if you'd go for it." I swear, Mitzy has a death wish.

"Ah, good." It was a joke. "I thought you were serious."

"I am." She corrects me and I hold back a groan. "I'm dead serious. You said it yourself. It's triple digits out there. If you want to protect Cara, we need to get her out of the heat as soon as possible. It just so happens, there's a superstore ahead of you. Park your Jeep. Re-provision. Backpacks would be best. Head to the train yard. It's less than a mile from the store. Do you think you can walk a mile in this heat?"

"Even that's asking for trouble. Cara already suffered from heat exhaustion, which only increases her risk of doing so again. That option is a no-go."

"When did that happen?" CJ cuts in, tone sharp, accusatory.

Shit, I was hoping to bury that little detail deep in the weeds of my after-action report. Guess that's not going to happen.

"Yesterday, but I took care of it. A mile is too far."

"Give me a second to check the schedules."

"And what'll prevent them from having a nice long chat with the conductor about unauthorized passengers?"

"I figured you jump on the train." Mitzy continues multi-tasking while I wait for Sam or CJ to jump in and tell her why that's a shit plan.

"Like a hobo?"

"Every boy wants to be a hobo. Consider this a bit of childhood fun." Her snarky comment finds me shaking my head.

I grit my teeth and debate a number of sharp replies that will only get me in trouble. Just when I'm about to open my mouth, Forest Summers's deep voice comes on the line.

"It sounds kind of out there, Chase, but I think it can work. Pack light. Carry extra water. Add more for good measure. Mitzy will send you all the info you need on the train schedules."

"Hop on a fucking train? And do what? Tour the countryside? Until we figure out how they found her, I'm not putting Cara on a train. Makes us easy targets with no exit strategy." I pull at my chin again, unhappy with the guidance Command gives me. A quick glance at the gas meter and I hold back a snarl.

"Listen, it makes sense. You hop a train, head to my retreat, and we'll work on what to do from there. Keep moving until we can make it work."

Again with the retreat. His retreat. Doesn't sound like a Guardian HRS asset.

Whoever's after Cara has the money and resources to match those of Guardian HRS. Maybe not match, but certainly come in a close second.

If they don't know who I am, they will once they run the plates on my Jeep. That leads to my credit cards. Which means we're on a cash-only basis from here on out.

Needing to completely re-provision will make that tight, if not impossible. I grip my phone and relay my concerns to my bosses.

Meanwhile, the gears in my head get to work.

I wasn't lying when I told Cara the best way to keep her alive is to disappear completely. Now, I'm thinking about how we can do that.

"Chew on it, Chase." Mitzy gives a little after my tirade about all the ways her plan makes little sense. "If you come up with something better, say the word. Meanwhile, I'm going to work on a supply drop for you at Forest's place in the mountains. New wheels. New identities for you both. All kinds of great stuff. All you have to do is get there."

Get there? I don't like it, but it makes some sense.

"I'll make it work." I'm not happy about any of this. Hop a fucking train? Travel to some retreat in the mountains? This is what the great minds at Guardian HRS come up with?

I do my best work alone, and while I'm technically a solo operator, there are several people over me who think their ideas are the best. With this being my first mission with Guardian HRS, I'm very well aware it may be my last if I don't comply.

Which I get. I'm expendable. Cara is not.

"I'll make it work."

"There you go." Mitzy sounds smug. "Was that so hard?"

"I'll let you know."

"Don't be a wiseass."

"Don't be so damn smug."

It may be my imagination, but I swear Sam and CJ, maybe even Forest too, chuckle at that comment.

"Send the location now." I pull up a map on my phone and type in a few search terms. Guardian HRS doesn't have all the answers. I still have a few tricks up my sleeve.

"Done. And, Chase?" Mitzy says.

"Yeah?" My hands grip the phone.

"Welcome to the team." The sass in her voice irritates me, but I admit her words warm my heart.

During my very short stint with the FBI, I felt like a nameless cog in a very big wheel. It didn't seem as if we were all working toward the same goal. I don't get that with the people of Guardian HRS.

They're doing anything and everything to make the world a

better place. This assignment may very well be the most difficult job I've ever had, but I love a challenge.

I end the call, then stare out the front of the Jeep.

Cara's grip on the wheel tightens; if that's possible. "Where are we going?"

"How do you feel about trains?"

FOURTEEN

Cara
___

"TRAINS?" I LOOK AT CHASE LIKE HE'S GOT A SCREW LOOSE. "What does that mean?"

"It means exactly what I said." He folds his arms over his chest and leans back, providing nothing further in the way of an explanation.

Which pisses me off.

This is my life that's in danger. There's no reason to withhold anything from me. After that rather lengthy conversation with his team, they had to have said something more than *trains*. Obviously, Chase doesn't think I deserve to know whatever it is they're planning.

I grit my teeth and tighten my grip on the steering wheel. It's the only thing keeping me from lashing out at him in anger.

We head down the highway. Which direction? Hell if I know. I just hit the pavement, turned left, and kept going. I feel sick to my stomach and try not to think about what happened.

Chase hasn't said a word about what happened. He killed eight men. Left them to bake under the sun. What kind of person does something like that?

Am I an accessory to murder? Is it considered murder? Is this like a hit and run? Where if you flee the scene of the crime that just makes things ten times worse?

Here's where it gets weird. As if seeing eight men shot right in front of me isn't weird enough, but how do I talk about it with Chase?

Do I console him? Ignore it?

Hell if I know.

I want to talk about it. Hell, I *need* to talk about it. It's not something I can just ignore and go on with life as if nothing happened.

Eight men are dead.

My former handler, Hank, killed men in the line of duty, but as a U.S. Marshal, those kills were justified. Does that same protection cover Chase? If he goes to jail over something like this, I won't be able to live with myself.

What if I go to jail for not reporting it?

Several minutes after I ask my question, Chase deigns to speak. "Command is coming up with ideas for us to disappear." The pointed look he gives my grandmother's watch puts a hitch in my breath. The urge to cover the watch and protect it comes on strong, but I grit my teeth instead.

I can't give it up.

I won't.

It's not just my grandmother's watch. It's the last thing my father did before he died. He told me to keep it safe. That he was sorry. He practically shoved the thing into my hand, as if it was something vitally precious to him.

"Bravo team said I could keep it." I dig in and fortify my defense. "They said no one could track it."

"And yet, someone did." Chase keeps his voice flat.

"I can't lose it." My grip on the steering wheel tightens. "It's the only thing I have left from my life. My real life." I don't know what else to say.

"The watch goes." He's tight-lipped and firm.

"You don't understand. It's all I have left."

We lapse into a strained silence for a moment, but then Chase finally breaks the tension.

"I know the watch means a lot to you, but at the end of the day, it's just a thing. A thing with too great of a risk. We can't assume anything. The risk is too great to make an assumption that could cost you your life." Our eyes meet for a moment before he looks away.

There's a duality to his tone. On the one hand, it says this is nonnegotiable. On the other hand, he knows what the watch means to me. He understands the pain of losing something precious.

I'm not going to win this argument, but maybe I can negotiate terms?

"I don't have to get rid of it forever, do I?"

"Not if I can help it." He reaches out and touches my arm. It's the first time he's touched me since this morning.

I don't know what to make of it.

His one rule.

He gives a little flick of his fingers, gently asking me to surrender the watch willingly.

I take a deep breath and let it out slowly. With the hole in my heart growing, I unclasp the watch and place it into his open palm.

He takes it with great reverence, running his finger lightly over the engravings. The admiration in his eyes is real.

The watch is a work of art. Age and wear have made the leather band smooth to the touch and buttery soft. The lustrous shine of the metal casing remains and its intricate swirls flow with grace and elegance. Tiny crystal stones adorn the delicate hands of the clock face; each number penned by a master calligrapher.

It's delicate, feminine, and there's no doubt it was made to adorn a woman's wrist. To me, there's a feeling of reverence about it, like being in the presence of something greater than myself. It connects me. Grounds me.

"Here, take your grandmother's watch."

"But, Papa…" Tears sting my eyes as my father struggles to breathe.

"Take it. Keep it safe. Never take it off."

"But, Papa…"

"My sweet angel, my dearest Angelique, the watch is…"

Those were my father's last words to me. He used his last breath to tell me about the watch. Not to tell me he loved me, but to keep the watch safe.

It's much more than a simple watch.

It connects me to my father. As evil as he turned out to be, no matter the crimes he committed against so many, he was still my father.

My *papa.*

I know he loved me, and he wanted me to have this watch. To keep it *safe.*

It's too important to just give it up to strangers.

"It's not forever." Chase holds the watch in front of him, before tucking it safely away in his pocket.

This isn't goodbye forever, but sadness tugs at my heart. Saying goodbye to this piece of me feels like saying goodbye to home, to family—to everything I left behind when I was forced to go into hiding.

I furrow my brow and grit my teeth. "What, exactly, are they going to do with it?" My tone is accusatory, heightening the tension swirling between me and Chase, and I don't feel bad about that at all.

"Command wants to look at it." His reply is gruff, flat, and lacking any real answer.

Like he couldn't care less what happens to something important to me.

"Why?" There may be a bit of a sarcastic tone laced within my words, but he could give me a more in-depth explanation as to why, and what, they're going to do with it.

Of course, I know why. It's all about keeping me safe. I can't fault them for doing their job, but I'd appreciate a bit more explanation, especially considering what it is I'm giving up.

"To see if there are any trackers planted in it." He raises an eyebrow as if it's obvious.

Which it isn't. It isn't obvious to me.

"This watch has never been off my body." Not since my father gave it to me. Suddenly, I feel sick to my stomach. Did he do something to the watch? Did he insert something that would lead his enemies directly to me? The thought makes me choke up and tears prick in my eyes.

"Never?" His disbelief is clear, and he lifts both eyebrows, giving me a look.

I shift uncomfortably and twist the truth. "Well, I take it off when I shower." That should be obvious. "But it's never out of my sight."

"They'll take good care of it. I promise." He points to an upcoming exit. "Let's stop and get gas while I figure out what our next step should be."

"Okay." I take the exit with a sense of emptiness growing in the hollow of my chest where my heart used to be.

The things my father did are horrific, but I refuse to believe he would sacrifice me. Or put me in danger. My father loved me. Of that, I'm sure, but how did those men find us?

I pull up to the gas pump and Chase jumps out to fill up while I continue to obsess over what Guardian HRS is going to do with my grandmother's watch. I slide out of the Jeep, feeling my muscles loosen up as I rotate my neck and shake out the kinks in my body. The tank guzzles up the fuel, and the numbers on the pump tick higher and higher while I wait.

Once finished at the pump, we head inside the small, run-down station and make our way over to the restroom. I step inside and Chase takes up position beyond the door, watching for anyone who might pose a threat. When I'm done, we stock up on snacks and head back out.

I'm eager to hit the road again. Not because we have a destination in mind, but because the need to keep moving is a driving force. If we're constantly on the go, no one can catch us.

No one can kill me.

FIFTEEN

Cara

THE SUN CREEPS HIGH OVERHEAD AS WE DRIVE THROUGH THE desolation of the desert. We hit one sketchy gas station after the next, and with each stop, Chase scopes out the area before allowing me to exit the vehicle.

I appreciate his vigilance and am grateful for his protection, but it feels like he's intentionally placing distance between us. I can't help but feel like there's a disconnect growing between us.

And while he's not speaking to me, he certainly seems to carry on a long conversation via text with his employers. He's got plenty to say to them and nothing to me.

Me.

The person who watched him kill eight men. I want to talk about it. I need to talk about it.

Chase?

It's like it never happened and he couldn't care less about how it might affect me.

What happened?

I climb out of the Jeep and stretch while the tank fills with gas. The pungent odor of gasoline irritates my nasal passages and mingles with the lingering exhaust from the Jeep after Chase killed the engine. The barest whisper of a breeze dries the perspiration on my skin, cooling me for only a moment before the intense heat returns.

In less than twelve minutes, we're back on the road. Total number of words exchanged between the two of us?

Zero.

The rumble of the Jeep's engine punctuates the quiet of the barren landscape and fills the silence that settles between me and Chase. We drive for hours, stopping for food, fuel and pit stops at the most rundown gas stations we come across.

Each stop now comes with a routine.

He surveys the area, pumps the gas, then escorts me inside. Total words exchanged?

Zero.

I may get a grunt or a gesture, but that's it.

I'm not trying to be ungrateful. I appreciate him more than I want to admit. I want to feel grateful, but letting go of my irritation over this awkward silence isn't happening anytime soon.

"Can't we stop somewhere nicer?" My words come out sharper than I intend, filled with sarcasm, snark, and irritation.

It's like I'm trying to force an argument, if only to get him to respond. As for my question, I don't expect an answer. Or rather, I already know what he's going to say.

"No." He shakes his head without looking at me. His reply clipped without explanation.

Unwilling to push things further, I shrug and climb into the Jeep. Once again, we set off down the desolate highway, driving in silence for what seems like hours. The never-ending road extends to the horizon with nothing but the barren wasteland of the desert to mark the miles.

An hour later, Chase breaks the heavy silence. "Take the next exit."

There's no please, just a barked command that rubs me the wrong way.

"What about the freeway?" Confusion rises inside me. I dislike non-communicative people.

"We'll get back to it." His reply is completely devoid of any information, which only irritates me further.

"Fine." I try my best to keep any sign of annoyance out of my voice and fail miserably.

"It's the safest way from point A to point B. Trust me."

Trust him? Hard to do when he barely speaks to me, but after a few moments of driving, my curiosity wins out and I open my mouth, demanding an answer.

"Where are we going?"

He holds up a manilla envelope and shakes it. When our eyes meet, his hardened features soften considerably. Maybe he realizes he's being a dick?

"Need to get this in the mail." He keeps his voice flat and emotionless.

"And what is that?" My expression betrays my irritation. I glance away as the tension builds between us.

"Your watch." He looks at me like I'm an idiot. As if it should be clear. Which, in his defense, it is.

I'm just crabby, cranky, and annoyed. His tone softens and there's something of the old Chase still there. "I need to overnight it, which means we need a post office or UPS. Our tech team will look and see if there's any evidence of a tracker in it."

My heart drops as I process his words.

"Oh." I feel bad for being abrupt, but I can't pull that back now.

Eyes on the road, I turn my attention to the arid land and squint into the distance, shading my eyes from the intense sun. We continue on with only the hum of the engine disturbing the silence hanging between us.

"Turn here." He points toward a long, straight road, not a bend in sight.

What an inhospitable place.

"And where are we going?"

"There's a town ninety miles out with a post office."

That kind of distance feels oppressive. With nothing to break the monotony, it's going to be a very long time with no conversation.

"I'm going to catch some sleep," he says. "If anyone comes up behind us, slow down and see if they pass. If not, wake me."

Obviously, the silence doesn't bother him.

"Okay." There it is again. The one-word answer I'm relegated to using.

With an uneasy nod, I head down the straight stretch of pavement, heading into the unknown.

Within moments of him speaking, Chase's eyes droop, and he drifts into a deep sleep. Soft snores soon fill the inside of the Jeep.

With no air conditioning, I lower the window and let the hot, dry air evaporate the sweat on my body. Ninety miles seems a long way to go before finding a post office, but an hour later, I understand why.

We travel in a barren, godforsaken land of nothing but rock, scrub, and the occasional tumbleweed. Overhead, the sky is as blue as blue can be—a deep, vibrant color that disappears into infinity.

After what seems like forever, bumps on the horizon slowly resolve into what look like foothills bunching up at the base of the mountains. Thin wispy clouds gather over the foothills, crowding together as if they snag on the hills.

Combined with the soft, diffused light of the setting sun, it's one of the most beautiful sights I've ever seen. Beside me, Chase sleeps like a lamb, and as for any cars following us, I've never traveled a more empty road.

Ninety miles down the road, the town of Dry Rock consists of six lonely buildings—none over two stories high—and one post office. One long road arrows through the center of the town, and the post office, with its faded blue siding and red shutters, stands out amongst the muted sandstone browns of the rest of the town. Afraid Chase made a mistake, I gently nudge him awake.

"We're here."

"Great. Pull over."

He jumps out, leaving me with the Jeep. Moments later, he returns without my watch.

I continue through what little there is of Dry Rock and head back down the lonely highway. We spend the rest of the day passing through one small town after another; each one a near replica of Dry Rock.

The hours slowly pass.

I shift in my seat, exhausted by a long day of driving, and cover my mouth with my hand as a yawn slips out. I can't stand it any longer and break the silence.

"When are we going to stop for the night?"

"We're not."

"We're not?" My eyes widen in surprise. "But it's getting late." I protest his decision.

"We're driving straight through."

"Straight through?" My face must be a mask of confusion because my mouth gapes and my eyes widen in surprise. I'm tired, cranky, sweaty, irritable, and the last thing I want to hear is we're spending more time inside the Jeep. By now, I'm done with it.

"Yup."

His one-word reply has me biting my tongue.

"What about food?" Maybe he'll listen to reason?

The monotony of the road is getting to me.

Has gotten to me.

Chase stares at the screen of his phone, tapping furiously at the keys. Curiosity gets the better of me, but I refuse to ask what he's doing.

"Well, I've been driving since this morning, and I need a break." Maybe if I make it an ultimatum, he'll listen. "Either we find a motel, or we pull off the road and camp for the night."

"Can't stop," he repeats himself, more dismissive than before, while I wonder what happened to the charismatic man who teased me at the little river, then spent the night showing me the constellations, wishing upon shooting stars, and curling his massive frame around mine while I slept.

What happened to that man?

"Chase…" My frustration builds. "I'm done driving and need a break."

"We've been taking breaks all day."

"Stopping at run-down gas stations is not taking a break. Can't we grab dinner at least?"

Obey his one rule.

I'm trying my best to be congenial and sweet, but there are limits to my patience. Chase tests that limit right now.

"Can you hold out for another hour?"

"Fine." Which means anything but fine. My jaw clenches, and my fingers curl around the steering wheel.

Soon enough, we arrive at another no-name town, where we find an old diner on Main Street. The sign out front proclaims, "The Cactus Cafe—All Are Welcome!" Without asking, I make an executive decision and park out front.

"What are you doing?" Chase looks at me in surprise.

"Taking a break. Getting food." Screw his one damn rule. I'm tired, hungry, and way past being congenial and nice to a man who's said less than ten words to me all day.

He pauses for a second, mouth hanging open, but he snaps it shut. Whatever he's about to say will remain a mystery. He does, however, surprise me by getting out of the Jeep and gesturing for me to join him on the curb.

"Dinner sounds wonderful." He wraps an arm around my waist like we're not at odds with each other, which means it's my turn to gape and avoid yanking out of his grip.

But I don't say all the nasty things swirling in my head. Hunger drives me into the diner, and it feels amazing not having to point the Jeep down the featureless road.

Inside, the restaurant is small and cozy, with a handful of rustic wooden tables and booths tucked into the corners. The laminate tabletops are worn smooth by years of use, while the booths have seen better days. Most are empty, although a few are occupied by truckers and other hardworking locals.

Burgers, hot dogs, and fries fill the air with their aroma, along with a hint of coffee from the diner's pot brewing away in the background.

The waitress brings us to a booth in the corner and takes our order with a warm and inviting smile. We order sodas, and she leaves to get our drinks. I look at Chase, and he glances at me, completely nonplussed.

"Interesting place." I try to open up a conversation with Chase after a day of little to no words, but he remains distant.

"Small, out of the way town. It works." He glances around the diner, taking in every detail.

"Do you think we can spend the night here?" I know he wants to drive straight through, but I'm tired and need a bed if I'm going to be functional in the morning.

"We shouldn't." He shakes his head and glances at his phone. The man seems to be glued to the thing, making me wonder what the content of his conversation with Guardian HRS holds.

Whatever it is, he's not happy.

Which leaves me to reflect on the frustrating mystery of the incredibly handsome man beside me.

We've exchanged less than a handful of words, and any of that heat between us—those tantalizing sparks of attraction—are either gone entirely or put on the back burner and reduced to a slow simmer.

Frankly, I don't care. I chalk off any thoughts I may have had toward Chase as messed-up madness in my head.

"Shouldn't or can't?" Maybe if I nail him down, he'll give in and let us take a break from this endless drive?

"Shouldn't." Another one-word answer.

"If they're tracking my watch, it's far behind us. What are the chances they'll find us here?"

"Slim."

"Slim enough to justify a stop?" We're both tired, and we still haven't talked about what happened earlier.

He gives it a moment, mulling it over in his mind, then finally agrees with a nod.

When the waitress returns, we order our food, then eat in silence once she brings it to the table. Chase clears his plate while I pick at my food. When he signals the waitress to bring the check, I take that as a sign to finish or spend the night with an empty belly.

Back on the road, again, we stop at the next town, this one

significantly larger than the last, but still nothing to brag about. We find an old motel advertising a vacancy. I wait in the car while he talks to the manager. He comes back a few minutes later with a room key in hand.

One key.

One room.

I don't know why I thought he'd get two rooms, but I was hoping to put physical distance between us.

Maybe there are two beds inside?

I cross my fingers and hope. The thought of spending another night sleeping beside Chase fills me with conflicted emotions. Putting those thoughts aside, I focus on what's important.

We're both exhausted. I'm relieved to have somewhere to stay for the night, and the moment my head hits the pillow, I'm going to fall into a dreamless sleep. I won't care that he shares the bed.

Except, that's a lie. I care very much.

I follow Chase into the motel room, where I'm pleasantly surprised by how clean it is—then cringe at the single queen-sized bed.

Despite being weary from such a long drive, my mind refuses to switch off as my thoughts return to Chase's strange behavior today. All of it leaves me confused about how to behave around him.

"Do you want to take a shower?" He gestures toward the bathroom.

I shake my head. "I'm tired and just want to sleep."

"A shower might help you feel better." He's trying to be helpful, but I'm not sure what to do.

The last thing I need is to be refreshed. All I care about is crawling into that bed and falling into a dreamless sleep. Not to mention, there are dangers to stripping down in front of him.

Am I making things up? Finding issues where there should be none?

Truthfully, I'm scared.

I'm scared of how he makes me feel.

I'm scared of this overwhelming need building within me.

I'm scared of what will happen in that bed, or what won't happen in that bed.

That's the worst part.

After all the uncertainty throughout the day, the awkward silence, and the distance between us, the thing I worry about the most is whether he's still interested in me.

I feel like a teenager, agonizing over a boy. Am I over-analyzing? Making a mountain out of a molehill? I don't know. I don't know anything anymore.

"Earth to Cara?" Chase's brows tug together.

"What?"

"The shower?" He cocks his head to the side and waits for an answer.

"No. I'm good. I just want to sleep." I hope he doesn't push the issue.

"Okay, I'm going to take a shower. You can have the bed."

"I'm sorry, what?" Did I hear that right? He's not going to sleep with me? Not that I want him to sleep with me—which is another bald-faced lie—but why doesn't he want to sleep in the same bed as me?

"Where will you sleep?"

"The floor?" He shrugs like he couldn't care less and turns away from me, pulling off his shirt and tossing it over the single chair in the room.

"You don't have to do that." I pat the bed, knowing I'm going to regret this later. "There's plenty of room on the bed. More than on top of your Jeep."

"I'll be fine," he says, walking over to the bathroom. He closes the door behind him, leaving me alone with my thoughts.

That's exactly where I don't need to be—alone with my thoughts.

The bed brings the last two nights rushing to the forefront of my thoughts. There's no way I misinterpreted what happened, and while I'm being completely honest with myself, why not address the elephant in the room?

I'm not just attracted to the man. I crave him on a cellular level.

I want to curl up next to him and breathe in his scent. I want to feel his arms around me and gaze into his deep brown eyes. I want to feel his lips on mine and discover all the secrets he's been keeping hidden away.

I can't deny it any longer. Chase drives me insane. I want to curl up in his embrace and never leave.

The deeper I dig, the more I talk myself into the unthinkable. There's something called the five-second rule. Where if you don't act on a thought within the first five seconds, you'll miss an opportunity.

Five.

Which way will I jump?

Four.

Dare to do something crazy.

Three.

Lord, I must be out of my mind.

Two.

I crawl out of bed.

One.

I strip out of my clothes and head to the bathroom. My hand shakes on the doorknob, but I don't hesitate.

What I'm thinking is crazy, and the risk of rejection will sting, but I can't live with this strained silence anymore. I need to know if he feels the same way about me as I feel about him.

I twist the knob and push open the door.

The steam from the shower fills the room. Chase stands with his back to me; head bowed as if in prayer.

I take a deep breath, hoping he can't hear my heart beating out of my chest. A wave of emotions washes over me, and I hesitate a moment, not wanting to interrupt, but also not wanting to miss this opportunity to take a leap of faith due to fear.

I take a deep breath and step forward. The sudden sound of my foot on the tile breaks the trance, and he turns to me. That's when I see his hand wrapped around the shaft of his very engorged, and erect, cock.

Holy hell, that was no prayer.

His eyes widen in surprise and then soften as he takes in my presence. His gaze travels down my body and then back up to my face. The tension between us escalates. That simmering heat returns in an effusive blaze.

Well, I wanted to know how he felt, and now I know he feels the same way as I do.

His lips part, "Cara…" Deep and husky, his voice vibrates heavily with his need.

"Chase, I…" Staring at his fully engorged cock, my words catch in the back of my throat.

"Don't." He doesn't turn around.

From his stance, it's clear what he's doing. My lips press together, imagining his powerful hand wrapped around the root of his cock.

I lick my lips in anticipation.

"Don't, what?" My voice shakes.

"You know what." His eyes glaze over with lust.

"Don't you want me?"

"You've been driving me crazy all day. Of course I want you."

"Then don't ask me to leave." I straighten my spine, digging in. After the silence of today, I need an explanation, but first, I need him.

"Cara…" Strain fills his voice. "We can't."

"I'm pretty sure we can."

Don't back down.

I give myself a pep talk and force myself to hold my ground.

"We shouldn't…"

"Tell me to leave, and I'll leave."

Please don't make me leave.

"You don't understand."

"What don't I understand?"

"If you don't leave right now, I won't be able to stop."

SIXTEEN

Chase

THE MOMENT CARA STEPS INTO THE BATHROOM, I FEEL HER ON A visceral level. With my hand on my cock, a primal, sadistic need overwhelms me. It's an *I want her, have to have her, going to devour and destroy her* kind of primal energy.

My cock swells and jerks in my hand.

With frustration tugging on me all fucking day long, I needed relief and figured a quick hand job in the bathroom would take enough of the edge off to allow me to spend the night with her in this moldy motel room.

I fully intend to sleep on the floor. Put me in a bed with Cara and my control will snap. It's not a matter of if, but when.

As for today, and my frustration, something weird shifted the energy between us. After I killed those men, Cara couldn't look me in the eye. She kept her eyes glued to the road and refused to look at me.

The heat between us sputtered and faltered. It went out like a light. To see the fear and disgust in her eyes gutted me. Yet, I continue to ache for her.

All that heat between us disappeared in the blink of an eye. It happened the moment she saw the cold-blooded killer in me. It changed everything.

The worst part is there's nothing I can do about it. I am what I am, and if she can't come to terms with that, then I have no choice but to turn the other cheek, take the rejection like a man, and find limited relief in the palm of my hand.

It sucks fucking monkey balls.

I'm good enough to protect her, but if I kill to protect her, suddenly I'm no longer desirable?

What did she think I did for a living? Didn't she understand lethal force is part of the job?

Not my fault if she can't handle it.

Maybe it's a blessing in disguise? I knew we were getting too close. We let the attraction between us build until it became something real.

That's on me. I never should've blurred personal and professional boundaries, but as hard as I try to convince myself this is for the best, my body isn't on board.

It craves Cara.

She turns me into a raving lunatic with a fucking hard-on, and I couldn't escape into the bathroom fast enough to rub one out. All I needed was a little relief.

My feelings haven't changed.

My body craves a taste of her flesh. My dick aches to sink into her wet heat. All I want is to make her mine, but all day, that silence between us thickened and smothered the heat sparking between us.

My cock stands proud, stiff, engorged, and hungry.

I want to abandon all reason and lose control as I torment her with sensation, drown her in passion, and ruin her for any man who might come after me.

Fuck that. I want no other man to come after me.

She's mine.

My heart bursts into a reckless sprint, forcing blood to race through my body and rush into my groin. My cock swells, hardens, throbs, and weeps for her.

For Cara.

I'm more engorged and hungrier than moments before as images of her flood my mind.

And now she's here. Naked. Standing in front of me with fear etched into her delicate face.

But fear of what? Surely not rejection. I don't have the willpower to say no.

The feelings she unleashes within me are powerful and overwhelming. They're dangerous.

When she takes a step toward me, my breath hitches and my cock jerks. When she places her delicate hands on my chest, I grit my teeth, barely holding on. When her sweet lips press against my breastbone, I about come right then.

My desire for this woman is visceral, but it's not based solely on lust. There's far more than an overwhelming physical attraction pulling me to her. It's in the brightness of her smile. The way her entire face lights up when she looks at me. It's in the absolute faith she places in me to keep her safe. It's in her every breath, every beat of her heart, and in her incredible strength to survive.

Right now, it's the way her intoxicating presence seeps into my pores, fills my lungs, and makes my heart pound.

"What if I don't want you to stop?" Her soft lips press against the tip of my shoulder. "Tell me to go, and I'll go, but you'll break my heart if you make me leave. I don't want to go."

"You don't understand." I thought she no longer wanted me. I'm so fucking confused. What happened to the woman who stoically clung to her silence all fucking day?

But I'm too desperate to refuse her advance. That's the kind of strength I don't have.

"What don't I understand?" Her fingers trace a delicate path down my arms.

"You don't want to have sex with me." I'm amped up enough that I'm more likely to hurt her than love her. It's that confusion about today.

"Why not?" Her tone bites and challenges.

So, I give it to her straight.

"I'll hurt you." My jaw clenches with the truth hanging in the air.

I'm too far gone. My mind boils with nothing but animalistic lust and that feral nature to rut and fuck.

Her fingers trace over my hip and curl around my stomach. They dip toward my groin and my entire body tenses.

"Cara—don't." It's the last warning she'll receive.

When her hand wraps around the shaft of my dick, right above the root where my hand clenches tight, a hiss escapes me. My toes curl, and my eyes close. The last fleeting bits of my restraint fall away.

Heat erupts in my core and blasts through my aching dick. Then she does the unthinkable. With a hint of challenge in her eyes, she kneels before me. Her lips part, forming an O. While I fight against my need to come, she leans forward. Breathless and overtaken by her courage, my entire body shakes as she lays claim to my cock with her mouth.

"Holy fuck." My hand whips out and tangles in her hair. My toes curl as her soft lips, hot mouth, and rough tongue push me right to the edge.

But there's no way I'm rushing this. My grip tightens on her hair, a show of dominance as I drag her off my cock. I stare down, waiting for her to look up.

Goddamn, but that's a sight to see.

When her lids flick and she gazes up, I widen my stance and harden my eyes. In that flash of a second, her eyes flicker with alarm, then soften with the barest nod as she cedes control to me.

I guide her in, forcing her to take me all the way into the back of her throat. She doesn't pull away. I pull her off my cock, just to the tip, then surge forward with a thrust of my hips. I force her to take me so fucking deep before catching myself and forcing myself to slow the fuck down.

If there's heaven on earth, I've found it in the impressive talent of her mouth. I release some control and allow her to suck and lick as I bask in the sensations flowing through me. She traces out the veins and ridges with her tongue. The roughness of her tongue on the sensitive underside of my glans brings a guttural groan to my lips and nearly buckles my knees.

Her hands begin a short exploration over my thighs, ending on my balls, where I face an overload of stimulation. Panting, grunting, sounding like a fucking animal, I fight against my release.

When I come, I'm going to come hard. Fuck, I might just blackout from the agonizing pleasure racing through me. Not yet. I grit my teeth and barely hang on. I never want this to end, but the urge to come is too powerful to resist.

With the relentless flicks of her tongue, the sultry heat of her mouth, and the way she swallows me down, there's no fighting the inevitable.

I have to have her. Fuck her. Kiss her. Taste her pussy. I need to touch her everywhere and leave my mark on her body. I fuck her throat until the burning need within me makes it impossible to delay the inevitable.

My balls draw up. Tighten. Heat builds. My skin feels like it's on fire as the pressure inside my cock erupts in the most violent and satisfying orgasm I've ever experienced.

I buck and jerk, groaning through the waves of pleasure coursing through my veins, unable to stop until the last aftershocks ripple through my body in tiny, flickering pulses of pleasure.

The moment my body stops shaking, I reach down, collect Cara in my arms, and carry her to the bed. I lay her out on the mattress and go to my knees. Her breasts lift and fall with the quickening of her breaths as I lift her legs and wrap them around my shoulders to fully expose her pussy to me.

But I don't start there.

Oh, no. There's too much to explore. I lower my mouth to her breast, loving her tiny gasp as I capture her nipple in my mouth. Using my tongue, I flick and torture the tiny peak until it tightens and her body thrums beneath the skill of my hands and mouth. My one and only intent is to ruin her for any man but me.

She grabs the back of my head and arches her back as I gently bite down on her nipple. A gasp of pain escapes her, and her entire body grows still as I increase the pressure, merging pain and pleasure into one sensation. Her body stills, but then trembles, as I show her what it means to belong to me.

My lips move from one breast to the other, where I repeat exactly the same thing, bringing pleasure first, layering on pain, then merging the two together. And I show her one important thing.

It's the only important thing.

Her pleasure is mine to give. There will be no taking from me.

As I kiss and suckle, she burns beneath me. Her breaths quicken and stack, turning to mewling pants of pleasure. The heat of my mouth, along with the expertise of my tongue, brings her to the edge and holds her there.

She's not ready to come.

Not yet.

From her neck to her hips, and her breast to her mons, I lick her with relentless strokes, inch by inch, staking my claim over her body. Her fingers twine in my hair, tugging at the roots, knuckling against my scalp as she arches her back and shoves her tits into my face.

Her entire body shakes with fine tremors, and I lose count of how many times she moans, except I want more. I need her surrender. Her submission.

Knowing she's close, I bury my mouth between her thighs. Surprised, she practically levitates off the bed, but I place my palm between her breasts and hold her down.

She tastes like heaven and I ravish her pussy, eager to taste and lick and destroy. Those moans of hers get louder and more insistent. They turn hoarse and frustrated as she tries desperately to come. Each time she tries to force it, I back off. It doesn't take long before she understands she is helpless to force any of this.

The moment she gives in to me, I bury my tongue inside of her and place my thumb and forefinger on her clit. With a bit of pressure and a twist, her entire body tenses as her climax builds.

This time, I eagerly bring her to orgasm, loving the way her body shakes and her pussy pulsates. Crying out, she grabs my hair and pulls me up her body.

"Fuck me. Fuck me now."

The desperation in her voice isn't something I can ignore.

"God. Please. Don't make me beg." Her demand turns to begging, and how can I refuse when she begs so nicely?

I barely have time to sheath myself as she gasps beneath me. With the broad tip of my dick notched at her entrance, I hold her gaze, push past her opening, and thrust as deep as I can. If she wants me to fuck her, then I'm happy to oblige.

Thick and engorged, I hiss as the heat of her body wraps around me. Sensation explodes. Shocks of pleasure tingle and spark. Heat in my groin builds as my balls draw tight. I try to control my thrusts, but Cara buries her face in my neck and begs.

"Oh my God, just fuck me already."

"Harder?" I'm already pounding in and out.

"Yes."

"I don't want to hurt you."

"Hurt me. Just fucking fuck me." Her entire body shakes with the aftershocks of her orgasm and the steep climb toward a second. "I want to feel you fucking me."

Well, fucking hell. Who am I to refuse a lady?

My entire body shakes, but I no longer control my thrusts. I pound into her, slapping our bodies together, stimulating her clit, determined to push her toward another orgasm. She squirms beneath me as her orgasm shudders through her. The moment she comes, a switch flicks in my head. My heart pounds as my orgasm sweeps through me.

I collapse over her, my chest colliding against her breasts. Our limbs tingle in a mess of spent sexual need. Then, I lift up and gaze deeply into her eyes. She wraps her arms around my neck, and our lips clash in a crazed fever of post-fuck delirium.

We lie in bed, hearts pounding and breaths coming in ragged gasps. Cara meets my gaze with her seductive eyes. Heat radiates off her body, and a thin sheen of perspiration is all that's left of our lovemaking. Our first time together is an unforgettable experience.

Never in my life did I imagine sex could be like that.

Feel like that.

He wraps his hand around the back of my neck and pulls me in for another kiss. This one lingers far longer than the rest and cements the connection growing between us.

SEVENTEEN

Cara

_____

MORNING COMES ALL TOO SOON.

"Good morning, princess." Low and husky, his voice rumbles in the back of his throat.

A grin fills my face, and I fight against the urge to look away in shyness. Instead, I let the heat simmer between us. If it were up to me, I could lie in bed all day long. In the quiet of the moment, a profound sense of safety and security overcomes me.

"Good morning." The smile on my face must be miles wide, and the heat in my cheeks must burn like the sun. I'm a blusher. Always have been. For the first time in my life, I don't mind.

"You want to hit the head?" That low husky growl of his makes my toes curl and my belly flutter, but I scrunch my brow in confusion.

"Excuse me?"

"The bathroom." He gives a jerk of his chin toward the tiny bathroom.

"Oh." Disappointment lingers in my voice. "I guess so."

When I pull away from him, he grabs my wrist, holding me fast. "Princess, I would spend all day in bed with you, but we don't have that luxury. We've already spent more time here than I'd like. Use the facilities and take a quick shower. We need to get back on the road."

He reaches out and touches my face, brushing a strand of hair away from my eyes. His tenderness is a balm to my soul.

"Right." I retreat to the bathroom in a funk.

Which is both funny and weird. Weird because I feel instead of being sent to bed without supper, like a kid, I'm grumpy because I'm an adult being forced out of bed and all the fun things that happen there.

He's right, of course. We need to move on. Where that might be is anyone's guess. Last night, there was talk of trains and leaving his Jeep behind.

Is that still the plan?

Part of me cringes at the idea of hopping on a train and riding it like a hobo. Another part of me secretly entertains the idea. It could be exciting, and it's the perfect time of year for it. Early summer, it's neither too cold nor too hot. Not to mention, it would be fun to see parts of the country very few people ever get to experience in a lifetime.

In the bathroom, I crank the water up to as hot as I can stand. I'm a sucker for steamy showers. Once the water's hot enough, I get in.

Hot water hits the top of my head and pours off my neck and shoulders. After the heat of the desert, I take advantage of the shower and use all the contents of the tiny shampoo and conditioner bottles.

The pressure of the spray is intense, which is a good thing considering the thickness of my hair. I soap up, rinse, and repeat. On the second round, conditioner goes on my hair. The floral aroma of the conditioner fills the room, intermingling with the steam, as I breathe in the fresh scent and let the lather from the soap carry the dirt and grit of the desert down the drain. I revel in the luxury of being clean, but not so much as to hog the shower.

When I step out of the shower, the small bathroom is a fog of steam. I wrap a towel around myself and exit. Sitting on the bed, Chase is already dressed.

"Don't you want to take a shower?" My brows furrow at the oddity.

"Princess, I took a shower while you were sleeping. Wanted to save all the hot water for you." The corner of his mouth crooks up in a grin.

"You did?" Odd that I'd sleep through that. Although, I was pretty tired after the events of the previous day and the epic sex we enjoyed.

A car door slams in the parking lot outside, making me jump. Chase bolts to his feet and places a finger over his lips, telling me to be quiet. He snaps his fingers and points to my clothes. I get the message and get dressed as fast as I can. He grabs his pistol and crosses the room in a few quick strides. He inspects the gun, checking to make sure it's loaded and ready to fire.

He places his back against the wall next to the window and takes a few breaths in and out real slow. His body tenses, and his eyes narrow. Another of his snaps snags my attention.

He points to my shoes, and I put them on. Then I throw our meager possessions into a bag and wait. Meanwhile, his entire demeanor shifts, like he's getting ready for a fight.

The voices outside grow louder. There are several men.

My attention focuses in on Chase. He's a fighter. A survivor. He's my Protector. He'll do whatever it takes to protect me, but can he stand against several men alone?

His eyes narrow with intense focus, almost as if he's running through several options in his head. With a nod, Chase seems to come to a decision because he snaps his fingers again, telling me to stand in the corner of the room behind him. I do as he says and stand there, my breathing loud and erratic.

Suddenly, the men's voices cut off. I strain my ears, listening for anything that will tell me what they're doing outside, but I can only make out muffled conversations.

With his free hand, Chase motions for me to crouch in the corner. With nowhere else to hide, it makes the most sense, so I do as he says while he points his pistol at the door. We wait for what seems like an eternity. Just then, a loud boom splits the air. The door flies off its hinges, crashing onto the floor, and a man barrels into the room.

Chase fires, taking out the man who kicked the door in. The man's head erupts in a burst of red as he falls back, his body crumpling to the floor.

Chase jumps into action. There's absolutely no hesitation on his part. Like back in the desert, with the eight men he killed, he takes out a second man, killing him instantly with a shot between the eyes.

And he doesn't stop there.

He flattens himself against the wall, gun raised and ready to fire while I cower in the corner. Gunfire sounds all around us as the remaining men outside return fire.

Bullets tear through the room. The concussive report of guns going off nearly ruptures my eardrums and thumps my chest as bullets fly and embed themselves in the wall opposite the door. I understand now why Chase positioned me where he did. I'm closer to the door, in my corner, and nowhere near where the bullets bury themselves in the wall.

Chase ducks around the doorjamb, fires off a shot, then ducks back, using the wall for cover. There's no doubt his shots are accurate and lethal, but they're not enough to take all the men down.

The men overwhelm our position, flooding into the room as Chase fires. This time, they don't go down as easily as the first two men. They return fire, and a bullet slices into Chase's arm. He seems oblivious to the wound and continues to take out the men.

A bullet whizzes by my head, so close the gunpowder irritates my nasal passages. I cover my head with my hands, as if that will stop a bullet, and feel something warm trickle down my neck.

Chase needs my help, but I'm scared. I can't move, and I don't know what to do.

A man reaches around the doorjamb and wrestles Chase's pistol from his grip. Chase dives out of the way as the man steps through and fires at Chase. The bullets go wide and dig into the carpet.

Unarmed, Chase pulls a knife against his attacker and slices the man across the face. That man cries out and clutches his bleeding face. Chase takes the man's gun and aims at his head. With zero hesitation, he fires, taking the man down.

Another man rushes into the room. He pivots, sees me, and raises his gun. I don't know if he's going to shoot me or Chase, but that can't happen.

Not sure what I'm doing, my survival instincts take over. I lunge for Chase's pistol and point it at the man. My finger squeezes the trigger, firing a shot in the man's direction.

The kickback knocks me flat on my ass, but the man drops his gun, screaming in pain. His hand's a bloody mess, and he clutches his gut where a red stain spreads across his shirt. He drops to his knees, mouth gaping. Eyes wide, it takes a moment for him to process what happened, but then he slumps forward and collapses on the floor.

Chase spares a glance and looks at me with a mixture of astonishment and pride in his eyes.

More gunfire erupts outside the room. A bullet shatters the glass of the window, and another hits the wall over my head, sending chunks of concrete flying in all directions.

I duck, covering my ears as more gunfire goes off. Scared beyond all reason, my mind races, and I don't know what to do. It's like we're in the middle of a war zone, and I'm completely helpless.

Chase fires again. Another man falls dead before he hits the ground, but more men keep coming.

How many are out there?

I don't know if I can shoot another person. I don't want to kill, but I will if I have to.

"Come on." Chase pockets the weapons of the fallen men. "We need to get out of here."

Out?

Like outside where whatever remaining men can shoot at us?

"Give me your hand." He reaches for me.

"What?" I say, confused.

"Give me your hand!" He grabs my hand, pulling me to my feet. Still dazed and confused, I don't know what's going on.

Chase is thoroughly insane. I stumble out of the room and sprint behind him, weaving through the gunfire. We make a beeline to the Jeep.

Gunshots sound all around us. Bullets whiz past my head, sounding like angry hornets. When we reach the cover of the Jeep, Chase spins around and takes out the remaining two men after another barrage of gunfire. Once the last men are taken out, he glances down at the tires.

"Fuck."

All four tires are flat; slit through their sidewalls.

"We've got to get out of here before they send anyone else." He glances around the carnage and grits his teeth. Without another word, he rushes to the back of the Jeep and pulls out several bags and a rucksack. "Here."

He shoves the rucksack at me and I shoulder it without thinking. Sized for him, I pull on the straps, making it fit my smaller frame.

"We have to go." Chase's tone is unyielding but filled with emotion. Battered and bruised, his face is a mess, but he's alive.

We're both alive.

"You're bleeding." I point to his arm, where the fabric of his shirt is stained red.

"So are you." He takes a moment to examine my temple, where a bullet grazed the skin. Another few millimeters, and I would be dead.

Talk about a literal brush with death?

Chase grabs me and pulls me close. He kisses my forehead and breathes out a sigh. I throw my arms around him, shaking with the aftereffects of the adrenaline coursing through my body. Profound relief fills me as I try my best not to think about what could have happened.

"Let's get out of here. We have a long way to go before we can rest." Chase holds me tight, his grip reassuring and familiar.

"Where will we go?" A feeling of renewed strength and determination fills me.

Together, we fought and survived. We're a team again, and we're back on the run. The only question I have is: how will we get to wherever it is we're going?

Chase pulls away and gazes up at the sky. "We'll have to find another mode of transportation." He looks at the men's vehicles with a determined glint in his eye. "I'm sure our friends can help us out."

EIGHTEEN

Chase

I QUICKLY GRAB OUR THINGS AND TOSS THEM IN THE BACK OF ONE OF
the cars. It's a temporary solution until I can find something better.
Maybe the whole train idea isn't such a bad idea?

"You ready?" I keep my voice gentle, not wanting to startle
Cara. I don't know how she's handling her first kill. She killed a man
to save my life, but now she displays classic signs of shock.

She nods, eyes wide, unblinking, like a deer in the headlights—
frozen in fear and unable to speak. A beat late, her reactions lag
behind where they should be and she moves woodenly and robotic.
The poor thing's on autopilot, her mind struggling to process what
happened.

"C'mon." I take her hand and lead her to the car. "We have to
get out of here before more men come."

She follows me silently, seeming to understand what's going on
without needing further explanation. I hold the door for her and she
slides into the passenger seat, fastening her seatbelt with a trembling
hand. She looks out at the carnage left behind with an expression
equal parts relief and horror.

I take off my rucksack and rummage through it until I find what
I'm looking for: a satellite phone full of Guardian HRS magic. I

connect with Command and Control to report the second string of bodies I leave behind.

"Any idea how they tracked you down?" Sam's tone is nearly as flat as mine.

"I'm struggling to answer that." I slip into the driver's seat and crank the engine. It roars to life, and I exit the motel parking lot as fast as I can. "It's not the watch. We left that far behind us. My primary concern is our little gunfight will draw the authorities. The one thing Cara can't afford is to be detained by the local police. That will attract even more attention."

"We'll make the appropriate calls," CJ speaks up, his Texan drawl the only thing distinguishing his deep voice from Sam's. "You're definitely setting a record for the highest body count during a mission."

"Definitely not my intent." The morbid statement finds me shaking my head. First assignment with the Guardians and Protectors and I'm already setting the wrong records.

Need to squash that fast.

"Sam's on the line with the local police." CJ clears his throat. "The shots were called in, and they're on the way. Best you vacate ASAP."

"Already on it."

"We'll manage the scene from this end. Meanwhile, do what you do best. Ditch the car. Find alternate transportation. And drop off the face of the earth."

Drop off the face of the earth.

"That's been the plan this whole time, but somehow, they keep finding us."

"Understood. I don't have any insight. Just do what you do best." CJ gives me my marching orders.

"Copy that."

I glance at Cara. She's back to the finger-twisting thing. I know her well enough to know that's what she does when stressed. A shadow hangs over her as she stares out the window. I can't tell if she's following my conversation with Sam and CJ or is completely zoned out.

Much like yesterday, we drive in silence; the only noise comes from the tires humming over the asphalt. Unlike yesterday, with our misunderstandings and lack of communication, this silence is different.

Cara stares straight ahead, her face pale and her body tense. I try to focus on the road, but I can't help but glance at her every so often. Her expression is a mix of shock and relief, though she doesn't speak a single word during the entire drive.

I need to get her talking and debrief what happened. If I let her stew too long with her thoughts, the trauma of taking a life will fester and rot. I turn my attention to Cara.

"Talk to me." I keep my voice low and soothing, praying her mental state isn't too far gone.

Her eyelids flicker, and she swallows hard. "What do you want me to say?"

"What happened back there was justified. You did nothing wrong." I reach over and place my hand over hers, giving her fingers a light squeeze. "The men who attacked you were there to kill you. You saved both our lives by taking that man's life. If it had been the other way around, we'd both be dead right now." My words seem to penetrate her foggy mind, and she relaxes slightly under my touch.

But she's not in a place to talk.

"It's never easy taking a life."

I give her hand another reassuring squeeze and want to tell her she's going to be all right, but that would be a lie. Not to mention, that isn't what she needs right now. I keep talking, my voice low and steady, letting her process what happened.

"You were incredibly brave and strong." My words slowly penetrate the fog of her mind, and she gradually responds with a sniff.

A tear trickles down her cheek, and she scrubs it away with the back of her hand.

"How do you do it?" Tears fill her eyes.

"Do you mean when I kill a man?"

"Yes."

"I don't focus on the life I took."

"How do you do that?"

"Because I focus on the lives I save instead. What you did back there was justified." I glance over at her tear-streaked face. "You saved me."

"How did they find us?"

"I don't know."

"What do we do now?"

"I'm figuring that out."

We drive in silence for a while. She doesn't speak for the longest time, which worries me. Hopefully, she takes the time to process what happened and will talk about it later.

While she doesn't talk about what happened, she's calmer now —significantly so—though still quiet compared to her normal self. My hope is our conversation, as short as it was, helps her accept her actions. She's still shaken, but no longer paralyzed by fear or guilt.

Finally, I break the quiet, offering a small smile.

"I don't see signs we're being followed." I check the rearview mirror and see nothing but an empty road behind us. "We need to stop."

"Stop? Why?" She gasps as panic seizes her.

"I need a new shirt, and you need something to bandage your temple." I tap my temple in the same spot where a bullet grazed her skin.

She lifts a hand to explore the wound, grimacing with a sharp intake of breath. "What about your arm?" Her attention shifts to me.

"It's just a flesh wound." My grin cocks up on one side, but she doesn't appreciate my attempt at making a joke.

"It's more than that." She winces as she looks at the wound. "Mine is just a flesh wound." She flips down the visor and inspects the abrasion along her temple.

Another millimeter, and she'd be dead.

"It was too fucking close."

My arm is another matter. The bullet bit into my flesh, punching a hole through the muscle. I think there's an exit wound but haven't had time to check. I barely felt it when I was hit, but the wound throbs now, and that throbbing intensifies. I wince and try to push back the pain.

"We need to do something about your arm. Is there a local drugstore or something?" She peers out the window, but there's no place to stop.

"We're not stopping here."

"It's bleeding." She points at my wound, then tugs at the hem of her shirt. After a few seconds of trying to rip it, she lets out a frustrated huff.

"What's wrong?" I'm not exactly clear what she's trying to do.

"I was gonna rip my shirt and use it as a bandage to wrap around your arm until we can dress it properly."

I take a second to respond, and I don't know why. But then it hits me. Cara is no helpless female. She's strong, resilient, and thinking more like a teammate than a client. And she's absolutely right. I need to stop the bleeding.

"Use my knife." I shift, lifting my hip with the intention of handing her the blade stowed in my back pocket, but my wounded arm protests.

"Surely we can stop for a second?" She looks at me, expression grim but determined.

I get it, and she's right. The next town is forty miles from here. That's a long time to let a wound bleed. With my senses on high alert, I make a concession.

I pull over to the side of the road and let Cara fish my knife out of the back pocket of my pants. She doesn't waste any time slicing a strip of fabric from the bottom of her shirt. Pushing up my sleeve, she's not the least bit squeamish about blood.

Before I know it, she ties a secure knot over the bullet wound, which seems to stop the bleeding.

"There. That's better. I need first aid supplies to do a better job, but it'll work for now."

"Thanks. Did you see an exit wound?"

"It looked like the bullet went right through. I'm assuming that's a good thing?"

"Hopefully."

"What does that mean?"

"Only that I'm lucky the bullet missed any arteries and punched straight through the muscle. But that doesn't mean it's a clean wound."

"But there's no bullet. I don't get what you mean by clean? It went all the way through."

"There's also a hole in my shirt. Think of the bullet punching through my shirt. It punches a hole in the shirt, and that bit of fabric can lodge itself in the wound."

"What happens if that's the case?"

"If that fabric is in the wound, it's going to get infected."

"Then we need to get you to a hospital."

"No hospital."

"But you said it'll get infected and…"

"Hospitals are required by law to report knife and bullet wounds to the police." I cut her off to explain. "We can't afford to take that risk."

"Oh." She leans back and blows out a breath. "Then what do we do?"

"Hope it doesn't get infected."

"That's not good enough."

"We'll stop at the next town and get some first aid supplies to do a better job. And antiseptic to clean it."

"I still think a doctor would be better."

"It's simple. All we need is to irrigate the wound and flush out the fabric, if any is in there."

"Irrigate? With antiseptic?"

"Yup."

"That sounds incredibly painful."

"Pain is merely a state of mind."

"Said no human ever." She gives me a look like I'm crazy, but that statement's partially true.

With enough focus, I can push back the pain. Not that I'm doing a good job of that now, but it's possible.

I don't stop until we reach the next town. With the blood

saturating my shirt, I send Cara in for first aid supplies and to grab a clean shirt for me, as well as one for her.

In the parking lot, we perform basic first aid on each other. Like I suspected, her wound is superficial, covered easily by a Band-Aid. Mine is more complicated.

Using the antiseptic—aka alcohol—she flushes the wound while I do my best not to make a sound. She's thorough, and it stings like a motherfucker, but she finally decides it's clean enough to wrap it in a bandage.

"Are you sure you're going to be okay?" She places the back of her hand over my forehead, feeling my temperature.

"I'm sure. Thanks to you." I lie, even though I'm not sure at all. I don't want to worry her more than she already is. "I don't have a fever."

"I know, but I want to know what normal feels like in case it gets infected."

I'm not sure whether to be surprised she's thinking ahead, worried she's thinking about the worst thing that can happen, or simply blown away by how calm she appears.

Bottom line—Cara's fucking phenomenal.

"I'm going to be okay, but we need to keep moving." I smile, grateful for her support.

"Want me to drive?" She points toward my injured arm.

There's a super quick debate in my head where I argue the merits of whether I should drive, or if putting her behind the wheel makes sense. Ultimately, I decide she needs the distraction that comes with driving to get her mind off killing a man back there. My arm hurts like a motherfucker. I could definitely use the rest.

With Cara behind the wheel, we set out again.

NINETEEN

Chase

MY ARM ACHES AS I SETTLE INTO MY SEAT. THANKFULLY, THE BULLET punched right through my bicep, but I'm not out of the woods. If I'm lucky, no remnant of my shirt remains in the wound. I'm hoping the bullet took the tiny bite of fabric with it when it flew out the other side, but I've learned not to rely on luck.

As for luck, we're back on the road, watching the desert fly by, and there's no sign of anyone on the road. No one in front of us, and no police chasing us.

Once again, we ride in silence. I'm trying to strategize our next move while Cara appears lost in her thoughts. A few minutes later, however, she takes a deep breath and lets it out in a rush.

"I feel like I'm going crazy."

"Why would you say that?" I sit up straight, then regret it when the wound protests being moved.

"This isn't supposed to be my life." She furrows her brows and purses her lips.

"How's that?" A rhetorical question, I ask only because I'm interested in what she envisioned for her life before any of this happened.

"On the run. Men who want to kill me? I can't believe this is happening. I'm a nobody." Her voice quivers as she stares out the front windshield, almost as if ashamed to look at me.

"You're not a nobody. You simply had the misfortune of witnessing your father's murder." I purposefully keep my voice soft.

Cara shuts her eyes and her shoulders slouch forward. She takes in a quivering breath and slowly nods. Her crestfallen expression guts me. She doesn't deserve any of this.

If I could, I would wish it all away, but wishes are for fools. I'm here for a purpose, and that purpose is to keep the assholes who want her dead from turning that into a reality.

"There is that." She takes a deep breath and lets out a long sigh. "Is it bad I don't know how to feel about my father's death?" Her lips tremble, as if she's trying to hide her feelings.

We haven't talked much about her father. Part of that arose out of necessity. There simply hasn't been time to delve into the deep, emotional mess of her life.

"It seems like maybe you need someone to talk to about it with. I happen to be free and have plenty of time to listen."

I make the offer freely and hope she feels comfortable enough to open up to me, which seems an odd thought considering where my mouth and dick were not too long ago. But sexual intimacy and emotional intimacy are two very different things.

Our chemistry may be off-the-charts hot, but we've only known each other a handful of days.

We're practically strangers.

"There is that." She dips her head and her hair cascades to the side, hiding her face from view.

"I'm serious. Tell me about your father." I do my best to prod gently. The thing is, I'm curious and want to know everything about the woman driving beside me.

"What do you want to know?" she mumbles softly, her voice barely audible.

"Mitzy has a saying." I smile with encouragement, hoping she'll open up.

"What's that?" She's curious enough to tilt her head and glance at me. A glimmer of hope returns to her eyes. It's clear she needs to talk.

"She says the best way to tell a story is to start at the beginning and keep going until you reach the end."

"Which beginning?" She blows out a puff of air that lifts her hair away from her eyes. The strands gracefully dance in the air before they slowly settle back down on her shoulder with a gentle bounce. She then sucks in a deep breath.

That's her way of stalling.

"How about the very beginning? You were born." I try to take the stress off.

If I can get her started, she'll eventually get around to talking about her father.

"We're going that far back?" Her lips curve, slightly amused by what I said.

"Call it general curiosity."

"Curiosity? You're curious about my birth?" Her eyes widen as she tilts her head thinking about what I said.

"I'm curious about everything when it comes to the woman I slept with. I have to say last night was epic." I flash her a cheeky grin and the color in her cheeks deepens in a blush. What a wonderful reward for a little bit of teasing.

Cara has the prettiest blushes.

"Lord…" Her eyes widen as she places a palm against her cheek. "I hate that. I blush so easily."

"It's sexy."

"Sexy?" She glares at me, but it's done in fun. Her left eyebrow arches in challenge. "I'm not sure I agree."

"Trust me. It's very sexy." I debate whether to tell her where else she blushes, but decide she's not ready for that. Instead, I steer our conversation back to her father. "Tell me your story, princess. You were born."

"Yeah."

"Any brothers or sisters?"

"None." She pauses and looks away to focus on driving. Her

eyes mist with tears as her shoulders and arms tense, clearly lost in the memories of her family.

"A single child then. I bet your parents doted on you." My brows pinch, realizing I've never heard her speak about a mother.

"They did." A soft laugh escapes her, but there's sadness there as well. "I was my mother's little princess."

"Oh." I bite my lower lip.

The first time I called her princess, it was out of anger and frustration. She was acting like a snit and making assumptions about me that are patently untrue. Looks like I need to pick a new name and call her something else.

A smile curves my lips thinking about the first few hours after Bravo team delivered her into my care. I remember thinking why couldn't she be a middle-aged, overweight man, instead of the stunning beauty she is?

Now, I wouldn't trade her for the world.

"Did your father call you princess?"

Please say no.

If so, me using that moniker is creepy as fuck. Not that I'm a big fan of nicknames. I actually cringe when I hear couples calling each other *baby* or *cupcake* or any of a hundred other things. *Sweetie?* I could try that?

"My father never called me much of anything." Her eyes dim and she averts her gaze.

"Were you close to your father?" I remember her saying her father was her hero at one time.

"We were exceptionally close—once." Her lids flicker and her body tenses.

"Exceptionally?" An odd choice of word.

"Not in a creepy, abusive kind of way, but I was his little girl. I was very much a daddy's girl. He gave me anything and everything I ever wanted, and after my mother died, he doubled down. I'm very much a spoiled princess." She murmurs that last bit, as if embarrassed, then bows her head as a sudden wave of grief overcomes her.

It's clear she's yet to grieve her father's death. No matter what she learned about him in the end, she loves the doting father he once was.

"I'm sorry. I didn't realize your mother passed. How old were you?"

She takes a deep breath. "I was barely eight." Her voice cracks and her pain feels fresh. Still raw.

"I'm sorry for your loss." My heart aches for her loss, and I give her nothing but a pathetic, sympathetic smile. She deserves a hug.

"Thank you, but it was a very long time ago." Her smile is sad. It's the kind of expression someone gives when they've lived with their pain for a very long time.

"The grief from losing a parent never goes away." My hand instinctively covers my heart, as if I feel her pain.

Not that I would know what that kind of grief feels like.

My mother is an old battle axe. When death tries to take her, she's going to go down fighting, and she's scrappy enough she might just win. My father is no different. He may have left his career in the Merchant Marines to raise me, but he's definitely a man's man. He's got the heart of an angel, the temper of the devil, and is as stubborn as a mule. He's also fiercely protective of those he loves, and he loves his family very much.

"And I've lost both of mine." She rubs at her breastbone and an ache that will never go away.

"If I may, how did your mother pass?" I watch her closely, concerned about her mental state.

"It was an accident." Her voice trails off and I'm not sure whether to push or wait for her to continue.

"Oh." I let the heavy silence stretch, unsure how deep to dig.

"A boating accident." When she finally speaks, her words are shaky, as though struggling to maintain her composure. Poor thing is barely holding it together.

"Really?" I blink, surprised. That's not what I expected.

"It was the second year my father was stationed in Nicaragua."

"He was military? I thought he was a diplomat?"

"Yes, and yes. He was a former Marine and served four years. He met my mother in college, using his GI benefits. They were both

PolySci majors and dreamed of spending their lives overseas as diplomats."

"I see."

"My mother got pregnant with me her last year in college and never joined the diplomatic ranks. My father, however, got assigned as a protocol officer overseas. I spent my first four years in Germany."

"An interesting place to grow up."

"I don't remember much, but I do remember being happy." A faint smile forms on her lips.

"That's good. You have some wonderful memories."

"I do. And my father loved her. He loved her so much. His second assignment was to Costa Rica."

"From Germany to Central America. An interesting path. I'm surprised he didn't stay in Europe."

"I don't know why he was reassigned. Whether he requested it or not, but Costa Rica was an amazing place to grow up. There were a lot of restrictions as the kid of one of the embassy personnel, but it was amazing."

"So you do have happy memories of your father?"

"I do. As a protocol officer, his hours could be unpredictable, but he showered me with gifts when the long days turned into late nights, or when work took him away for days at a time. I went to a private school with all the embassy kids. Learned to speak Spanish. Toured everywhere. It was amazing."

"How long was he assigned there?" My information pins her father in Nicaragua, not Costa Rica.

"It was just before my mother died. This time, instead of hopping continents, he requested reassignment to Nicaragua. I think he was settling into his role and establishing ties with the local movers and shakers."

"You lived in Nicaragua a long time."

"From the age of eight until I went to college. My father took us on a family trip along the coast. He and my mother went out diving while I stayed behind with my nanny and played in the sand." Her expression darkens and I give her space, knowing this is a sad memory.

Cara sniffs and swipes at her cheek. Her grip tightens on the wheel and she stares down the long and lonely highway for a few seconds before continuing.

"I didn't know what happened until the morning. They were late returning. My nanny took me to our bungalow. We had dinner. Watched some movies. She let me stay up late. Not once did I sense something was wrong."

"Did your nanny know?"

"She did, but she didn't want to upset me. I later found out there was a search party looking for my mother. My father never really told me what happened, other than she got separated from the group of divers and never surfaced. They searched for days, hoping to find her, but eventually had to give up."

"That had to have been horrific."

"I won't lie. It was very hard, but my father got me through it. I'd bonded with our nanny, and with my mother gone, my father didn't want to separate me from Lola. He stayed in Nicaragua until…" She chokes up. "Well, until the end."

"I feel like you need a hug." I twist in my seat, but with my bum arm and the restriction of the seatbelt, that's not happening.

"Thanks. I appreciate it."

"When did things begin to sour with your father?"

"Oh lord." She flicks her eyes to the roof of the car as if thinking. "I would definitely say when I hit puberty."

"That's a rough age for anyone."

"For him in particular. I'm thankful for Lola because she helped me through all the awkward firsts. My father—I don't know what happened, but from the moment I started developing breasts, he grew distant and fiercely overprotective. I was no longer his little girl, but an unruly teen he wanted nothing to do with. To me, he was an uncompromising tyrant. But isn't that the way it is for everyone?"

"I'm sure he wasn't that bad. Just a father looking out for his daughter."

"Perhaps. Things just kind of changed. I don't know what it was… Well, I know now." She rolls her eyes and I lean forward. "As the Director of Protocol, my father worked with the A-list of who's who in Nicaragua. From the ambassador, and other high ranked U.S. officials, to the president of Nicaragua, prominent political players, and notable business executives, he rubbed elbows with anyone and everyone involved in Nicaraguan politics. That's where it all started."

"What started?"

"Well, my upstanding father, former Marine, protocol officer, and then director of protocol, rubbed elbows with the wrong men. Granted, it was his job, but corruption is rampant in Central America. Eventually, it rubbed off on him."

"What did he do?" I know this story, but feel like she needs to tell it. Speak it out loud. Maybe that will help with some of her grief. I can do this for her. Listen, that is.

"Well, my father got too cozy, or too greedy, or something snapped in his head. My memories of him as a girl are so different from the man he became."

"And what was that?"

"My father went to several parties at the Minister of the Interior's residence where…" She chokes up.

I know what she's going to say but want to hear it from her point of view.

"Th-they sold women at the parties. Rented them out to the guests. Kind of like a trial run, then sold them to the highest bidder. Maximus Angelo, the Minister of the Interior partnered with Artemus Gonzalez to acquire the women."

Bravo team's been active down in Nicaragua lately. Most recently, they raided the Minister of the Interior's estate where the man ran a human-trafficking operation. Artemus Gonzalez was his partner.

"And your father?"

"He supplied a steady stream of wealthy clients to Artemus Gonzales. He fed the machine, and profited from it."

The depravity in this world never shocks me.

"If he supplied the clients, why did they kill him?"

"Crisis of faith."

"Explain."

"Like I said, he called me out of the blue and said he needed to talk." She tips her head back and taps the steering wheel with her thumbs. "I flew home that night."

"When you met him, did he tell you then?"

"Not at first." She shakes her head. "Said he would tell me over dinner. Hank was there."

"Your handler?"

Hank was her former handler in the WITSEC program. He died protecting Cara, but not before telling her to contact Guardian HRS. I didn't realize he knew her father.

"My father's handler, then mine. That night, my father told me about the human trafficking and how he got involved supplying clients. He told me everything."

"Everything?"

"All of it." She curls in her lower lip. "He introduced me to Hank, said Hank was putting him into witness protection to testify against Artemus Gonzalez and Nicaragua's Minister of the Interior. Hank was there to extricate him that night. My father said I would never see him again and gave me my grandmother's watch. Said he needed me to have it. That if anything happened to him, he needed me to have the watch." Her voice cracks. "That's the night he died."

"How did that go down?"

"There was a raid by Artemus Gonzales's men. Hank hid me behind the bar. They shot my father in the chest. Shot Hank in the leg. One man stood over them and delivered a message."

"What was the message?"

"They told my father that men who crossed Artemus Gonzalez didn't live to talk about it. That's when they killed him."

The way she recounts it—so matter-of-factly—makes me cringe. She definitely hasn't processed her grief. How do I help her through something like this?

"And you heard all of this?"

"Heard and saw." She pauses, then takes in a deep breath. "There was a mirror where I saw everything."

"I'm surprised they let Hank live, to be honest."

"After they killed my father, they told Hank to tell his superiors to drop it."

"It?"

"The case I suppose. Although, with my father dead, there was no case."

Something doesn't sit right with me. I feel it in my bones, even if I can't put it into words.

"But they're after you? Why not take you out at the same time? No offense, but it's what I would do."

"That's what Hank said." She glances outside, looking away from me. "He told me *the dead don't talk*."

"Unfortunately, that's true, but it doesn't explain why they didn't kill you."

"I'm very good at hiding and not making noise. Gonzales's men left. Once they were gone, Hank called it in. Within fifteen minutes, the place was swarming with embassy personnel, Marines, FBI, CIA, and some other agency I've never heard of. Hank debriefed everyone. When he mentioned me, they decided my life was in jeopardy because I heard the men mention Artemus Gonzales by name."

"Still doesn't explain how they know about you. Not to mention, the U.S. doesn't have jurisdiction for a murder that occurred on Nicaraguan soil. Not to be too blunt about it, but you're not an asset."

"My father told me what he did. That's why Hank protected me."

"On the surface, that makes sense, but it's not admissible in court."

"What do you mean?"

"What you have is hearsay. It's not independent recollection of fact. It's inadmissible. I get they want to protect you, but once you left Nicaragua, you're no longer of interest to Gonzales. Or shouldn't be."

"Then why are his men after me?"

"It has to be something else."

There's a worm in my ear. Something she said earlier I can't pin down. The more I try to bring it to the forefront of my mind, the more it slips through my fingers. I leave it and let my subconscious mull it over. It'll come to me when it comes to me.

"Well, Hank said I needed protection and hitmen are after me. I don't know what to make of what you said, but Hank believed there was a leak in their organization. He got me out of Nicaragua. Flew me out in a military aircraft and put me directly into the FBI's WITSEC program. If I have nothing of value; hearsay? Is what you called it?"

"That's right."

"Then it doesn't make sense."

"We're missing something important."

"I don't know what it could be. I've told you everything I told Hank. The FBI said they wanted to protect me, that I'd be called upon to testify at trial. Hank insisted on staying with me, which I agreed to. He was the only face I knew. But after they raided the first safe house, Hank said something felt off."

"A leak?"

She's mentioned this multiple times.

"It got to where he trusted none of his contacts." She tucks a strand of hair behind her ear. "He told me about Guardian HRS. Said if anything happened to him, I was to call your team."

"Someone found you."

"They did. He couldn't figure it out. We went all cash. Avoided public places. He didn't report in to his superiors. He couldn't figure out how they knew where to find me. The gunmen. Not his superiors."

"Let me get this straight. Gonzales's men have been tracking you the whole time?"

"Yes."

None of this makes sense, but there's definitely a pattern. Gonzales's men found her in the safe house. Tracked her wherever Hank took her when he went off the grid. Found her at the airport when Bravo team picked her up. Tracked us in the desert. Then found us this morning in the hotel room.

What am I missing?

"I guess, but I don't know how."

"Or how they knew to look for you."

"That's right. And that's why Hank felt there was a leak in the FBI. He mentioned several of the men my father introduced to Artemus Gonzales were high ranking U.S. government officials. All I can think is that maybe one of them is in the FBI and is trying to…" Her voice hitches and I finish her sentence.

"Tie up loose ends? That's exactly what I would do." I can't help but be blunt.

Cara's no delicate flower. She doesn't need me to sugarcoat anything. In fact, the one thing I'm learning about her is she does best when she has all the facts.

"Yes."

"I don't know what's happening, but we're going to strip you down one last time."

"Hmm…" Her brow creases in a frown.

"What's wrong?"

"That doesn't sound like the fun way."

"Sadly not." I can't help but smile. It's good to see her making a joke. It shows healthy adaption to extreme stress. Which means I don't have to worry about her becoming catatonic on me. "But they're tracking you somehow. We need to figure out how they're doing that."

And for that, I need Mitzy's expertise.

"Well, it's another lonely road." She gestures down the arrow-straight highway.

Far in the distance, foothills bunch together at the base of the Rocky Mountains.

"No one in front of us and no one behind us." She glances at the rearview mirror. "Any idea where we're going? Or what we're going to do with this stolen car?"

"I'm working on that, but first, I want to call in to my team and brainstorm for a bit."

"Brainstorm?"

"Figure out how they are tracking you."

"Oh." She taps the steering wheel and shrugs. "I'm no help there."

I reach across and gently squeeze her hand, not wanting to let go once I touch her. "You'll get through this." I do my best to assure her things will get better.

She meets my eyes with a weak attempt at a smile before looking out the rearview mirror again. We both know that things will never be the same, but for now, she doesn't have to face it alone.

"Are you checking for someone following?" I can't help the upwelling of pride.

Maybe this is what she needs to regain control. Whatever it is, it's a significant change and impressive. No longer a passive actor, she's stepping up as a valuable partner.

TWENTY

Chase

THE DESOLATE DESERT SPREADS OUT AS FAR AS THE EYE CAN SEE. The sand and rocks shimmer in the heat and mirages on the road tempt with water that isn't there. The day is stunning and we're nearing the base of the Rocky Mountains.

"Is it weird there are no cops and nobody else on the road?" Cara points us down the highway, moving at a decent clip.

"Command is taking care of the authorities."

I respond to a text from my team, giving them an update on our plans and our injuries.

Doc Summers bombards me with a flurry of questions about my injury. I answer to the best of my ability, but it's clear she's not happy. There's a bit of back and forth, but ultimately my marching orders are given. Doc Summers wants to explore the wound and put me on antibiotics. Which means we're headed to the mountains and the private refuge of none other than Forest Summers, Guardian HRS's founder.

"Ah..." Her gaze shifts to her wrist where her grandmother's watch used to sit. "I'm sorry I got you into this mess." Her gaze flicks up to my injured arm.

There's that niggling itch again. I try to force whatever my brain's trying to tell me to the forefront of my brain, but the thought slips away.

"You have no reason to apologize to me. This is what I signed up for." I reach over and squeeze her hand.

"But you're injured, and you lost your Jeep." Her attention moves to my shoulder where blood stains my shirt.

"It's just a flesh wound."

"This is a flesh wound." Her mouth twists as her fingers tap the Band-Aid on her temple. "Your arm, however…"

"Is fine. I'm not stopping until we've put enough distance behind us." A lingering sense of unease twists my guts.

"What's going to happen to your Jeep?"

"Command will sort that out."

One of the things I love about Guardian HRS, and being a Protector, is I don't have to bother with minor details like that. They take care of all the extraneous things, allowing me to remain focused on my job.

Keeping Cara alive.

She squeezes my hand and turns to stare out the window. We drive in silence, our minds focused on the task ahead. She's shaken, but strong.

Stronger than I ever could've imagined.

Resilient.

An hour later, we arrive at the next town, where I tell her to pull into an abandoned parking lot across from a bus station.

"Park out of the line of sight of the surveillance cameras." I point to the ones I see.

"Why are we stopping here?"

Is it the cameras? Is that how they're tracking us?

Mitzy's tracked people down before, using facial recognition and security cameras. It requires significant technical skills and access to the camera feeds. It's difficult, but not impossible. She also embeds worldwide locaters in Guardians and Protectors alike. A passive system, it allows her to track down Guardian HRS operators in the event something happens to us.

Security cameras and facial recognition may explain how we

were tracked to the motel, but not how they found us deep into BLM land.

"Chase?"

"Huh?"

"I asked what we're doing here?" Cara looks around the abandoned lot.

"Oh, sorry," I apologize for the distraction and answer her question. "We're taking a bus."

"A bus?" Cara's brows pinch together. "Is that wise? Can't they track that?"

Good girl, she's thinking all the right things.

"We're letting them think we're taking a bus."

"Huh?" Her mouth turns down in a puzzled frown while her gaze flicks from me to the parking lot again, her confusion evident in the scrunching of her forehead.

"We're going to purchase tickets that hopefully take them on a wild goose chase."

"I don't get it?"

"I want them to follow the bus, not us."

"And where are we going?"

I climb out of the car and grab my things. "We're going to grab supplies, hitch a ride, and head into the desert."

"Um, that didn't work very well the first time around." She cocks her head, trying to puzzle it out.

"You're right. We're headed toward the mountains this time."

"And how are we getting there?"

My phone pings with a message from Mitzy, along with the coordinates I need. "We're hopping a train."

"A train?" Her voice is uncertain and tinged with disbelief. "I thought that was a joke?" Seriously confused now, her face twists, perplexed as she questions me.

"No joke. We're taking a train."

"To the mountains?" She glances around the vacant lot and over at the bus terminal with one lonely bus. "Wouldn't a bus be safer?" A sheen of perspiration coats her face, making her skin glisten.

"Last time I was out in heat like this, it didn't go very well." She wipes her brow and purses her lips.

My shirt clings to my skin while rivulets of sweat run down my chest and back. I probably smell like a mule; sour and pungent.

"We're ten miles from the next town. We'll grab first aid supplies, a change of clothes, plenty of water, and hitch a ride."

"Didn't your mother ever teach you not to hitchhike?" Her face flushes from the heat, making me question my decision.

"My mother taught me the best way to get from one place to another for free. Merchant Marine, remember? She's resourceful."

"Well, that's ships, not hitchhiking."

"My mother is a wealth of unusual talents. Trust me. I know what I'm doing."

"I trust you." But her expression says exactly the opposite. "But if we get picked up by a serial killer, I'm never forgiving you."

"Don't doubt me, princess." I reach for her hand. "Now, let's buy a ticket we're not going to use."

"Aren't they going to know we didn't get on the bus?"

"Maybe, but then they have to figure out where we went. I aim to make that as challenging as possible and buy us the time we need to disappear for real."

She doesn't protest as I wrap my arm around her waist and lead her toward the bus station. It's nearly deserted, but there are a few folks waiting for the bus. Keeping an eye out, I scan the crowd and strategize.

"Wait here." I gesture to an empty bench seat.

"Where are you going?"

"Working my magic." Her eyes follow me as I make the rounds, canvasing potential leads.

In a town this small, people go to the bus stop for only one reason. Either they're coming home or shipping out. I'm looking for the latter and find gold when a middle-aged couple walk in with a kid sporting a wide-eyed stare and a botched military haircut.

Kid's barely eighteen and obviously shipping out for basic training. The only question is which service. From the anchor tattoo on the dad's bicep, I guess Navy.

I can work with that.

I approach with a warm smile. "Headed to Basic?"

"Yes, sir." The kid suddenly straightens, standing tall and proud, but waivers with the insecurity of youth. In his eyes, a mix of excitement, fear, and eagerness mingle together.

"Navy?"

"No, sir. Army." His voice grows bolder, prouder, but there's still a hint of fear in his young, naïve face.

"Army Ranger myself. Welcome to the brotherhood." I shove out my hand, curious why the kid isn't following in his dad's footsteps. The kid's eyes light up at that, and I continue before he makes a fool of himself.

It's the perfect way to open up a conversation and warm up to the kid's parents. He's got tons of hard work ahead of him. I tell him a little about my career and how I became an Army Ranger and Scout Sniper, then I give a few tips for surviving basic training.

Half an hour passes before the signal's given to board the bus. I step back, letting the kid say goodbye to his folks. This is the last they'll hear from him until the end of basic. His mom sheds real tears. The father tries to hide misty eyes. They're clearly proud of their son, and I give them space for last goodbyes. When the kid boards the bus, I move to stand next to them and wave goodbye to the young recruit.

When the door to the bus closes, the father looks at me in confusion.

"Aren't you getting on the bus?"

"Sadly no. My wife and I are headed in the other direction." I twist around to wave at Cara. She smiles brightly and waves back, almost as if this is something we rehearsed. I scratch my head and stare at the bus schedule. "We hitched a ride, and thought we could catch a bus, but luck is not on our side. We're headed east." I heave a heavy sigh, playing it up, while hoping our common tie to the military makes the man comfortable offering a ride.

It's not him, however, who suggests it. The wife grips her husband's arm. "We're headed that way. You can ride with us and you might find better luck in the next town."

"Ah, that would be…" I rub at the back of my neck, pretending I don't want to put them out. "It would be amazing. You don't mind giving two strangers a lift?"

"Isn't this how it is?" Walter laughs. "The Army is always asking the Navy to step up." He clamps a hand on my shoulder— thankfully, the non-injured one—and gestures toward Cara. "Get your woman and we'll give you a lift."

"Gee, thanks. That's very decent of you." I twist and gesture for Cara to join us. Once she's close, I pull her in and wrap an arm around her waist. "Walter, this is my lovely bride, Cara."

When I say her name, I gently squeeze her waist and hope she plays along. To my delight, Cara takes everything in stride.

"Nice to meet you, Walter." She thrusts out her hand and Walter returns a gentle squeeze.

"Bride?" Walter's wife's expression perks up. "You're newlyweds?"

"Only just." Cara rocks back on her heels.

"I'm Betty." Instead of greeting Cara with a handshake, Betty folds Cara into a hug. "Now, why are newlyweds hitchhiking?" She glances at me, arching a brow in question.

"My parents hate him and his parents don't know about me," Cara fires back seamlessly and I can't help but grin. She's fucking fabulous in her delivery. "Got married in Vegas and are trying to make our way home. If there's a home left to go to."

"Now that sounds like a story." Betty takes Cara's arm and steers her outside. "And I love a great love story."

Walter looks at me, and I look back at him. We both shrug, which makes him laugh. It's one of those deep belly laughs that just makes a person feel good.

"Sounds like you've got an uphill battle, son."

I love the way Walter switches to calling me son. I hate to use these kind people, but desperate times call for a bit of a white lie.

"She's worth it." I stare longingly at Cara and realize how truthful that statement is. Somewhere along the way, I've fallen head over heels for my mysterious charge.

We share a ride with Walter and his wife, traveling a hundred miles closer to our destination before they let us out and we part ways.

"What now?" Cara waves to the sweet couple as I glance at my phone.

It's late in the afternoon, which means the sun's due to set within the next hour or two. Just enough time to hike to where Mitzy placed a giant X marks the spot on my phone's GPS.

"We've got a half hour hike ahead of us. How are you feeling?"

"Feeling like I should say something about hiking into the wilderness to catch a train is a bad idea."

"It's the best place."

"Why not hop on board in a rail yard where the trains aren't moving?"

"Because closed circuit surveillance monitors those. Out here, there's nothing but us and dust."

"Us and dust?" She cocks a hip forward and sticks out a foot. "Did you really just say that?"

"I did."

"And how are we going to jump on a train when it's moving? I don't know how fast you think I can run, but it's not fast at all."

"Then you're in luck."

"How's that?"

"Because the train is pulling out of the station five miles from here. It'll be barely chugging along, building up speed as it goes. It'll be a lazy stroll."

"Says the Army Ranger." She shakes her head. "I'm skeptical."

"Don't be."

"Why not?"

"Because I'll be there to help."

"And what do we do once we're on the train?"

"Mitzy's got it all laid out." I glance at the phone and double check my instructions.

"Care to share?"

"The train will be at the coordinates in fifty-seven minutes."

"That's oddly specific."

"Trains run on tight schedules."

"Never heard of a train being on time."

"That was in the past. It's mostly automated now. Which gives us fifty-six minutes to hike two miles."

"Two miles?" She glances around the dry, baked ground. "Do you remember what happened last time?"

"Last time, it was pushing a hundred twelve. It's barely over a hundred."

"And you want me to hike?"

"There is no other way, and it's not like it's strenuous. It's flatter than flat. Just mind the snakes."

"You had to remind me of the snakes." Cara lifts her arms up in the air, for dramatic effect. She's playing it up, not really complaining.

"Come on, princess." I swat her ass and love the way she lifts on her toes and gives a little shriek. "I'll protect you against the snakes. Just watch where you put your feet."

"Great. Just great." She spins around, shading her eyes from the setting sun. "Which way?"

TWENTY-ONE

Cara

WE HEAD OUT OF TOWN, WALKING BESIDE THE HIGHWAY. I TAKE IN the vastness of the desert, feeling small in comparison, and not completely sold on the idea of catching a train while it's chugging along the tracks, but Chase hasn't let me down yet.

The hot air feels like I'm walking through an oven, but the temperature, while hot, is nothing like it was a couple of days ago. I remember feeling as if the desert was cooking me from the inside out. This heat isn't as intense. It's barely tolerable, but not impossible.

After a brisk ten minutes of walking, I'm at once covered head to toe in sweat, yet surprisingly dry. I guess that kind of thing happens in arid places where there's zero humidity.

Growing up in Central America, hot always came with oppressive humidity that thickened the air. Dry heat is something else entirely.

When I turn toward Chase, he holds out a bottle of water, which I take and empty to the last drop.

"How're you holding up?" Concern lines his eyes.

"I'm good, actually."

"Glad to hear. It's not much farther."

We head to the coordinates sent to Chase on his phone. At first, there's no sign of railroad tracks anywhere, but as we veer away from the highway, they suddenly appear, running at an angle to the road.

"Ready for an adventure?" Chase holds out his hand, and I take it, loving the way his hand folds around mine.

"As ready as I can be."

He points toward the tracks. "This is the closest the train approaches the road. Watch where you step. This time of day, snakes are out and about."

"Great." I hate snakes, but I pay attention to what he says as we venture onto the hard-baked ground.

Head down, I watch where I step, praying I don't meet up with a snake, but every now and then, I take in the scenery around me. Cacti and other desert plants dot the landscape. In between the scraggly vegetation, there's nothing but cracked dirt, pebbles, rock, and small lizards scurrying across the sand.

So far, no snakes.

I've spent enough time in the desert to appreciate its beauty. Nothing like the rainforests at home teaming with life. In the desert, life must be tenacious and determined to survive.

"You're really doing okay?" He's likely worried about the last time I was out in the heat and collapsed.

"I'm good. Still sweating." Evidently, that's a sign of heat exhaustion.

"The train's running on schedule." He checks his phone.

"Are we going to make it?"

"We have plenty of time."

We continue on, trading casual conversation here and there, but mostly we're silent. He's wrapped up in his thoughts and I'm wrapped up in mine.

Eventually, however, we approach the tracks. My heart races with anticipation. I'm going to jump aboard a freight train and ride it to the mountains. Just thinking about it makes me shake my head. Like I said to Chase earlier, how did this become my life?

Chase drops to a knee. He places his hand on the thick steel and closes his eyes. I stare at him, confused, but then he waves for me to join him.

"Here." He takes my hand and places it on the rail. "Do you feel it?"

"What am I supposed to feel?"

"The vibrations of the train. You can feel them long before the train comes into sight. If you put your ear to the steel, you can hear it coming long before you see it."

"Wow." I feel vibrations and glance down the length of the track. "How far is it?"

"The train just pulled out of the yard. It's two miles away."

"And how do we jump it?"

"We run."

"I thought you were going to say that." The vibrations under my hand grow stronger. Indeed, when I look up, the locomotive is visible and heading straight toward us. "Um, Chase?"

"Yes."

"I don't think I can jump that high." I may be able to run alongside the train, but there's no way I can make that leap.

"Don't worry. I'll jump on first, then give you a lift. Get ready. It'll be here before you know it." He moves to the edge of the tracks while I eye the train dubiously. It's moving faster than I thought it would.

The rumble of a vehicle echoes behind me. I turn to find a black SUV hurtling toward us. Its engine growls like a wild beast and its tires kick up rocks and sand as it hurtles toward us.

"Chase!"

The word barely escapes my lips before Chase wraps his strong arms around me, diving for the ground. We hit the ground hard. He cushions my fall with his body, landing on his back with a grunt. An eruption of gunfire sends bullets ripping through the air.

The sting of rock and debris pricks my skin. Trapped with no cover, the harsh sound of bullets flying around us rings in my ears like thunder.

Chase doesn't miss a beat. He rolls me to the side, shielding me from the onslaught of bullets with his body. Pinned down with no cover, the SUV's rapid-fire rattles all around us, making it impossible to think.

Chase, however, isn't paralyzed by fear. He pulls his gun and returns fire with deadly calm, retaliating with one precise shot after another.

The deafening report of his pistol pierces the air and strikes the SUV's windshield, shattering it on impact and leaving a spiderweb-like pattern on the glass.

But it isn't enough to knock out the driver.

Chase takes aim again, his pistol bellowing as he unleashes another shot. The air explodes with the violent report of his pistol. This time, the vehicle swerves out of control, kicking up a cloud of dust and debris.

The ground beneath my feet shakes as the train's deafening roar echoes over the land, drowning out all other sounds. The clacking of its wheels is deafening, matching the accelerating rhythm of my racing heart.

Chase takes one look at the SUV, then grips my hand tight as the train whistle pierces the air.

"Run. We have to take cover on the other side of the tracks."

Somewhere between fear and shock, I catch sight of a second man in the SUV with a gun pointed toward us. Chase doesn't flinch. He yanks me toward the tracks as the train speeds toward us.

The second man from the SUV peppers us with bullets as Chase and I leap over the tracks right in front of the train barreling down on us. Chase stumbles, nearly trips on the rails, but then is back on his feet with a sudden burst of strength.

"You good?" he shouts over the roar of the speeding train and his eyes search mine for an answer. "Are you hit?"

"I'm fine." I yell to be heard over the deafening roar of the train. Its sheer speed generates a powerful wind that whips through my hair and pushes me back. Caught somewhere between fear, surprise, and disbelief, the acrid smell of burning coal and screeching metal floods my nostrils and coats my tongue.

How the hell did those men find us out here? How do they keep tracking me?

I get why Chase had us cross the tracks. It puts the train between us and the shooter. It's the best protection against the hitman on the other side.

"Are you ready for this?" His grip on my hand tightens, almost painfully.

The sweat on my palms makes our grip slippery, but I yell loud enough over the roar of the train to be heard.

"As I'll ever be."

He explained the plan, and my stomach churns with nervous excitement. We have to run alongside the speeding train, doing our best to match its speed. He'll jump on board first, then hoist me up behind him.

Chase takes the lead, building up speed and pulling me behind him. My feet pound against the hardened ground as I push myself. My legs ache with the effort, but I push harder, gritting my teeth against the searing heat of the sun and the dry, hot air burning my lungs. With every step, the train's deafening roar grows louder. Its wheels click ominously. A single misstep could be deadly, but I don't focus on the ground blurring beneath my feet.

Chase picks up the pace. His fingers dig into my hand as he drags me along. My lungs burn with exertion. My breaths are nothing but ragged gasps.

He stumbles, and my heart skips a beat as I fear what would happen if he fell, but he recovers and pushes me to run faster.

The train thunders beside us and the wind from the passing cars hits my face like a wall, threatening to knock me off balance. I push myself, running harder than ever before.

As we approach the railcar, Chase lunges for a ladder at the back of the railcar with his free hand. My heart drops as he stumbles again, but he recovers quickly, hoisting himself onto the moving railcar. My lungs burn as I continue running. I double down on my sprint, doing my best to maintain his crazy speed. Then I'm suddenly lifted off my feet and swing through the air.

Chase deposits me onto the back of the railcar like I'm a sack of potatoes. My shoulder screams in protest, and I land with a force that knocks the air from my lungs.

For now, we escaped a fourth wave of hitmen sent to kill me. I'm safe. We're on the train, and as I sit here, catching my breath, something warm and sticky oozes under my hand. I look down at a pool of blood and Chase gripping his leg.

TWENTY-TWO

Cara

"HOLY SHIT. CHASE, WHAT HAPPENED?" MY HEART RACES AS I TAKE in the sight of him. Blood seeps through his pants, staining the fabric and pooling on the metal.

"Fucking asshole, got my leg." He grits his teeth against the pain and his face twists in agony.

"You're shot?" I twist around and confirm what I already know.

Chase gives me a withering look, then quickly unbuckles his belt and draws it free of his belt loops. My eyes widen as he wraps it around his thigh, just above the wound. He winces in pain, sweat beading his forehead as he tries to feed the end through the buckle.

"Help me." With his wounded arm, he can't do it himself.

I hesitate for only a moment while my mind races. This is bad. Really bad. But I need to keep a level head. I kneel beside him and cinch the belt even tighter, ignoring his sharp intake of breath, or the way his muscles twitch beneath my fingers.

As I perform a quick inspection, my heart sinks. "I don't see an exit wound." My voice is barely a whisper, and dread creeps up my spine.

Chase's face pales. "Well shit. This is bad." He tips his head back and closes his eyes. His breaths come in short, shallow gasps as he wrestles with his pain.

The sound of the wheels clacking over the joints of the train tracks is the only thing breaking the eerie silence. Suddenly, Chase fishes his phone out of his pocket, his expression hardening. My heart beats wildly as he takes my hand and we sit in silence.

"What do we do?" My voice trembles with fear. Why does bad stuff keep happening to me? I lost Hank and now Chase has been shot, not once, but twice.

"We don't panic," Chase's reply is firm and his grip on my hand tightens.

His eyes lock onto mine with steely resolve. I force myself to meet his gaze, trying to silence the rising panic within me. He releases my hand, then places it on my arm.

"Cara, look at me." Strong and steady, he sounds fully in control, but there's an edge of pain wrapped all around his deep voice.

I do as he says, swallowing down my panic.

"The bleeding's stopped. We're on the train. The shooter can't reach us. I'll call it in."

"And do what?" I swallow hard and do my best to suppress the bile rising in the back of my throat. "We're in the middle of nowhere, riding a train to lord knows where."

"We're headed to Colorado."

"Where? Where in Colorado?"

"Forest has a place there. We're meeting Doc Summers there. She'll look at my arm and my leg as well."

My mind reels, trying to make sense of how nonchalant he's being about getting shot. There's blood everywhere, yet he acts as if it's no big deal.

"How can you be so cavalier about this?"

"What do you mean?"

"Getting shot?"

"It's nothing." His tone is almost dismissive.

"Nothing?" My voice is incredulous. "That's a lot of blood."

"It's fine." Once again, his expression hardens.

"Fine?" I stare at him, dumbfounded.

"That's what I said."

"Chase, you've got a bullet in your leg. And your arm…" My words trail off as I look at him and the pain etched in his features. He's trying to be strong for me.

He's far from fine.

"I've seen guys with far worse. Trust me, this is nothing." He lifts a finger when someone answers the phone.

While he gives a brief rundown of everything that happened, I settle back on the warm metal at the rear of the railcar.

We're in for a rough ride.

There's a bit of back and forth as he describes his injury to the person on the other end of the line.

I shift to sit beside him and snuggle up against him. The train rocks side to side as we head toward the mountains. Finally, he hangs up the phone.

"They're going to meet us at the next—*stop*." The way he says *stop* makes me want to question him, but I bite my tongue and keep my response simple.

"And where is that?"

"In the mountains." He points toward the horizon.

"And how long until we get there?"

He flips his wrist and stares at his watch. "Eight hours."

"Eight hours?" I flip out. "They need to get here now. You need medical attention."

"I'm fine. It's just a flesh wound."

"You and your '*just a flesh wound*' routine." I shake my head. "What am I going to do with you?"

"Lean against me and enjoy the ride." The way he winks makes my heart flutter. "Come on. It's an adventure. Lean on me."

Which I do.

I snuggle closer to him, but my mind races with fear and doubt. Eight hours until we reach the next stop in the mountains?

What if his injury is worse than he's letting on? What if we don't make it in time?

As the train chugs along, the scenery outside slowly changes.

The desert gives way to rolling hills, which eventually grow into towering mountains. The train tracks wind precariously along the edge of steep cliffs, making my heart race with every twist and turn.

I try to distract myself by staring at the car in front of us. Or staring out the right side toward the mountain rather than the dizzying drop on the other side. I can't help but glance at Chase every few minutes. He's gone silent, like he's in deep meditation. His face contorts in pain with the worst of the jarring along the tracks, and sweat beads on his forehead.

"Are you sure you're okay?" I ask, for what feels like the hundredth time.

"I'm fine," he grits out his answer through clenched teeth.

But I'm not convinced. Snuggling up to him, I feel his body temperature rising, and his breathing grows shallower by the minute. When I reach out to touch his forehead, he flinches away.

"Don't."

"Why not?"

"Just let me focus."

"Okay." I drop my hand, and my mind does what it does best. It races with worst-case scenarios.

What if he has an infection? What if he needs surgery? What if we're too far away from help?

As the hours tick by, my anxiety mounts. Every time the train slows down, my heart skips a beat, willing it to go faster. Every time it speeds up, I feel a surge of hope. But the reality is we're still hours away from help, and I don't know if he can make it that long.

I lean against him, trying to steady myself, but as the train continues to rock and sway, I can't help feeling like we're careening toward disaster. And there's nothing I can do to escape or prevent it.

TWENTY-THREE

Cara

As we ride into the night, it feels as if I'm caught in a dream. The stars twinkle above us, but nothing like the stunning night we spent staring at the heavens while making wishes on shooting stars. The train chugs along and I hold on to Chase as tight as I can, never wanting this moment to end. And that's my greatest fear.

That this will end. We cross the gap between cars, moving away from the blood left by Chase's injury, and settle onto the small platform at the front of a grain car.

The rhythmic rocking and *clickety-clack* of the wheels lugging over the track lulls us both into a deep sleep, providing some small measure of relief.

I look over at Chase, and his gaze meets mine. For a moment, everything else fades away, and I realize how much I care about him.

How much he means to me.

How I can't afford to lose him.

As we catch our breath, the tension between us grows.

It changes.

Chase suddenly grabs me by my nape and pulls me into his arms. Our lips meet in a fiery kiss, and that tingling electricity is back, stronger than ever before. I run my fingers through his hair, pulling at the roots as his hands explore my body, traveling over every curve and dip.

I don't know if it's surviving another attempt on my life? Or the adrenaline of jumping onto a moving train? All I know is my soft moans speak for themselves.

He kisses his way down my neck, leaving a blazing trail of heat behind. His touch sends shivers down my spine, a stark contrast to the heat of his mouth that drives me insane.

Our bodies move together, but then my fingers brush against the leather of his belt and I pull back.

"Your leg."

"Princess, it's just a flesh wound."

I lean back and do my best to cool the heat simmering between us.

"It's a bullet in your leg."

"Doesn't seem to have any effect on the rest of me." He reaches between us and releases the snap on his jeans. A quick zip and some rearranging frees his cock.

"You really want to… Here?" I gesture all around us. "Now?"

He responds with a throaty laugh. "I've never felt more alive than when holding you in my arms, and if you're up for it…" He lifts me up and into his lap, facing him. "There's just one thing."

"What's that?"

"The bullet in my leg." His mischievous charm radiates outwards, transforming him from a mere rogue to irresistibly attractive and devilishly handsome. Add in his cheeky grin, and the twinkle in his eye, and he's impossible to resist.

"That's what I'm saying." I playfully thump his chest and lift out of his lap.

Or try.

His hands clamp hard around my waist, holding me in place.

"Not so fast, princess."

"But, you said…" I stammer. "The bullet? Your leg? We shouldn't…"

"You're absolutely right, princess, I shouldn't exert myself, but you're more than welcome to go for a ride."

"A ride?"

"That's what I said."

"Is that your version of talking dirty? Because if it is, it needs a lot of work."

"Is that so?" He reaches between us before I can blink. Those expert fingers of his flick the button of my jeans and slide the zipper all the way down. He works his fingers under the denim and cups my pussy. The heat of his hand makes me hate the denim that separates us.

Leaning close, his voice turns dark and husky. "Jeans and panties off, princess. I want your pussy wrapping around my cock. I want to watch your tits bounce as you fuck me. And I won't overly exert myself. You're in charge."

He lifts me, and despite the injury to his arm, he tugs on the waistband of my jeans.

Needing no further encouragement, I kick off my shoes and strip out of my pants. He lifts his ass and slides his pants down as far as they'll go.

Under his hungry gaze, I straddle him, but when I go to sit, he grabs my ass and he crushes my pussy to his face. The man has an expert tongue. He licks and sucks endlessly; the stimulation of his mouth turning me into a sex crazed animal.

I'll die from the agony of the pleasure he delivers, one lick at a time. Nothing exists except for his hot mouth, devilish tongue, and those talented fingers that seek, stimulate, and explore. I cry out as he lifts me to my toes. My legs tremble and shake as the overwhelming stimulation drives me insane. I hold on to a nearby railing while he licks, fighting the need to come, but I never want this to end.

But he's relentless and I can only stand so much. He sucks my clit into his mouth and delivers a devastating barrage of sensation until I'm a panting, moaning mess.

I can't stop my hips. My fingers grip his hair, and my fingernails claw at his scalp as he coaxes me up and up and up.

I need him. I need him to fuck me. Kiss me. I need to feel him everywhere at once. My arousal grows until I'm soaking wet. My pussy throbs as I thrust my hips into his face, gyrating for more stimulation.

He suddenly adds a finger, sliding it into me again and again. One finger becomes two. Two becomes three. He locates my g-spot and expertly massages the sensitive area until I cry out. My breath falters as he fingers me with relentless strokes. My neck arches. My head tips back, and my screams split the air as I tumble into oblivion.

He drags his tongue along my slit, flicking and teasing me through the orgasm as the world around me splinters into a million shards of intense pleasure. I feel like I'll tumble into his lap, or worse, fall off the train. But if I do, it will be a blissful end as he drowns me in pleasure so intense my body continues to spasm with the aftershocks of his fingers, his tongue, and those devilish lips.

Chase holds me, supports me. He keeps me from collapsing, but I slowly come down and straddle his legs, breathing hard, panting like an animal, wet and ready for more. With a rip of foil, Chase sheathes himself while I cup his cheeks and kiss him, tasting my essence on his tongue.

"I need you, princess." Husky and raw, eyes blown black with lust, there's no denying his need.

With a glance down, I wrap my fingers around his shaft, and with no further preamble, adjust the angle and slide down his cock.

His hips join the rocking of mine, thrusting up as I lower myself down. I can't believe we're doing this.

Here.

I've never needed a man like this. Never enough to throw caution to the wind and give into the need of feeling him deep inside of me.

Chase does this to me. He breaks the chains of my restraint, setting me free. Allowing me to give in to mindless pleasure.

I've never experienced anything like this.

My breaths turn to hoarse cries. His turn to husky moans. Hand on my ass, he pulls me up, slams me down. The heat of his mouth captures a breast, finds a nipple, and clamps down. The delicious burn brings a fresh scream to my lips and the unexpected pain morphs into the most delicious torment.

I continue to lift and rise above him, only to slam down until he's as deep as he can go. My heart pounds as the tumultuous sounds of our lovemaking fill the air. He releases my poor, tortured nipple, and looks at me with glazed eyes and fierce determination.

Our lips meet in a frenzy as our bodies become one, moving together in a rampaging firestorm of sexual heat.

Sweaty and breathless, pleasure builds within me for a second time. Somewhere along the way, I lose the rhythm of our bodies, but Chase takes over, barely missing a beat. He takes charge, sets the tempo, lifting me up, then thrusting his hips up as he slams me down his hard length.

The man is a wild animal, feral with the need to fuck. He pushes my knees out, giving him more room to go deeper.

I claw at his shoulders, bite his neck, and hold on to him as we fuck like animals. Wild and unhinged, this is what sex should feel like. A little dangerous too.

Rapturous.

My gasps get shallower as pleasure builds within me. For the first time in my life, I know what it feels like to belong to another. Chase lays claim to my body and my mind, but more importantly, he burrows deep into my heart.

My nipples ache, and a fluttery sensation builds in my belly. A man on a mission, Chase knows how to fuck, even with a bullet in one leg and one arm.

Breath abandons me as that fluttery sensation explodes into a white-hot heat that consumes every cell in my body.

Forget my heart. Chase leaves his mark on my soul.

As my release rolls through me, the chugging of his breaths deepens. His thighs tense. His body shakes. He bites down on my shoulder as his release ignites and explodes. He comes violently and it's all I can do to hold on and ride out his release.

Sweaty and breathless, we hold each other as the sky darkens, and the train takes us to our next destination. The heat of the air slowly disappears as we gain elevation and climb into the foothills of the Rocky Mountains.

We ride in silence, both of us catching our breath, before Chase speaks up. "Help will be waiting for us. We'll get off where the train has to slow before its descent back down the mountain. Then, we drive to Forest's place."

"That's what's going through your mind after sex?"

"Multitasking?" His swoon worthy smirk is deliciously unapologetic.

"You're impossible." I grip his chin and lift his face to meet mine, then I press my lips against his.

The kiss starts slow and gentle, but after a few minutes, it turns heated and raw. His cock hardens again, and this time, when we have sex, it's slow and gentle.

Until it's not.

Our mouths crash together.

Our teeth clash.

Our tongues war.

We find release and solace in each other's arms until neither one of us can ignore the exhaustion pulling at us both.

With night fully upon us, and after being thoroughly fucked, I climb off of his lap, pull on my pants, tie my shoes, and flip around to sit beside him. He yanks his pants back up while I take a moment to check his leg for any bleeding after our vigorous fucking.

"How's it look?" Chase takes my hand and holds it in his lap.

"Like you'll live another day."

"Ah, princess, one day won't nearly be long enough."

"For what?"

"For loving you."

The pitter-patter of my heart trips and stumbles. Surely, he's not professing his love. We barely know each other. Hopefully, darkness covers my surprise. Chase chuckles beside me.

"What's so funny?"

"Nothing."

"Nothing, my ass. Tell me." I playfully shove him in the shoulder.

"Fucking on a freight train was never on my bucket list, but now I'm definitely checking that one off." He brings the back of my hand to his mouth, kissing it gently, then he wraps his arms around me and holds me tight. "Cold?" he asks.

"A little."

He pulls me tighter and we snuggle in each other's arms, blissfully content, while staving off the encroaching chill of the mountains.

As we settle in for the night, I can't help but think about the events that brought Chase into my life. And as I drift off to sleep, my dreams fill not of Chase, but of the father I once loved.

It's the night he died, moments before the men barged in, changing my life forever. In the dream, I sit across from my father. He holds my grandmother's watch. Passed down from daughter to daughter, it's a precious heirloom.

It once belonged to my mother, given to her by her mother. If my mother were alive, she'd wear it today. It should've come to me after her death, but I was too young to safeguard it for future generations.

I'm surprised my father hands it over now. It means he finally sees me for the woman I am, rather than the child he loves.

"I need you to have this." There's no one in the dining room except for Hank, but my father whispers. "It's important you keep it safe. Remember, family isn't just blood. It's love, support, and sacrifice," he recites to me the same words my mother once said to me.

I take the watch and scrutinize it. This is a big deal—like a rite of passage. A beautiful piece with intricate engravings. The way he hands it to me makes me feel like it's more than a simple watch.

Which it is. The watch has a history, with stories to tell, but before I can ask my father anything more, Artemus Gonzales's men breach the outer security perimeter of the house. Hank barely hides me before the men rush into the dining room and take my father from me, leaving me an orphan.

Heart pounding, I wake in a sweat. Chase sleeps soundly beside me, and I check on his leg, making sure the bleeding's stopped after we had sex. I rub at my eyes, trying to shake off the dream and clear the cobwebs from my mind.

That watch is no longer in my possession, but headed toward Guardian HRS's headquarters to determine if it carries a tracker. I have vivid dreams, but none as real as this one. There's something about the watch my subconscious is trying to tell me, but for the life of me, I can't figure out what that might be.

I wish my father was still alive. I could ask him, but for now, I'm content with the memory and hold the dream close to me. He disappointed me in the end, revealing his involvement with despicable men, though I can't help but love my father. I wish he was still with me, so we could have one last chance to talk. A chance to let him know I forgive him.

Needing to clear my head, I scoot to the edge and dangle my legs over the side. The wind whips past me, messing up my hair and making the fabric of my shirt flap. It's pitch black. Stuck between the back of one railcar and the front of another, there's only a tiny slit of the sky visible, but it reveals stars twinkling above us. In the desert, we saw the entire sky. Here, it's nothing but a sliver. Regardless, those stars provide a sense of comfort and soothe my racing thoughts.

The gentle swaying of the train no longer frightens me and despite the danger and general discomfort, riding on the back of this railcar is the adventure of a lifetime.

I close my eyes and savor the wind on my face, the gentle swaying of the train, the rumble of the wheels along the tracks, and know this is a moment I'll never forget.

Especially since I share it with the man beside me. A yawn escapes me and I scoot back from the edge. Before curling up to Chase to share his warmth, I check his leg and his arm. Satisfied there's no sign of bleeding, I curl up to Chase and let myself drift into a dreamless sleep.

TWENTY-FOUR

Cara

A SUDDEN ROCKING OF THE RAILCAR JOLTS ME AWAKE. WE'RE slowing down. I grab onto Chase in surprise. The sun's up and the morning air chills my skin. When I exhale, my breath condenses in the cold air.

I never thought I'd be running from hitmen, leaping onto locomotives, or dodging bullets, but here I am, in the middle of nowhere, with the man I've come to love, doing all three.

"Good morning, princess." Chase leans against the back wall of the railcar and smiles at me.

"What time is it?" I stretch and rub the sleep from my eyes.

"Just past six in the morning."

"How long have you been up?"

"A few hours."

"A few hours? Did you get any sleep?"

"Enough."

Knowing Chase, *enough* means he stayed up all night keeping watch.

"What's happening? Why are we slowing down? Are we stopping?" A look down the length of the train reveals no station in sight.

"You woke up at the perfect time. Our hopping off place is just ahead." He makes a vague gesture outside.

"Is that why we're slowing down?"

"No."

"Umm—No?"

"The train is slowing down for a steep grade coming up. We're going to hop off before it heads down the other side of the mountain."

"Hop off?" Surely, I didn't hear right?

"Yup."

"Like jump?"

"Yes."

"Off the train?"

"Exactly."

"And how are you going to do that with your leg?"

"Carefully, I suppose." He leans back and folds his arms over his chest, looking smug.

"What does that mean?"

A crooked grin fills his face and I shove him again. It's like pushing granite. He barely budges.

"It's not funny. It's a serious question."

"We're hopping off to catch our ride." He looks at me like it's obvious, but it's not. Far from it.

"I get that. It's the jumping off part that worries me."

"The train is going to be basically crawling. Getting off is the easy part."

"And the hard part?"

"I guess it's the hard part as well." Chase stands, favoring his wounded leg. "Come on. Up you go. On your feet."

"You're serious about jumping off the train?"

"Absolutely."

In his defense, we've slowed down considerably since the train picked up speed last night. I don't know how fast trains travel. If I had a phone, I could look it up. But I don't, so I guess we were going between forty and sixty miles an hour. At least, the scenery seemed to pass by at about that speed.

Now?

We're basically crawling along. A few miles an hour at most. I can totally see climbing down the ladder fixed to this car and jumping off.

Easy for me.

But Chase with his leg?

"Ready, princess?" He gestures toward the ladder, but I hesitate.

We're in a small valley filled with long, wavy grass, wildflowers, an alpine lake, and a sentinel of towering pines. Crisp mountain air fills my lungs and a gentle breeze ripples the grass, carrying the scent of pine and damp earth to flood my senses.

The alpine lake shimmers like a jewel; its glassy surface reflects the towering pines standing guard at the base of the slopes. A small road meanders through the middle of the grassy meadow, joined by a small stream carving its way through the valley.

A black Jeep parks at the side of the dirt road, and two men wait for us. They stand beside the vehicle like guardians.

"Who are they?" I point toward the pair and try to keep my hand from shaking. Please let these men be here to help us instead of kill us.

"That is none other than Forest and Paul."

"Who?"

"Forest Summers created Guardian HRS and Paul is his…" Chase pauses as if grasping for the correct word, but there's no need. The power vibrating in the space between the two men unites them. "They're our ride." Chase points to the Jeep.

I stare at the ground moving below us and hesitate. My breath hitches in my throat and I take a hesitant step toward the edge.

"Um, you go first." I take a step back from the brink and slowly inch away from the edge.

"Sorry, princess, you gotta go first." He grins with mischief.

"Why?"

"Because, if you chicken out, I doubt I'll be able to jump back on." His gaze dares me to show some courage, and his eyes twinkle mischievously.

"I'm not going to chicken out." I bite my lip, because I totally want to chicken out, but then I raise my chin defiantly and square off my shoulders.

"Then jump." He leans in close and whispers in my ear. "I dare you."

"You dare me?" I raise an eyebrow and my lips twitch into a half-smile filled with amusement.

"Yup." He no longer contains his smirk. It spreads across his face as his eyes twinkle.

"You're serious?" I cock my head and cross my arms as if being defiant.

"I double dog dare you." His brows lift in challenge, making my stomach flip and my heart race.

My heart skips a beat. "Double dog dare?" I give him a teasing frown and shake my head. "This is getting serious." I feign fear, secretly enjoying our playful banter.

"You gonna jump, or do you need a little push?" His eyes spark as he waits for my answer. That smirk plays on his lips and reminds me of the incredible talent he displayed with those lips last night.

"Don't push me." I give an exaggerated shriek, savoring our lively repartee.

"What if I triple dog dare?" He leans forward slightly, both of us lost in the moment.

"Well, I can't back down from a triple dog dare." My expression turns serious as I listen to my words. Every part of me wants to prove him wrong and show him I'm brave enough to jump off this train.

I take a deep breath and step to the edge. The wind rushes past, blowing my hair back, and my heart pounds wildly in my chest. If I thought getting on the train was hard, that's nothing compared to jumping off.

When I look down, the ground rushes past, but I don't let that mess with my head.

Without another thought, I jump. For a moment, I hurtle through the air, but then I hit the ground. A surge of adrenaline rushes through me and I look up to see Chase grinning ear to ear as he leaps into the air.

But when he lands, his leg gives way, and his face contorts in pain. He rolls to absorb the impact and winds up on his back, clutching his leg.

"Shit, that hurts like a motherfucker," he hisses through gritted teeth.

The two men standing by the Jeep notice Chase's distress and sprint into action. They run toward us, one of them bellowing in one of the deepest voices I've ever heard. They approach in ground-devouring strides while I tremble before the sheer dominating force of these two men together.

"Is everything okay?" Forest comes to a halt and takes a knee beside Chase.

"It's his leg," I call out, thrilled they're here to help.

Paul crouches down as well, then looks to Forest. "Should've brought your sister." He loops one of Chase's arms around his shoulder. Forest does the same on the other side. Together, they lift Chase to his feet.

As I dust myself off, I take in the two intimidating men.

Forest is broad-shouldered and muscular, with a towering physique that dominates his surroundings. His shock-white hair is long and tied back with a leather strap. With his Nordic features, he bears a striking resemblance to the mythical god, Thor, with a rugged, chiseled jawline, and a wild and untamed look in his piercing, ice-blue eyes.

Painfully handsome in a rugged, masculine way, I could stare at him for hours if it weren't for the man standing beside him.

In stark contrast to the fair-haired descendant of Thor, although equally tall, Paul is all lean muscles and towering strength. Where Forest's hair is the lightest blond, Paul's is dark and wavy.

Like Forest, there's an aura of strength around Paul, but where Forest's dominating presence is due to his massive size, Paul's confident posture, and strong steady gaze commands attention and respect. He exudes authority and control of not just himself, but everything around him. As a pair, the men take my breath away with their brutal dichotomy.

"Can you walk?" Forest's concern is palpable.

"Probably shouldn't put weight on the leg. Doc Summers was pretty specific about that."

"You look like shit." Paul doesn't waste time with pleasantries. "Skye is going to be so pissed."

The two of them bracket Chase. He loops his arms over their shoulders and then they each grab under his knees and carry him to the Jeep.

We've officially left the dry and dusty desert behind us in favor of cool, misty mountains. I can't help but take in a deep breath, loving the crisp fragrance of wildflowers mingling with the towering pines all around us.

I walk behind Chase, Paul, and Forest as they make their way toward the Jeep. I can't help but worry about Chase's injuries and can't get Hank's death out of my mind. If I lose Chase like I lost Hank, I won't recover from the trauma.

My greatest fear is no matter how long I run or how far I go, Artemus Gonzales and his men will find me.

They'll kill me, and they'll kill whoever's with me.

I wish I knew how to make it stop. I still don't know why Artemus is so relentless in his pursuit, especially after what Chase said about any testimony I might provide being nothing but hearsay and inadmissible in court.

If that's true, why would Artemus Gonzales care what happens to me, or where I go?

Instead of focusing on things I can't change, I take a deep breath and focus on the present. This little valley is beautiful and I want to soak it all in.

I shiver, suddenly feeling exposed and vulnerable, and turn around, looking for any signs of danger, but there's nothing. Just the morning mist and the trees.

"Hey, you okay?" Chase reaches for me as he settles into the back seat of the Jeep. Although injured, he's still in Protector mode.

"Yeah, I'm fine." I try to sound confident, but my voice comes out shaky. I join Chase in the back and the vehicle rocks as Forest climbs into the passenger seat while Paul takes his spot behind the wheel. He cranks the engine and gravel crunches beneath the tires as we head out on the dirt road.

Before long, we're back on pavement, driving along winding mountain roads with spectacular views and towering trees all around us.

Despite the beauty, however, I can't help but feel a sense of unease. I lean my head back against the headrest and close my eyes. I don't know what's going to happen next, but I'm ready to fight for my life and for the people I love.

But I twist to look behind us, to see if we're being followed. My gut says more men will come, and so far, it hasn't been wrong.

TWENTY-FIVE

Cara

SEVERAL HOURS LATER, WE ARRIVE AT FOREST'S MOUNTAIN RETREAT. I can't help but gape. The fresh scent of pine is all around me, mingling with the pungent aroma of loamy soil. Add to that the crisp, clean air of the mountains, and I feel as if I've found heaven.

There's just something about the mountains that rejuvenates and refreshes a weary traveler. At just below seven-thousand feet, the air is thin enough I feel it in my lungs. Just a bit of exertion finds me tugging for air.

As for Forest's *retreat*, I imagined a small cabin in the woods— one or two bedrooms, a tiny kitchen, and a cozy hearth. The massive log home in front of me is that tiny cabin on steroids.

Lots of steroids.

It looks more like a corporate lodge than a private residence. It's big and bold like the man himself. Despite its size, the retreat is isolated, tucked well off the beaten path, if I'm to believe Forest; and I have no reason not to. There's literally no one around for miles.

I should feel relaxed, but I can't shake the feeling something's off. Chase and the others seem unconcerned, so I push those negative thoughts aside and focus on what's important.

The front door opens and three people walk out. One of them carries a stretcher in his hand. The others, two women, skip down the steps, rushing toward us. Like Forest and Paul, the dichotomy between them is striking. One's tall, nearly the same height as the man carrying the stretcher, and the other is more diminutive; short like me. From the way she leads, however, I guess she's the doctor Chase spoke to on the train.

Her long hair falls in gentle cascading waves down her back, framing her striking features, and bright eyes filled with determination. She gathers her long hair and ties it up and out of the way as she approaches the vehicle.

"How's my patient?" She comes to a standstill and props her hands on her hips, aiming her question at Forest.

"Bleeding all over my back seat." His deep, powerful voice sounds like boulders crashing together.

"I'm not bleeding all over your seat." Chase shakes his head.

The woman takes one look at Chase, then snaps her fingers over her head. "Tia, Ryker, get him on that stretcher ASAP and take him to the dining room." She steps out of the way while Ryker places the stretcher on the ground.

Paul helps Chase out of the Jeep and, with Tia's help, lowers him gently down on the canvas frame. Paul bends down, looking like he's going to take one end of the stretcher, but Tia gives a sharp shake of her head.

"I've got this." She pushes him aside, and I can't help but raise my brow at Paul's grin.

"Yes, ma'am." Paul gives a sharp salute, but there's a cheeky grin plastered on his face.

"Don't *yes ma'am* me. Help Forest with their things and let us do our job." Tia is a bad ass. I love the way she doesn't take any flack. I already like her.

Doc Summers takes one look at Chase and begins a cursory examination of his wounds. She examines his injuries first, her movements graceful and practiced, then she places her fingers to his neck.

"Strong and steady." She turns to address Chase. "Congratulations, you're not in shock."

"Only because I've got the best teammate on the planet." Chase's gaze cuts to me and it takes a beat before I realize he means me. "Cara stopped the bleeding."

I'm his teammate?

For some crazy reason, that fills my heart with a rush of warmth. Not that I contributed much, but it means more than I can say that he feels I've helped rather than hindered.

"Hi, Cara." Skye stands and dusts off her hands. "I'm Skye. Nice to meet you. This is Tia and Ryker. Ryker's my respiratory tech and Tia is my CRNA. We're going to take good care of Chase. Forest and Paul can show you inside and where you'll be staying. As soon as we're done with Chase, I'll give you an update."

"Um, nice to meet you." I glance at Chase, unwilling to be separated from him. "Can't I stay with him?"

As friendly as Forest and Paul appear, there's too much testosterone flowing between them, buzzing with insane energy. I can't put it into words, except there's a profound degree of intimacy between the two men, but also a powerful push back and forth. It's like they're involved in a constant battle of wills. I'd rather not be left alone with them.

"Skye's got a mini operating suite prepped," Tia speaks to me. "Best if you follow Forest and let us take care of your man."

My man?

First teammate and now he's my man? I press my hand against my breastbone, not sure how I feel about that. Both Ryker and Tia give me friendly smiles, then they lift Chase on the stretcher while I stand back.

"I'd really rather stay with Chase. I promise I won't get in the way."

"I'm okay if she stays." Chase reaches for me and I clasp his hand, unwilling to let go.

Tia glances toward Skye, leaving the decision up to her. I breathe out a sigh when Skye nods.

I walk with them up the steps and into the massive log structure, too overwhelmed to take in the breathtaking beauty of the place. We head down a long hallway and into a cozy dining room with a long table in the middle, covered in white sheets. Tia and Ryker set the stretcher down on the table and help Chase transfer off the stretcher and onto the table.

I find a corner and press my back to the wall, trying to make myself small and unobtrusive. Medical instruments and other supplies sit on a smaller table at the back of the room, still in the rugged cases they were brought in.

The three of them work efficiently as a team. Tia begins an IV while Ryker sets up an oxygen mask for Chase. Meanwhile, Skye heads to a connected washroom and scrubs up. When she returns, her long hair is tied out of the way with a surgical cap covering it, along with a mask over her face. Tia helps Skye into a surgical gown and sterile gloves, then masks up along with Ryker.

"Here." Tia wanders over to me, holding out a surgical mask. "You picked a good spot. Skye's going to be doing minor surgery, and you need to wear a mask and cap if you're going to stay in the room. Are you squeamish when it comes to blood?"

"No." I take the cap and mask, putting them on the same way Tia did.

"You sure? Last thing we need is to have you fainting."

"I won't faint." After what happened in the motel room, I'm not worried about a little bit of blood.

"If you feel light-headed—" Tia points toward the door, "just excuse yourself."

"Thanks."

"No problem." She twists around to check on Chase. "We're giving him extra oxygen for the procedure, but there's no reason to knock him out."

"He'll be awake during the whole thing?"

"Yes. We'll extract the bullet from his leg, then irrigate the bullet wound in his arm . Patch anything that needs patching and give him a hefty dose of antibiotics. Shouldn't take long."

"Want a stool?"

"No, I'm okay." With that, Tia leaves me.

She and Ryker work seamlessly together, but it's clear they're in more of a support role. Skye Summers, who works solo, does the actual surgery.

As she operates, the small crease in her forehead shows the depth of her concentration. She's completely focused on the task at hand, and it quickly becomes clear she's an accomplished physician. A wave of relief washes over me, knowing Chase is in expert hands.

With a practiced hand, Skye removes the bullet from Chase's leg and irrigates the wound. From where I stand, her touch appears gentle, yet firm. Chase doesn't appear to be in any pain, and all the tension in his body slowly dissipates under her care.

One hour turns to two and I shift on my feet, curious to know what's going on. Skye keeps a running conversation, telling Chase what she's doing and why, but I'm too far away to hear anything but a word here and there.

At the end of the second hour, she finishes with his leg, dressing the wound, then turns her attention to his arm. Like his leg, she irrigates that wound, then grabs one of the surgical instruments and goes digging inside Chase's arm.

My brows pinch together, and I lift on tiptoe, trying desperately to see. Finally, she pulls something from the wound, examines it, then tosses it into a metal tray beside her. Then she finishes stitching the skin and dresses that wound as well.

Finally, she looks up at me and gives me a reassuring smile. "He's doing great. Almost done."

Happy Chase is finally out of danger, I take in a deep breath and blow it out real slow, not realizing how tense I've been these past two hours.

Skye steps away from the table and pulls off the surgical gown, along with her gloves, then she pats Chase on the shoulder.

"You're good as new, but please try not to put much weight on the leg for the next seventy-two hours."

Chase pulls at the oxygen mask over his face to speak. "Three days? How am I supposed to get around?"

"With good old-fashioned crutches. Although, I'm putting you on mandatory bedrest." Ryker pulls out a pair of metal crutches and sets them up for Chase.

"What about my arm?" Chase glances at the crutches with narrow eyes.

"You're allowed to hobble to and from the bathroom. Other than that, your ass should be planted on a couch or in the bed," Skye answers with a smile, but it's clear those are Chase's marching orders.

I step out of my corner and move to stand beside Chase. "How long until he can walk?"

"He needs three days of downtime for the wounds to heal; a full week before he's ready to push it. The arm is a clean wound. It'll heal fast. The leg wasn't as bad as I thought. If he takes care of it, there's no reason he can't be up and about within a few days. A week would be better, but I've learned Guardians and Protectors rarely pay attention to medical advice. Give me three days, Chase." She turns her attention to Chase. "After that, start slow and take things easy. Your body needs rest to heal."

"Received and understood." Chase returns a wry grin. "I'll give you twenty-four hours."

"It's three days, and that's a hard line in the sand. That applies to *all* activity." Skye winks at me. "In and out of bed."

An immediate rush of blood heats my cheeks, but Chase's throaty laughter fills my heart with joy.

"I knew I hated doctors." He reaches for my hand and I take it, loving the way our fingers intertwine and our hands fit perfectly together. When Chase lifts my hand to his lips and plants a featherlight kiss on the back of my hand, there's a fluttery sensation in my belly.

"Thank you," I express my gratitude to Skye and her team.

"Make sure he follows doctor's orders and he'll heal up without any problem." Skye returns a small smile, and I know Chase is going to be okay.

"Will do." I do my best to reassure her, but Chase is going to do what he wants.

Tia helps Chase to spin around on the table while Ryker sets up the crutches. It takes a moment to get the height right, but then Chase is on the move, at least until we're shown to our room. Skye watches over him until he crawls into bed.

"Three days." She holds up three fingers, emphasizing her point.

Chase rolls his eyes, but dutifully settles into the bed.

TWENTY-SIX

Cara

THE NEXT TWO DAYS PASS AGONIZINGLY SLOW. TO MY SURPRISE, Chase obeys Skye's orders to the letter. He spends most of his time on the couch, his leg propped up on a pillow. We binge several TV shows, read books, or fool around. When not on the couch, we're in bed together, either sleeping or getting to know each other better.

I do my best to keep his mind off being confined to bed. When binging TV, reading, or playing cards isn't enough, I strip down and distract him with sex. The bedrest sucks, but the sex is fun.

The best thing about it is for the first time in a very long time, I feel like I can catch my breath. We're not on the run or being chased by men who want me dead. It feels as if we finally escaped that madness.

When we're not having sex, reading, or watching TV, Chase and I talk about anything and everything, enjoying each other's company in a way we haven't been able to since his mission started. When Chase falls asleep, I hang out with Forest and Paul, who are incredibly interested in me. I answer what I can, deflect when I don't want to dwell on anything, then share about the desert and getting to know Chase. I mention how I can't wait to meet his ball-busting mom, mention he's adopted, and let it slip he had an older sister in the wreck. Forest seems interested in that, asking details about when, how, and where. I do my best to answer what I can, but that's really for Chase to share, not me.

As the third day approaches, however, Chase gets restless.

"I'm tired of this damn bed."

"You sure about that?" My gaze shifts to his groin. "Because if you're tired of being in bed…" I leave the rest unsaid, but Chase gets the hint.

He grabs me under the arms and pulls me up the length of his body, as strong as ever. "I will never get tired of you in my bed, but it would be nice to get out of it now and then."

"It's only one more day. You can do it," I do my best to encourage him. His arm appears fully healed, but I worry about his leg.

We spend the rest of the afternoon playing board games and watching TV, but his restless energy only grows. When there's a knock on the door, we both visibly relax. Any distraction would be good.

"Can I come in?" Forest pokes his head inside.

Chase looks up from the book he's reading.

"Sure." I wave for Forest to join us.

"How are you feeling?" Forest paces the room, his long stride gives him only four steps before he's forced to pivot and spin around.

"Better, thanks." He shifts, trying to get comfortable. "Hopefully, Doc Summers will let me out of here soon." Chase looks at me and smiles.

"He's tired of being laid up in a hospital bed, and I don't blame him." My voice is chipper and hopeful that Skye finally gives Chase the okay to get out of bed after her exam.

"You've been taking good care of him." Forest's gaze shifts to Chase. "Listen, can I talk to you for a minute?" Forest runs his fingers through his white-blond hair.

"Sure. What's going on?" Chase sits a little straighter, looking concerned about Forest asking him a question.

Forest takes a deep breath before speaking. "I was just looking through your file and something caught my eye."

"What kind of something?"

"Maybe nothing, but…" Forest brings his pointer finger to his temple and taps the side of his head. "Ever have a thought in your head that won't leave you alone? Like a worm niggling at your brain?"

"Definitely." Chase turns to me, eyes narrowing with concern. "The one in my head right now is how Gonzales's men keep finding Cara."

That's all Chase thinks about. We talk about it night and day. Only it's been two days since we arrived here and so far, no one's shown up and tried to take me out. Maybe Gonzales is finally tired of running through his men and gave up?

My gut says that's not the case, though I can't help but wish it to be true.

"We're all trying to figure that one out, but this is more of a curiosity. I'm probably really off base, but can you tell me a little about your family?"

"My family?" Chase shifts to a more comfortable position, favoring his leg.

"If you don't mind." Forest stops his pacing at the foot of the bed. I press back in my chair, awed by the powerful presence of the man before me.

"There's not much to tell. Single kid. Happy childhood. My parents are amazing. Met in the Merchant Marines. The only really interesting thing about them is my father quit his job to raise me. Mom's still kicking ass and taking names."

"Not your adoptive parents. Sorry, I should've been more clear. I meant your birth parents."

"My birth parents?" Chase's eyes widen in alarm.

"That's right."

"Sadly, there's not much to tell. They died in a car accident when I was a baby. I was adopted almost immediately into a loving home. I have no memories of my birth parents."

"Was it just the two of them who died?"

"Why are you asking? Is there something wrong with my file? Some question about my security clearance? It's all in there."

"Not all of it." Forest scratches his head.

"I'm not hiding anything." Folding his arms across his chest, Chase gets defensive.

"That's not what I'm saying. Sorry. I'm doing a piss-poor job of this."

"Of what?" Skye Summers breezes in with her stethoscope slung around her neck.

Something about Skye's presence makes Forest react. He turns and gives her a look that stops her dead in her tracks.

"What's wrong, beanpole?" She lifts a hand as if to touch his arm, but falls short with her hand hovering in the air.

"Tell Chase about your parents." Forest's deep baritone makes the air rumble.

"Why?"

"Just do it," he snaps at her, popping off an order.

From the way she bristles, two things are clear. First off, this isn't the first time Forest's been abrupt with her. Second, she's not happy with the question.

"I'm sorry." She pivots and those words are meant for Chase. Not Forest. "My brother can be a bit obtuse at times. I generally ignore him when he gets like this. He doesn't know how to be subtle or polite, or how to ask questions nicely. I hope he hasn't been bothering you?"

"Dammit, Skye, I'm not being obtuse. Tell Chase about your parents."

"Why would I tell him about that?" She stares down Forest. "And why are you bringing it up? Let the dead lie in peace. Leave it alone."

"Just do it." Forest rolls his eyes in an Oscar-worthy performance.

"Fine. Geez, what bug crawled up your butt?"

"Skye…"

"My parents are dead." She delivers her answer in a monotone, but her words are short, clipped, and angry. "Happy now?"

"And why are they dead?"

Chase and I exchange a look. Forest's beating a dead cat and Skye is less than amused.

Talk about uncomfortable.

"Because they died in a car accident." Her anger rises and her words tear through the tension building between her and her brother. "Thanks for digging up old pain, beanpole. What the fuck is wrong with you?"

Chase and I exchange confused looks, unsure where this line of reasoning is going. Neither of us speaks, because neither of us wants to get our heads bitten off, or our asses chewed out. Neither one of us wants to be between the siblings at all.

From the tension escalating between Forest and Skye, chances are pretty damn good that might happen.

Once again, Skye turns toward Chase. "Just going to listen to your chest, check the bandages, and if all looks good, I'll give you the go ahead to get up and around." She purposefully ignores Forest, which pisses him off.

"Tell him who else was in the car?" Forest grinds out the words while gesturing to Chase.

"You're being an ass." Skye yanks her stethoscope from around her neck and puts the earpieces in her ear. "How about you leave and let me do my doctor thing with my patient?"

"For the love of God, Skye, answer the fucking question." When Forest roars, the very ground shakes.

I curl against Chase, wishing I could leave. Which I would do if not for the fact Chase is stuck where he is.

"And what question is that?" Skye leans over Chase and makes a show of pressing the diaphragm of her stethoscope against Chase's chest, ignoring Forest.

"Who else died in the accident?" Booming now, his voice is like a clap of thunder.

I shrink back at the power in his voice.

Forest is a towering giant of a man, a Viking chieftain, or Norse god, transported to the modern day. He's imposing, frightening, and absolutely terrifying when he yells.

Skye straightens and scowls at Forest. She flings her arm out wide, pointing to the door. "Get the hell out of here."

"Not until you tell Chase about your baby brother."

"Fuck you." Skye's eyes mist with tears.

"Tell him."

"Fine, although I don't see why you're dragging them into this." She props her hands on her hips and faces Chase. "Forest is a fucking asshole for digging up painful memories. My parents died in a car crash when I was young. My foster father used to tell me my baby brother survived. He used that to…" She chokes up and takes a moment before continuing. "He threatened to hurt him if I didn't… If I didn't do the things he made me do. I found out years later my brother didn't survive. He died in the accident. And all those threats…" She swipes at her eyes and glares at Forest, but doesn't finish whatever she was going to say.

Chase's grip on my hand tightens painfully.

"After all this time?" Skye stomps her foot and turns to Forest with tears in her eyes. "Why are you asking about him now?"

"Because…" Forest runs a hand through his hair and turns to me. "Cara was talking to me earlier and causally mentioned something I can't get it out of my head."

"Me?" I speak for the first time and point to my chest. "What did I say?" I shrink back beneath the intensity of Forest's gaze.

"Now, you're scaring her." Before Forest can reply, Skye continues berating her brother. "You can be such an ass."

Forest completely ignores the derision in Skye's tone. "Chase, tell Skye about your family. Not your adoptive family, but your birth family." He stares at Chase and I swear his entire body trembles. Which is a weird word to use for a man his size.

Chase releases my hand. He looks at Skye, then bows his head. "My parents died in a car crash. Me and my sister survived. We both went into foster care, but because I was a baby, I was adopted. My sister wasn't."

"How old was your sister when it happened?" Forest's voice cracks and all color in his face drains out. He comes around the foot of the bed, visibly shaking, to stand behind Skye.

"She was twelve." Chase looks up, meeting Skye's gaze.

Her eyes widen and her entire body goes rigid with shock. "I was twelve." She takes a step back, faltering, and falls against the solid wall of muscle that is Forest Summers. Her head doesn't even reach the middle of his chest. The man is that imposing.

I glance around the room, trying to take in everyone's reactions.

Skye stares at Chase. Forest stares at Skye. Chase stares at Skye, but his grip on my hand tightens. I look between Skye and Chase, searching for any resemblance between the two of them.

Is it possible?

He has the same eyes and hair, but that's it. They could be related, but it's not something that stands out. Nothing that screams siblings.

Maybe I'm a hopeless romantic, but hope flares inside of me. After a lifetime lived apart, each thinking the other was dead, can it be?

Wouldn't it be wonderful?

A million questions race through my mind, but it's Skye who covers her mouth with trembling hands to keep back a sob. Tears glisten in her eyes as she stares at Chase.

"Skye…" Forest's voice softens as he places his hands on her shoulders. "I think Chase is your brother."

"The odds are astronomical," she says. "It's not possible."

"You sure about that?" Forest asks.

"But Clark Preston said… He told me…"

"He lied about so many things. Why not this as well?" Forest wraps his arms around Skye, supporting her. "The more I think about it, the more it makes sense. Chase's sister was twelve. Your brother was a baby. You were twelve when the accident happened. Shouldn't we at least explore the possibility your baby brother is Chase?"

Chase's eyes look like they're about to pop out of their sockets. He's too stunned to speak.

But Forest speaks for them both. "You and Chase share the same blood. You look like brother and sister."

Skye shakes her head, then steps away. She points to the door with a shaky hand. "Can the two of you excuse us? I need to talk to Chase alone." Her gaze remains hard for Forest, but softens when she looks at me. "Please?"

Forest nods. He looks at me and gestures toward the door.

"Chase?" I don't want to leave. Not if any of this is true.

"Give us a minute, princess." He takes my hand and kisses my knuckles. "Please?"

"Of course." I move toward the door, not wanting to leave, but knowing I need to give Skye and Chase this time. If what Forest thinks really is true, it changes everything.

TWENTY-SEVEN

Cara

"COME." FOREST GESTURES FOR ME TO FOLLOW HIM AND CLOSES the door to Chase's room until it latches shut. "Let's give them a moment."

"Do you think it's true?" I crane my neck to look at him. "Is it possible?"

"Anything is possible. I hope for Skye's sake it is."

"Why?"

"The man who…" His voice catches. "What do you know about our past?"

"You and Skye?"

"Yes."

"Not much."

"The Cliff's notes go something like this. A man named Clark Preston fostered Skye and me. He abused us: physically, sexually, and emotionally."

"Wow. I didn't know."

"It gets worse."

"Worse than that?"

"Far worse."

"I don't know how Chase is going to handle that."

"What do you mean?"

"He had a happy childhood. Loving parents." My heart warms with the stories he shared about his mother and the love showered upon him by his father.

"Skye did not." Forest leads me through the estate until we wind up in the great room where a massive stone fireplace occupies an entire wall. It seems as if he's going to say more, but Forest comes to a sudden halt.

"Why are you building a fire?" Forest's deep voice booms. "We're in the thick of summer. It's hot as fuck outside."

"We're in the mountains." Paul feeds the beginnings of a fire at the hearth, adding kindling to a small flame and doesn't let Forest's words affect him.

"And it's summer." Forest appears eager to argue.

"And tonight it's going to drop to the forties. And why the fuck do you care? I want a fire tonight, so I'm building a fire. What bug crawled up your butt?"

"No bug crawled anywhere." Forest dismisses him with a sniff. "What is it with butts and bugs around here?"

Paul checks me, then selects his next words with great care. "Perhaps we can address this later?" The timbre of Paul's voice changes. His words are innocent enough, but there's definitely a shift in the air.

Forest stiffens beside me and his breath catches. He doesn't respond, except for the slightest dipping of his head.

Paul turns toward me, and his gentle smile suddenly cuts through the tension clotting the air. "Can you tell me what's up Forest's butt?"

"Nothing's up my butt," Forest mumbles, keeping his voice low, but Paul catches what he says and ignores it.

I jump in, only because I don't understand the relationship between the two men.

"We were with Chase and Skye." I hook a thumb over my shoulder. "Forest thinks they might be siblings."

"Siblings? Is this true?" Paul glances at Forest.

My words change the weird vibe between the men.

"Might be." Forest shrugs but doesn't elaborate.

Paul is on his feet. "You look like shit." Paul pulls Forest into a close embrace. "You look like shit a lot lately, but this is worse than your normal shitty look."

He murmurs something in Forest's ear, something I can't hear, then grasps Forest's cheeks with his hands and presses their foreheads together. The two men stare at each other, carrying on an entire conversation without words.

Feeling like an intruder on an intimate moment, I back away from the men and curl up in one of the many plush leather chairs that practically swallows me whole.

The revelation Skye might be Chase's sister is a lot to process. I know we talked about it before. How Chase wanted to look for his sister, but then joined the Army. How he secretly hoped she was dead because it was easier to believe she was dead than knowing his sister was alive and never bothered to look for him. But before I can make sense of this strange change of events, a blaring alarm goes off all around me. Paul releases Forest and the two men separate.

"What's going on?" I leap out of my comfy chair, heart racing, as I frantically look for the source of that alarm.

Forest glances at me, but there's no surprise on his face. "It's Mitzy. She always sets off the perimeter alarms just to make sure they work, and to annoy me."

"Mitzy?" I pull at my ear, nervous to meet even more of the Guardian HRS gang. "She's your technical lead, right?" At least, that's what Chase told me. Chase sent my grandmother's watch to Mitzy.

"She's a fucking bad ass. A girl geek nerd on steroids. She's almost better than me when it comes to computers, but if you tell her I said that, I'll deny every word. We were expecting her later tonight. She said we needed to chat about your watch."

"What did she find?"

"She didn't elaborate. Want to meet her outside?"

"Of course." I leap at the chance. Not so much because I'm eager to see Mitzy, but because Chase and Skye have yet to emerge from whatever conversation they're having about their potentially shared past.

Paul thumps Forest on the back of his shoulder, seeming to conclude whatever private conversation they exchanged without words. Forest gives a nod; perhaps saying he's okay, then marches toward a bank of security monitors, where we watch a helicopter land in the middle of the meadow out front, but it's not just Mitzy on the helicopter.

Six men jump out behind her; four of whom I know. There's Alec, Hayes, and Rafe who met me at the gate and Zeb who drove the car. I don't know the two other men, but they're clearly Guardians like the rest.

Six Guardians are an impressive sight, but the six men are nothing compared to what follows them out of the helicopter.

Six black robots the size of large dogs, or sheep, maybe wolves, march behind the men. Each walk on nimble legs, has a rectangular body, and then there's something that's an arm, or a head—maybe both—that swivels in all directions as they follow the men to the front door.

As for the men of Bravo team, they come armed for bear. Before reaching the expansive wraparound porch, the robots peel off and disappear, heading wherever they're supposed to go. Dumbstruck, I turn my attention back to the armed men.

And when I say armed, I mean armed to the teeth as if they expect to fight a war.

"Come on." Forest gestures for me to follow him. "Let's greet our guests."

I trot behind Forest, barely keeping pace. We pass back through the great room, where Paul coaxes a raging fire to life in the hearth. Forest reaches the foyer just as Mitzy opens the massive front door.

"You're six hours early," Forest chastises a diminutive woman who's nearly the same height as me.

She ignores Forest and turns her attention to me. "You must be Cara." She holds up my grandmother's watch. "This has turned into quite the mystery."

It's a struggle not to snatch the watch out of the air. I hang back instead and wave like an idiot.

"Hi."

Mitzy stomps until she's toe-to-toe with Forest. Her psychedelic hair shimmers in every color of the rainbow and the short pixie cut sticks hair out in every direction.

"As for being *early*…" She makes air quotes and shakes her head. "You're lucky we got here when we did."

"How's that?" Forest doesn't back down. He stands exactly where he is and stares down at Mitzy.

I don't know what's funnier, watching her crane her neck to look up at him, or watching him try to tuck his chin far enough to glare down at her.

"This isn't a tracker." She lifts my watch until it's right below Forest's nose. Her attention shifts to me, but it's fleeting. "Which means…"

I'm really confused, but Forest just shrugs. "What?" he asks.

"Think about it?" She gives Forest a moment, but rushes to answer the question herself. "If this isn't a tracker…" She looks at me. "And those assholes have been tracking Cara…"

"No way." Forest's eyes widen.

"Yes way." She nods as if winning this round. "Which is why Bravo team is here and why I brought the RUFUS *pack*." The way she emphasizes *pack* makes me wonder if she refers to the robot dogs.

"Was wondering about that." Forest finally takes a step back and to the side.

"I'm sorry, but what are you talking about?" I can no longer hang back and pretend they aren't talking about me as if I don't exist.

Mitzy tucks my grandmother's watch into her pocket and props her hands on her hips. "It means the outer perimeter alarms are down."

"Down?" Forest jerks in surprise.

"You heard me. Someone cut the feed. Pretty smart how they

did it. I'll give you one guess." She ignores me and goes back to Forest.

He thinks about it for a moment, while the men of Bravo team slowly file in. I wave to Rafe, Hayes, Zeb, and Alec, surprised to see them in full tactical gear. Each man carries more weapons than I can count, which only escalates my fear something is horribly wrong, and increases my frustration no one's answering my questions.

"I'm sorry, but can one of you explain to me exactly what's going on? Why is Bravo team here, looking like they're ready to fight a war? What the hell are those robot things? What does it mean my watch isn't a tracker, and what does it mean someone cut the feed? What feed?"

"Now this one asks great questions." Mitzy turns her attention to me. "The robot things are my Rufuses."

"Rufi!" Hayes, Alec, and Zeb all shout in unison, correcting Mitzy.

"I'm not calling them that." She shakes her head and rolls her eyes.

"And what is a Rufi?" My questions remain unanswered.

"Rufuses. Not Rufi. It's short for Robotic Ultra Functional Utility Specialists. R-U-F-U-S. Think of robotic sentries that are all plugged together and work as one."

"Like a pack of dogs?" I ask.

"More like a pack of wolves. Those Rufuses are armed and capable of…"

"Wait. They're armed?"

"Yes, but not autonomous when it comes to shooting humans. That's what Jack is here for." She points to another man climbing out of the helicopter. Unlike the Guardians, he's significantly smaller in build. Much younger too. Early twenties? High teens? Lord, he's young.

"I'm confused."

"Jack authorizes any kill shots, but the robots decide how to patrol and how best to defend." Mitzy continues as if I should understand. But I don't. I'm completely lost.

"Defend? Against what?"

"Who. Not what," Mitzy corrects me, then shifts back to Forest. "I summoned the team and flew out as fast as we could. You've got twenty plus armed men crawling through the woods. After seeing the helicopter, they might decide to put caution to the wind. I'm assuming they were counting on a night attack. As for your defense, they used drones to disable the cameras." Mitzy takes a step back and stretches her neck.

She shakes her head. "Didn't write that into the programming when they went in. Now, we have to rethink everything. The bad guys are getting smarter every day. Anyway, that's why Bravo is here. The Rufuses will hunt the men down and herd them toward Bravo team. Meanwhile, the rest of us should probably retreat to the safe room." She looks at me again and flashes a bright smile. "Forest doesn't like calling it a panic room. So we had to go with safe room instead, but we should probably go."

"I'm sorry." I take a step back, eyes wide, and gape. "What's happening?"

More men? Will this nightmare never end?

TWENTY-EIGHT

Chase
_____

THE BLARE OF AN ALARM RUDELY INTERRUPTS MY CONVERSATION with Doc Summers. My older sister? That's incomprehensible.

She wants me to call her by her first name, but that feels weird.

"What's that?" I sit up in bed, hating the way it confines me.

"That's the perimeter alarm." Skye gestures to the door. "Come on, up and out of bed."

"My leg?"

"You gave me three days. I only needed two. Go ahead and put weight on it." She gestures for me to get out of bed. "I have a feeling they're going to need you."

"Me?"

Skye gives me a look. "You _are_ Cara's Protector? Time to get out of bed and do what you do best." Skye waves toward the hallway, urging me to go ahead of her.

I don't hesitate, but the moment I put weight on my leg, I know it's going to be a hindrance. I hobble down the hall, stumbling toward the great room, then run into Cara coming toward me.

"What's going on?" I stop Cara in the hall and take her hands in mine, then pause when Mitzy follows on her heels.

"They found me." Fear rims her eyes.

"Hey, it's going to be okay." I pull her into my embrace and squeeze her tight. "Where are you taking her?" I direct the question at Mitzy, but she doesn't answer my question immediately. Instead, she gives a mini SITREP.

"There are twenty plus men in the woods, moving in on the cabin. I brought Bravo team along with six of the Rufi—um Rufuses." Mitzy corrects herself, as if annoyed.

"And *where* are you taking Cara?" My voice firms because there's no way in hell I'm leaving Cara's side. She's mine. Mine to protect. Mine to hold.

Mine.

Mitzy gives me a look, then nods as if she understands. "Skye, Cara, and I are going to hole up in the safe room. You and Bravo team…" She looks toward Skye. "Along with Tia and Ryker are on defense." Mitzy turns toward Skye. "Forest and Paul are as well."

"Forest?" Skye shakes her head. "He's in no condition to…"

"If you think you can get him to stand down and join the women in the safe room, by all means." Mitzy gestures toward the great room.

"No." Skye shakes her head. "He's being a stubborn mule, pretending nothing's wrong."

"Paul is going to be by his side. If anyone can protect Forest, it's Paul." Mitzy tugs on Cara's sleeve. "We really need to get downstairs and let the muscle do what they do best. Besides, I want to talk with you about something."

Cara grips my shirt and lifts on tiptoe. "I don't want to lose you." She presses her lips against mine. A fleeting kiss. It doesn't last nearly long enough, but I sense the urgency in Mitzy's tone.

I hold Cara tight. "I'll be back before you know it. In the meantime…"

"In the meantime…" Mitzy tugs on my sleeve. "We need to get to the safe room so the guys can focus on what needs to be done."

Letting go of Cara is the hardest thing I've ever had to do, but I tug her tight to my chest, wrap my arms around her one last time, and breathe in her light floral fragrance, before tasting her lips for what I hope isn't the last time.

They found her again.

The question is how?

The three of them head deep into the estate, to the safe room that will keep them safe. Meanwhile, I join Bravo team in the great room and plan to defend Cara with my life.

"Ah, there you are," Brady Malone, Bravo-One, welcomes me. "We don't have much time." With that, he begins the briefing, identifying the threat against us, the resources we have at our disposal, and his plan to negate the threat.

My leg gives me pause, but Brady takes the injury into consideration, stationing me on the porch with Tia and Ryker in support. We'll be the last line of defense.

"Everyone know their positions?" Brady glances around the foyer at the end of the short briefing where Bravo team, myself, Doc Summers's medical team, and Forest and Paul gather.

Bravo team's decked out in tactical gear: full-body armor and integrated heads-up displays. They brought extras, giving one each to me, Tia, Ryker, Paul, and Forest. We're eleven men strong. I count Tia among that number.

She and Ryker aren't technically special ops soldiers, but they are former members of a special ops surgical team trained to perform life-saving operations while behind enemy lines. Which means they're as proficient with their handguns as they are with providing medical care in the field.

Forest and Paul have no military training, but Forest spent the last few years with the Guardians—he's been checked out with both pistol and rifle—and Paul seems to know his shit, making me wonder what he did in a previous life.

The five of us are the last line of defense. Forest and Paul will guard the rear entrance, while Tia, Ryker, and I hold down the front approach. Bravo team will deploy into the woods. Going with them are six of Mitzy's Rufi, who are supposedly armed.

I head outside with Bravo team, joined by Tia and Ryker. Forest and Paul go through the house to take up their position at the back of the estate.

"See you on the other side." Brady grips my arm, then leaves me to prepare our last line of defense.

Despite the sun being high in the sky, there's a cool nip to the mountain air. A light breeze rustles the leaves. It's a beautiful day to die. Not that I plan on dying today.

I make a circuit of the wraparound porch, then stop behind a woodpile.

"I'll set up here. Anyone who steps foot in the clearing, I'll take out. You and Tia…" I turn to scan the deck. "Ryker, you take left, and Tia, you take right. That should give us good crossing fire. Take out anyone I don't hit."

Not that I'll fail.

It doesn't escape my notice the number of men sent to kill Cara continues to increase. Two in the car following Cara from the airport. Eight men in the desert. A dozen at the motel. The truck by the train. Now, Mitzy's drones count twenty plus.

I take a deep breath and push away the pain in my leg. It's been three days since I got shot. Three days since I've been on my feet. Doc Summers lifted mandatory bedrest literally minutes before now, making me promise to '*take things easy*,' but there's no time to take things easy.

Not when we have a mission to complete and I have a woman to save.

With Tia and Ryker by my side, we take cover. Bravo team hooked me up. I carry a sniper rifle for the long-range shots and a handgun for up close and personal engagement.

Tia and Ryker will take out anyone who makes it past Bravo team and the bullets from my sniper rifle. Behind us, the estate is locked down with steel reinforced doors and blinds, bulletproof glass, and several nasty surprises for anyone who makes their way inside.

Meanwhile, Bravo team splits up, heading into the woods to hunt down twenty hired mercenaries. Along with the rest of the team, both indoors and out, I keep track of Bravo's movements through the HUD.

Bravo team creeps through the woods, staying low, deadly, and silent with weapons at the ready. The six-man team breaks up into three teams of two and fan out. The Rufi fill the gaps, ghosting silently through the forest. Their job is three-fold: scan the area for attackers, herd them toward Bravo team, and take down anyone who gets past our first line of defense. Overhead, a dozen of Mitzy's dragonfly drones search for the heat signatures of the men advancing on our position.

After several minutes of quiet, gunfire erupts in the distance.

The battle begins.

Bravo team takes cover and returns fire. The Rufi dart back and forth, harrying the enemy and pushing them toward Bravo team. A pair of the robotic dogs charge two men after locating their targets. They gallop after the terrified men, leap onto their backs, and tackle the men to the ground. I watch them through my HUD, impressed and amazed at the technology behind the Rufi.

Brady and Hayes exchange fire with the enemy and take cover behind a fallen tree. Brady takes out two men when they attempt to rush the position he holds with Hayes. Rafe and Zeb circle around the back of the cabin, looking to flank the mercenaries. Booker and Alec take out two men, then provide covering fire for Brady and Hayes, freeing them from their position. The four men break apart again, following directions given to them through the drones to take out the next group of attackers.

After that, the battle turns chaotic. In between the Rufi running men down, and Bravo team taking them out one by one, they work seamlessly to pick off our enemy.

Meanwhile, I wait.

Bravo team takes out the mercenaries with methodical precision, filling the woods with the sharp report of gunfire and the screams of men.

The moment an attacker steps foot past the tree line, I take aim and bring him down.

The battle rages on with Bravo team and the Rufi methodically closing in on the mercenaries. Through my HUD, I watch the chaos unfold. My heart wants to race, spurred on by the adrenaline flowing through my veins, but I take deep measured breaths, a technique to steady my aim.

Each burst of gunfire sounds closer, making me fear Bravo won't get to all the men in time. I stare through the scope of my rifle and ignore the throbbing in my leg. It protests every movement, but I refuse to let it slow me down.

A second man creeps out of the trees from the west. I take aim at the asshole and line up my shot. My breathing slows as my finger tightens on the trigger.

The rifle fires with a loud crack and the man drops to the ground, motionless. He won't be getting up from that.

Tia and Ryker focus on two men who slip past Bravo team. I swing the barrel of my rifle over to assist, but there's no need. They're both deadly with their handguns.

The three of us work well together, holding the front line, taking out any enemy who dares rush the cabin. We move from cover to cover, keeping our heads down as the men return fire.

Out of the twenty-some-odd who attack, six make it through the Rufi and past Bravo team. Honestly, I expected far less, but Bravo has a lot of ground to cover and they're outmanned three to one.

The battle reaches a fevered pitch. We've taken out nearly all the men, but a few remain. Alone and cut off from their team, they're getting desperate, and know they fight a losing battle.

I always find this part the most interesting. If they turn around and decide today is not their day to die, what waits for them at home? Are they getting paid enough to risk it all?

Will Artemus Gonzales turn his mercenaries into targets to teach the rest a lesson?

Shouts in Spanish reach my ears and give me pause. Barely audible over the gunfire, it tells me much. Those men aren't locally grown, and by local, I mean U.S. born and bred. They're native Spanish speakers, which makes me think they work directly for Artemus Gonzales. That means they're likely cartel members rather than hired mercenaries.

Which makes them far more dangerous. They won't run from

this fight. Their honor and allegiance to the cartel won't allow it. They're in this to the death.

Suddenly, a loud explosion rips through the air. The ground shakes beneath my feet, and I look up to see a plume of smoke rising from the woods.

"Bravo took out the last of them." Mitzy's voice comes through the comms channel. "The drones are making another sweep, but I don't see any more heat signatures."

I wait for the all clear. My body shakes with a mixture of relief and exhaustion. My leg is nowhere near field ready and will remain a liability for several more days. I lower my sniper rifle and turn to Tia and Ryker.

"The two of you are amazing."

"Thanks." Tia checks her weapon, clearing it, then tucks it behind her back.

Ryker clears his weapon, then comes over to thump my shoulder. "Looks like your woman is safe."

"For the time being." I can't help what I say. "Next time, he's going to send more."

"More?" Tia's brows scrunch in confusion.

"They're cartel. Not mercenaries. Each time he sends men after us, he doubles the number. Don't know what we're going to do if that happens."

"Hmm…" Tia pulls at her chin. "I'm sure we'll figure it out. Until then, it was nice working with you." She shoves out her hand.

"Likewise." I shake Tia's hand then do the same with Ryker, truly impressed with their skill and their cool demeanor while under fire.

Ryker thumps me on the back after we shake. I may be a solo operator, but that doesn't mean I don't enjoy working with a team of top-notch professionals.

With the battle won, Bravo returns two by two, making their way back to the cabin. Mitzy opens the house, retracting the reinforced steel doors and the steel shutters covering bulletproof glass. Her drones return, flying overhead, heard first by the low whine of their engines, then seen as tiny specks in the sky.

Rufi emerge from the forest, running one by one back to the porch where they stand at the ready, silent and deadly. Mitzy mentioned they're armed, but I don't remember any of the Rufi firing during the engagement.

Paul's voice comes over the comms. "We're still holding the rear. Are we done?"

"All clear." Mitzy's high-pitched voice brings my shoulders lifting to my ears, but damn if those aren't the best two words I've ever heard. "Unlocking the house. You can come in now. I've got something to show you."

First out of the front door, Cara runs into my arms, her body trembling from the adrenaline and fear. It may be my imagination, but her heart pounds against my chest, which makes me hold her even tighter. I'll explain to her later how running out the door is a bad call.

As I breathe her in, tears stream down her face and wet my shirt. I stroke her hair gently, whispering sweet nothings in her ear, trying to calm her down and assure her everything is going to be alright.

We stand for a minute, holding each other, lost in the moment. The chaos of everything else fades away. There's cleanup to be done. Authorities to call. But, all I can focus on is her: her warmth, her softness, and her scent. I'm grateful she's safe, but not so complacent that I don't usher her inside the safety of the building. Who knows if there is one last man out in the woods with a sniper rifle trained right between her eyes.

Best not to take chances.

Once inside, she pulls back slightly and looks at me. Her eyes fill with gratitude and love, but there's something else there as well.

Fear.

"Hey, it's okay. Everything's going to be okay."

"How is your leg?" She turns her attention to me and I love how much she cares for me.

"Just a flesh wound."

"Just a flesh wound?" She smacks me playfully in the arm, my non-wounded arm, and shakes her head. "What am I going to do with you?"

"Love me?" I smile, feeling my heart swell with emotion. At that moment, I realize a profound truth. Somewhere along the way, I fell deeply in love with this amazing woman and I can't imagine life without her. I'll do anything to protect her, to keep her safe, and to make her happy.

"I do too."

"Huh?"

"I love you too." Her smile is wide and her eyes are bright.

I lean down and kiss her gently, feeling her respond to me with passion and tenderness, and don't care one bit that we do it in front of a crowd.

Or that they're clapping.

As we break apart, I loop my arm around her shoulder and keep her tight to my side. Her cheeks turn the prettiest shade of pink, while I rock back on my heels.

"If the two lovebirds are done swapping spit, I've got something to show you." Mitzy gives another one of her Oscar-worthy eye rolls. It seems to be something she does a lot because everyone laughs.

"You guys chat while we deal with the cleanup outside." Brady Malone gestures to his team and the six men file out the front door.

This is the second assist the men of Bravo team provide me and I couldn't be more thankful, but Mitzy herds all of us into the great room where Paul's earlier fire sputters on a bed of dying coals.

TWENTY-NINE

Chase

——————

PAUL HEADS TO THE STACK OF WOOD BY THE HEARTH AND FEEDS THE dying fire while Mitzy stands in front of everyone and lifts something shiny.

"What's going on?" I whisper in Cara's ear, wanting to get the short version of whatever it is Mitzy is going to say.

"She found something," Cara whispers back, snuggling close.

"The tracker?"

"Not exactly." Cara leans back, saying nothing more, which leaves me frustrated. Not that I stay frustrated long.

Despite her high-pitched voice, Mitzy knows how to quiet a room and make her voice carry. She holds the watch shoulder level and lets it sway, slowly, back and forth.

"As you all know, we took Cara's grandmother's watch, thinking it had a tracker embedded in it. Despite routine safety measures, men could still locate Cara here and at the motel. That's after Chase mailed off her watch. We divested her of everything she brought with her." Mitzy looks around the room, taking in each of us in turn.

"Artemus Gonzales's men followed her from the airport. Bravo team shook the tail, but when Chase took her into the desert, more men came. That got me to thinking we were missing something. The only thing she still carried on her person was this watch. I assumed it held a tracker, and you know how I hate assuming anything."

Mitzy hands the watch to Paul, who gives her a look. After a nudge, Mitzy tells him to pass it around the room like we're having show and tell. Once the watch gets to me, I stop that in its tracks and return it to Cara.

"Did you find the tracker?" I can't help but ask, knowing Mitzy wouldn't be grandstanding if that's the case. Like everyone else in the room, I'm curious.

"We didn't," she delivers the answer deadpan, which makes me do a double take.

"What do you mean, you didn't?"

"I mean exactly what I said."

"Then how did they find us at the motel? How did they track Cara here?"

"We'll get to that. In the meantime, while we didn't find a tracker, we found something else."

"Something else?" Clearly confused, I scratch my head. I also take note that I'm the only person who's confused. Evidently, everyone else is used to how Mitzy makes a point.

Cara takes the watch and cups it in her hand. She brings it to her chest as if touching her heart.

"What did you find, Mitzy?" Forest breaks the silence with his deep baritone. "'Cause you wouldn't make us sit through this if you didn't find something juicy."

"As always, you steal my thunder." Mitzy props a hand on her hip. "I found something."

"Then spit it out already." Forest leans back and pinches the bridge of his nose, looking tired and pale.

"She's getting to it, beanpole." Skye blows out a breath and settles into the couch beside her brother.

Her brother.

After the bombshell Forest dropped earlier, that takes on a whole other meaning. What if it's true? What if Skye is my sister? What happens next?

"Yes, I'm getting to it. Or trying to." Mitzy shifts on her feet.

"I'm all ears." Forest gestures for her to continue.

"We didn't find a tracker. We found something else. Something unexpected." Mitzy turns to Cara. "Tell them what your father said when he gave you the watch."

"Um, it was right after he told me what he'd done." Cara grips the watch and places her hands in her lap.

"What did your father do?" That question comes from Paul. "Sorry, but not all of us are in the know."

"He connected wealthy men," Cara explains. "Americans mostly. He made introductions to Artemus Gonzales who then arranged for the men to attend one of the galas at the Minister of the Interior's estate just outside of Managua. Those were introductory parties where Artemus and Maximus Angel, he's the Minister of the Interior, showcased the women they were trafficking. My father brought them their buyers." She chokes up and shakes her head.

"Wait a second." Again, it's Paul who speaks. "Artemus? Why do I know that name?" He turns to Forest for the answer.

"Artemus Gonzales is Maximus Angelo's business partner. Maximus is Carmen's father. Artemus is who Maximus arranged for Carmen to marry."

"The fucker who took Isabelle?"

"None other." Forest's tone sounds more like a growl than words.

"Didn't your Guardians raid his estate and shut it down?" Paul's brows bunch with confusion.

"We did, but Carmen's father is a powerful man. They never charged him, despite taking him. Fucker is out there right now, probably still destroying lives. He and Artemus are two of a kind, and thick as thieves. I have no doubt they're back at kidnapping women and young girls, then selling them to the highest bidder."

"I don't get the connection between Cara and Artemus." Paul glances around the room.

Again, it's Forest who answers. "Cara's father was the Protocol Director for the U.S. Embassy in Nicaragua. He spent a few years in Costa Rica, then moved to Nicaragua. He's been under investigation for years, but the FBI found nothing to pin on him. But then he initiated contact with them."

Cara gasps. "All this time, I thought they caught him. I thought that was why he was going into witness protection."

"From what I could find out from my contacts, he initiated communication with the FBI." Forest turns to Paul to fill him in. "The night he was supposed to enter witness protection, Artemus had him murdered. Cara's father called her home to give her the watch. She was there when he died. Sorry, Cara, I didn't mean to be insensitive."

"No, it's fine. I always wondered what changed? Why, after so many years, did he decide to… Well, it doesn't matter now."

"Tell Forest what your father told you," Mitzy says. "Not about the human trafficking, but about the watch specifically."

"Well, he held out my grandmother's watch. It's an heirloom in my family, passed from mother to daughter for generations. It belonged to my mother, given to her by her mother. Because I was so young when my mother died, my father was keeping it safe until I was old enough to hold on to it for the next generation."

"Tell them the words he used," Mitz presses.

"Um…" Cara closes her eyes, then tips her head back to stare at the ceiling. "He said… I need you to have this. It's important you keep it safe."

"I don't get it." Forest looks to Mitzy. "None of that is earth-shattering. What are you hearing that I'm not?"

"It is when you take it in context, and after we x-rayed the thing."

"Please share," Forest tells Mitzy to continue.

"He didn't tell his daughter he wanted her to have the watch. He *needed* her to have it. He also told her it was important to *keep it safe.*" Mitzy uses air quotes for emphasis.

"Not exactly damming words," I jump in, trying to make sense of whatever Mitzy's trying to tell us.

Skye says nothing. Presumably, she already knows. Paul sits quietly, taking it all in. Only Forest and I appear to struggle with what Mitzy's trying to tell us.

"I'm not following." I give up. "Her father gave her the watch. Of course, he'd want her to keep it safe."

"True, but not because it's an heirloom." Mitzy gestures to her technician, Jack, who hovers in a corner. I didn't even know he was in the same room until he moves to join Mitzy in front of the hearth.

He reaches into his pocket and holds up a small Ziploc baggy with a tiny square of metal inside.

"What's that?" I pinch my eyes, trying to see what it is.

"That is a microchip." With the revelation, Mitzy's eyes blaze in victory. "A microchip hidden inside the inner workings of the watch. A microchip with no business being inside a hundred-year-old watch." Mitzy points to the microchip. "If I'm right, and I know I am, he needed Cara to keep the watch safe because he made a copy of whatever evidence he intended to hand over to the FBI to secure whatever deal he negotiated."

"You think?" Forest crosses the distance to the hearth in three long strides. He yanks the baggy out of Jack's hand and lifts it to the light. "You haven't read it yet?"

"Well, that's a problem." Mitzy pulls at her ear.

"How so?" Forest looks at Mitzy.

"I tried. The thing's encrypted. He obviously didn't want anyone reading it. I'm thinking it was an insurance policy, but he also had to know Artemus would do anything to silence him. Which is exactly what happened. I think he put whatever information he had on the microchip and made sure he gave it to Cara. Then I think he did what he could to tell her the watch was important with his dying breath."

"You think Cara knows the password?" I drape my arm around Cara's shoulder. "Do you?"

"I don't know." Her voice sounds tiny. She shrugs. "Honestly, we didn't get that far, but I already told Mitzy, I don't know. My father never mentioned it. He just gave me the watch. Didn't say there was anything hidden in it, and he definitely never gave me a password."

"He probably did that to protect you." Forest continues to stare at the microchip. "It might explain why Artemus is dead set on taking you out of the picture."

"I thought it was because he figured my father told me what he'd done, but Chase says none of that is admissible in a court of law. You think Artemus knew my father gave me the microchip?"

"It makes sense," Mitzy says. "Your father wouldn't have gone to the effort of hiding the chip, and knowing Artemus put a hit out on him, he had to believe you could figure it out. It has to be something personal. Something memorable. Something that's important enough to you both that it would be obvious." Mitzy spins toward Forest. "What do you think?"

"There's one problem," Forest says. "I don't see a protocol officer having the knowledge to encrypt information, let alone put it on a microchip. Someone did that for him."

"What about putting it inside the watch?" Cara stares at the watch. "He would've needed help with that."

"Maybe, or maybe not. That might be why Artemus is after you. Maybe whoever helped your father drew the attention of Artemus?" Forest runs his hand down his chin. "If Artemus discovered your father made a record of whatever information he had about the clients he supplied, it explains the relentlessness of the attacks against you. It's exactly the kind of information that can damage any political hopes Maximus Angelo has to take power in Nicaragua. I would bet Artemus needs the political power Maximus can pull. Those two are tied at the hip. More so than we ever thought."

"You're making a lot of assumptions, Forest." Mitzy shakes her head, clearly not pleased with Forest's logic.

I place my hand over Cara's trembling fingers. "We need to figure out how he's tracking Cara, because each time he fails, he doubles the number of men he sends. We have to assume he knows about the microchip and believes Cara has it."

"I agree," Skye, who's been silent until now, speaks up. "And while it would be great to break the security of the chip and see what's on it, I'm worried about the next wave. If we rely on past experience, it takes a day or two for him to round up more men to go after Cara. I'm not saying we don't need to know what's on the chip, but we need to figure out how he keeps finding her before he sends an army down on top of our heads." Skye turns to Forest. "Love your little cabin, beanpole, and we did well against twenty men, but what if he sends forty? Fifty? Or a hundred more?"

"Bastard's going to run out of men. Or money." Forest props his chin in his hand and cups his elbow with the other.

"Actually…" I speak up. "Those men are cartel out there. We'll know after Bravo ID's the bodies, but if they're cartel like I suspect, it's not money that drives them, but loyalty. Artemus doesn't need money when he has hundreds, if not thousands, of loyal men willing to die for their leader."

"Well, shit." Forest spins around and stares at Cara like she's a puzzle he can't figure out.

Cara withers beneath Forest's pensive scowl.

"We've ruled out everything." Mitzy shrugs. "Almost everything."

I listen to the conversation, trying to think of anything we might have missed. Then it hits me like a thunderbolt. Something so obvious I kick myself for not thinking of it before.

I clear my throat. Everyone looks at me. "We're looking in the wrong place."

Mitzy raises an eyebrow and shares a look with Forest, almost as if the two of them already figured it out.

"He's not tracking something she's carrying, because we've taken everything from Cara… Except one thing."

"I think he figured it out." Forest turns his heavy gaze on me, but his comment is to Mitzy.

Cara looks to me, confused, but hopeful I have an explanation.

"Cara…" Skye's eyes brighten like a lightbulb going off. "He's not tracking *something* she's carrying. He's tracking her."

"Exactly. What if he embedded a tracker in her body without

her knowledge?" I look around the room, hoping what I say makes sense.

Cara's face pales at the suggestion. "How is something like that possible?" She looks from Mitzy to Skye, then back at me.

"It's very possible. And after ruling everything else out, it's the only thing that makes sense." Mitzy steeples her fingers and rests her chin on the tips of her fingers. "All of our Guardians and Protectors, even some of our support personnel, have trackers embedded in their bodies. Two actually. The trackers I use are the size of a grain of rice. It's totally possible he's doing the same thing."

"It's the only thing that makes sense." I know I'm right. "We've eliminated everything else."

We all exchange glances, realizing the implications of what we're saying. Meanwhile, Cara's eyes widen in horror.

"How did he put it in her without her knowledge?" Forest asks.

"I always knew this day would come." Mitzy shakes her head and pulls at her pixie hair.

"What's that?" Curious, I can't help but ask.

"The day our enemies caught up to us. A tracker embedded in Cara? Drones that disabled the perimeter sensors? They're getting better and better with their tech. More sophisticated by the day."

The room falls silent as we consider the possibility. Finally, Skye speaks up, "We carry a portable ultrasound in our medical gear. I should be able to detect a subcutaneous tracker. Cara, would you be up for that?"

Cara shivers next to me. "If there's something he put inside of me, I want it out. Now. When can we start?"

THIRTY

Cara

"LET ME GET THE ULTRASOUND OUT OF OUR GEAR." SKYE LOOKS AT both Chase and me. "If you and Chase want to meet me in the dining room, we can do it there. Or we can do it in your room?"

"Which is easiest for you?" I know my preference. The room Chase and I have been staying in comes with a door that locks. The dining room doesn't have doors. Anyone can walk in. Not that anyone would, but still.

"The dining room is best. We'll drape it with a sheet, grab a pillow to keep you as comfortable as possible. I've never done a full body scan before, but we'll want to be as thorough as possible. It won't take long."

I follow her back to the dining room. It's the same place she performed minor surgery on Chase's arm and leg. After a few days, his arm's darn near fully healed, but he walks with a limp. He follows me into the dining room, providing support by merely being by my side.

Skye digs through the cases of medical gear they brought with them and pulls out the ultrasound machine.

"Will it hurt?" I can't help my nerves.

The idea there's something inside of me, something placed without my knowledge, without my consent, sickens me.

"Not at all." She looks at me with a reassuring smile. "Have you ever had an ultrasound before?"

"No."

"Well, it's the same device used to scan pregnant women and their babies. There are a ton of uses for ultrasound these days. We look at hearts, heads, and bellies. We even use it to identify blood vessels and help with the insertion of IVs. It's perfectly painless."

"I won't feel anything?"

"The only drawback is the gel can be cold, and the cleanup can be messy, but other than that, you won't feel a thing." Skye lifts a tube of gel and squirts clear goo out on her palm. She holds out her hand. "See? It's gooey and cold. That's all."

"Okay."

Skye turns to Chase. "Do you mind grabbing the sheets for us? And a pillow. I don't know how long this will take. I want Cara to be as comfortable as possible."

"Not at all." Chase gives my hand a squeeze. "Back in a bit, princess."

"Thanks." I watch him go, my mind spinning with questions about what happened outside. The fact Chase and the others are back tells me more men died. More men sent to find me.

Kill me.

Terrorize me.

It's no longer possible to count how many men have lost their lives because of me, and I hate it. I absolutely hate there are people dying because of me. Even though I did nothing—well, nothing other than breathe—there's still a piece of me that feels at fault.

I know what Chase would say. Heck, I know what everyone around me would say. Each and every one of them would tell me it's not my fault. While I know it intellectually, my heart still aches for the men who've lost their lives because of me.

"What are the sheets for?"

"One to cover the table and one to cover you."

"Me?"

"We don't know where they may have placed a tracker, if it's there at all. Which means I need to search your entire body. Everything should come off."

"Even my bra and panties?"

"Yes. Don't worry. I'll keep you as modest as I can. Think of it as getting a massage, only with goo instead of body oil. To be honest, the best place to implant a tracker is in the fattier parts of the body. Breast tissue is perfect."

"And you're sure that will detect it?" I point at the ultrasound machine.

"It should."

"So, I should get undressed?"

"Wait until Chase returns with the sheets. No one will walk in on us, but you'll probably feel more comfortable being draped."

"Thanks." But I don't wait for Chase to return. While unbuttoning my blouse, I can't help but ask the obvious. "How would they have inserted a tracker?"

"That's a good question and all we have is speculation."

"After my father died, I was immediately put into witness protection. They took all my identification, credit cards… Artemus wouldn't have had a chance to implant a tracker. Unless… Is it possible I could've swallowed it? Like if someone slipped it in my food?"

"Good thought, but not likely. Anything you swallow comes out the other end. It's not a permanent way to track someone."

"Oh. Boy, do I feel stupid, but still. Then how?"

"Someone had to do it beforehand."

"How so?"

"I don't know. We'd have to assume a lot of things, and if you didn't pick up on it out there, Mitzy hates when any of us assume anything."

"Why is that?"

"She says it puts your brain in a rut. The more you assume, the harder it is to get out of the rut and shift lanes. She says you lose perspective and the ability to see things from different angles."

"I guess that makes sense."

"If I were to *speculate*, rather than assume." Skye lifts a finger in the air and winks at me. "I'd say it had to have been placed earlier. The embassies are not so advanced that they've resorted to that kind of tech. Usually, they use the cellphones of their employees to keep track of them. They rarely do that for dependents, and rarely for anyone who isn't the immediate family of the ambassadors. But that's where I would begin."

"I see that."

"So, *speculating*…" She makes use of air quotes and grins again, as if we share an inside joke. "If we assume the embassy didn't do it, and I highly doubt they're sophisticated enough, then that leaves your father. He must've done it."

"How?"

"Have you ever had any surgeries while overseas?"

"No."

"Had braces, dental work, anything where you would've received sedation?"

"No."

"Vaccinations?"

"Definitely vaccinations." I rub at my arm, remembering the slew of vaccinations we were required to take.

"If we assume… Sorry, if we *speculate* they inserted the tracker without your knowledge, and rule out any medical or dental procedures where you would've been sedated, then vaccinations are a potential. Like Mitzy said, the ones she uses are the size of a grain of rice. Most are inserted just under the skin. Were all your vaccinations in the arm?"

"Arm and butt." My cheeks heat talking about my butt. I hate the way I blush so easily, and it's not like Skye isn't a doctor.

"Butt?"

"Yeah."

"Interesting."

"Why?"

"None of the vaccines we use today go in the buttocks."

I can't help but brush my hip and slide my fingers around to the rise of my hip. "A chip in my ass?"

Of course, Chase wanders back into the room at that exact moment.

"There's a chip in your ass?"

"We're just speculating." Skye saves me from embarrassment. "Haven't started yet. Go ahead and spread a sheet on the table. Cara, time to strip. I don't like to assume, but am I right that you don't mind if Chase stays? If you'd rather he didn't…"

"No, it's okay. I prefer having him here."

There's a knock on the door and Tia pokes her head inside. "Heard you were checking Cara with the ultrasound. Need any help?"

The tall brunette is a stunning woman. She reminds me of an Amazon queen with her lustrous black hair, towering presence, and uniquely feminine hourglass shape. Tia is the epitome of female power. She's strong, smart, sultry, and sexy. It's a unique combination.

"That would be great." Skye waves Tia in while I divest myself of my clothes.

While I've spent most of the past three days naked and in bed with Chase, stripping out of my bra and panties, in front of him, with two other women in the room, is exceptionally awkward for me.

Chase immediately picks up on my unease, lifting the spare sheet to provide privacy. He continues holding it in place while I climb up on the table and lie down. Then he lets the cotton sheet slowly float down to cover me completely, except for my head.

"Lift up." His uniquely masculine voice sends shivers down my spine. He helps me up and tucks the pillow under my head. "Comfortable?"

"Not in the slightest. Just the thought of something inside of me gives me the creeps."

"It's not so bad."

"How would you know?"

"All Guardians and Protectors have two chips."

That's right. Mitzy mentioned it. I'm just too shocked to retain any information right now.

"Two?"

"One to find and one to hide."

"What?"

"In case something ever happens. I guess it matters *why* it's there. For me, it's nice to know there's a backup in case anything happens. Not to mention, I consented to the whole thing."

"I have a feeling I don't want to know what kinds of things can happen." I take in a deep breath, feeling incredibly exposed, even while fully covered.

Skye connects the ultrasound device to power, and it chirps to life. "We'll do the scan in pieces, keeping you covered as much as possible. The gel is cool, and I don't want you getting chilled."

"Okay." I try to sound like going on a hunting expedition for a hidden tracker in my body is an everyday occurrence.

"I'm right by your side." Chase picks up on my unease and leans down to kiss my forehead. Somehow, that makes me feel a million times better.

"We'll start with your left arm." Skye squirts some of the gooey gel onto the tip of the ultrasound probe while Tia comes over and pulls back enough of the sheet covering me to expose my arm. "I want you to relax as much as possible. Tia will manipulate your arm so I can reach everything."

"Okay." I take in a breath and blow it out nice and slow, only realizing how incredibly tense I am when I resist Tia's touch.

"Relax, sweetie." Tia's voice soothes me. "We'll let you know everything we see and tell you what we're going to do before we do it." Her touch is warm as she takes my wrist and rolls my arm until my palm faces up. A moment later, cool gel hits the skin on the inside of my elbow and I flinch.

"I know it's cold." Skye runs the probe up and down my inner arm, and the cool gel warms against my skin. "I'm going to go slow. Just close your eyes and pretend this is an all over body massage."

I close my eyes, but there's no relaxing as Skye begins her scan. As she works her way up and down my arm, my heart pounds and my mind races. I hold my breath, praying she doesn't find any hidden trackers inside of me, but also hoping she does. If she finds one, we can remove it.

But what if she's not able to remove it?

THIRTY-ONE

Cara

_____

"Nothing in the left arm." Skye begins her diligent exploration of my body with the ultrasound probe. "Everything looks good so far." Skye moves from my arm to my leg, running the probe all the way to the tip of my toes.

She squirts out more cool gel. This time, when it hits, I'm prepared for the sensation. She's right about the scan feeling like a mini massage. I let my eyes drift closed and imagine myself on a beach, listening to the waves crashing against the shore and a gentle breeze blowing through my hair.

It does nothing to ease my anxiety.

"I'm going to move to your abdomen now. You doing okay?" Skye's bedside manner is beyond amazing. She makes me feel like she really cares.

I nod, unable to find my voice. While afraid she's going to find something, that's not nearly as overwhelming as what happens if she finds nothing at all.

We have to figure out how Artemus Gonzales keeps tracking me down.

As Skye applies more cool gel to my belly, my muscles tense. Tia's touch comforts me as she adjusts the sheet to expose my midsection for the probe. I'm tense and frightened, but these women make me feel like I'm in capable hands.

"You're doing great," Tia comforts me with her soothing alto.

I try to focus on the sound of her voice and the steady movement of the probe, but every time the thing passes over a sensitive area, I can't help but flinch.

After my belly, Skye moves to my breasts and then my neck. Tia helps with the sheet, exposing the part Skye needs to work on, while covering up the areas already scanned.

Tension builds inside of me and I try to focus on Tia's warm touch and her soothing voice rather than my fear.

Suddenly, the probe stops. My heart skips a beat and I open my eyes to see Skye's attention glued to the screen.

"What? What do you see?" My voice trembles and the tension in my body escalates, turning into a mini panic attack.

"There's something here." Her tone turns serious and her brow furrows in concentration. "It's not like the trackers the Guardians and Protectors have."

"What do we do?" My heart skips a beat, and I try to keep as calm as possible.

"Remove it." Skye glances at Tia. "Can you get me my instrument tray? We'll need to numb her neck."

"On it." Tia covers me with the sheet and moves off to the side.

Without hesitation, Chase takes my hand and gives it a reassuring squeeze. "Don't worry. I'll be right here with you, every step of the way."

"Actually..." Skye interrupts. "If you could get Mitzy, please? Once I get this out, she needs to examine it."

"You okay if I leave?" Chase turns to me, asking what I want. I love that about him. He's always thinking about me first.

"Yes." I don't want him to leave, but Skye's right. Mitzy's going to need to look at whatever this thing is in my neck.

"Be right back." Chase leans down and places a soft kiss on my temple. Then he slips out of the room as Tia approaches me.

"Cara, I'm going to inject a numbing agent around the spot

Skye needs to work on. You'll feel a light pinch and a burn, but that's the worst of it. Are you okay if I inject the anesthetic?"

"I am." My toes curl and I fist my hands, steeling against the prick and burn, but first, Tia rubs something cool over the side of my neck.

"Just cleaning the area with alcohol. I'm going to inject two spots on your neck. Then Skye will sterilize the skin and extract the chip."

With Chase gone, Skye places her hand over mine. "It'll be over before you know it. Roll your chin to your shoulder. I'll need you to hold still."

"Okay." I roll my chin to my shoulder and breathe deeply as Tia injects the numbing agent into my neck.

The pinch and burn she mentioned are minimal, but the thought of Skye digging around in my neck makes me sick to my stomach. I do my best not to jump, or flinch, or do anything that'll distract her, but it's hard. At least until Chase returns with Mitzy. With him by my side, all my fear slips away.

"How're you doing?" He brushes back my hair and runs his fingers through the strands.

It feels heavenly.

"Better now that you're back."

It occurs to me getting a chip removed from my neck pales compared to having a bullet dug out from his leg. Perhaps it was a good thing I didn't think too much about the surgery Skye performed on his leg? In my defense, however, Skye seemed inherently capable and confident. It never occurred to me to worry.

So why am I worrying now?

The way Chase's fingers run through my hair, pulling softly on my roots, helps me relax.

Skye's voice is calm as she sterilizes my skin. The tension in the room is palpable when she pulls the instrument tray close and prepares to extract the chip.

"Feel anything?" There's the slightest tugging on my skin, but nothing sharp.

"No."

"Good." Somewhere along the line, she put on a surgical mask and gloves.

I hold my breath as her fingers press against my neck. There's a bit of pressure, but no pain. I wonder how long it's going to take, when…

"Got it." Skye pushes back from her chair and lifts a tiny square chip for me to see.

A wave of relief washes over me, knowing the thing is out of my body. Skye places the chip in a metal bowl and hands it to Mitzy.

"This doesn't look like any tracker I'm familiar with, but let me run some tests." Mitzy cups the metal tin like it's precious and backs out of the room.

"You did great, Cara." Tia assists Skye as they clean the wound and place a bandage over the spot on my neck.

"But we're not done." Skye takes a step back, removes her gloves, and tosses them in the trash. "We still have the other half of your body to go. I want to be as thorough as thorough can be. Then we'll flip you to your stomach and check your backside."

As Skye resumes her examination, tracing the probe along my right arm, Chase continues to run his fingers through my hair, distracting me, and turns it into a scalp massage that finds me closing my eyes, enjoying his touch.

I focus on him, the steady rhythm of his breathing, and his loving touch. After Skye finishes with my arm, she moves to my leg, and then I flip to my belly for her to complete the exam. When the cool gel hits my back, I can't help but shiver, although, other than that, my anxiety almost disappears. The entire time, I take comfort in Chase's steady presence while Skye completes her exam.

"That's it. Nothing else is there." She gives the all clear.

"That is the best news I've heard in a very long time." I prop my chin on my hands and gaze up at Chase, who stares down at me with a smile.

"Why don't you take a shower to get the gel off? By the time the two of you get back, hopefully Mitzy will have something for us."

I don't know what to make of Skye assuming Chase will go with me, except there's no doubt he will. I flip over and jump off the table.

"Whoa." A wave of dizziness suddenly overcomes me as the room spins around me, but Chase is right there by my side, steadying me.

"Easy, princess. Don't want you falling over." His low, throaty chuckle fills the room. "Come now, let's clean up all that goo."

I'm grateful for his strength and his support: physical, moral, and emotional. There's no way I could get through any of this without him.

We slowly make it down the long hall that ends at our room. Each bedroom in the estate is a suite, which means the bathroom is private and the shower luxurious. He turns on the water while I peel the thin sheet off my body. It sticks where the ultrasound gel dried against my skin.

Chase watches me with open admiration, then comes over to me. He pinches my chin and tilts my face back while he closes the distance between us. His lips lightly brush against mine as the heat between us builds.

"Want some help?" Low and throaty, the way his voice vibrates sends delicious sparks dancing over my body.

"Definitely."

Steam fills the room as he slowly removes his shirt, dragging it up and over the chiseled perfection of his washboard abs and broad chest. With a wink, he tosses the shirt on the floor and kicks off his shoes. He steps out of his pants while I drink him in.

I'm grateful for his presence, the easy flow of energy between us, and the depth of intimacy we share.

I step into the shower and let out a contented sigh. The warm water rushes over my skin, washing away the remnants of the gel and the tension in my body. I close my eyes and tilt my head back, letting the water hit my face.

Chase steps in behind me. His brawny arms wrap around my waist and he rests his chin on my shoulder.

"How're you feeling, princess?"

"Mmm, much better with that thing out of me." I lean back into him, feeling the hard planes of his chest against my back. Turning my head slightly, I press a soft kiss against his jaw.

He nuzzles my neck, and his hands trail up and down my sides. The hard length of his erection presses against my back. We both know where this is going, but neither of us is in a hurry.

He massages my neck, easing the lingering tension bunched in my muscles. His hands move down my arms, a gentle caress. Then he turns me to face him. I wrap my arms around his neck and lift on tiptoe to meet the hunger of his kiss.

His tongue traces the seam of my lips before delving inside. I moan against him and he deepens the kiss. He cups my face, his thumb slowly tracing along the angle of my jaw as any lingering tension in my body disappears.

Acutely aware of him, my body responds with every nerve ending coming alive. His hands slide up and down my body, and his kisses move from my lips to flutter gently along my jawline. Heat pools deep in my belly as he kisses the soft spot behind my ear. He continues to shower me in feather-soft kisses until I squirm beneath the heat of his mouth.

I revel in the sensation of his wet skin against mine as my desire flares and takes over. When he pulls back, his eyes smolder with desire, and I'm right there with him. My body hums with desire. Need pulses through me, hungry for more, turning more ravenous by the second. Chase breaks our connection long enough to put on a condom, then he pulls me close.

Our bodies come together, fitting perfectly as one. His lips brush against mine as we move in sync with each other. In no hurry, we explore each other as if we have all the time in the world. His hands move with purpose and familiarity. My skin sparks and flares as his fingertips dance along my skin, sending pleasure shooting through my body.

His touch starts out gentle and slow, building up the tension between us, stoking the passion heating the air. My breathing turns ragged as my desire builds and I ache with the need for more.

His hands wander, moving inextricably lower, tracing the curves of my breasts, my slim waist, and the flare of my hips, until he finally cups my ass.

In one fluid display of masculine prowess, Chase lifts me off my feet, his grip on me sure and strong as the hard length of his erection presses against my folds. He cups my ass while I grab his neck and wrap my legs around his hips, eager for him to take the reins.

He kisses me again, but where there was no need to rush, his pent-up urgency can't be denied. I'm right there with him. My thighs wrap around his waist while I claw at his neck. Our lips smash together in a reckless clash of hunger, desire, and the need to erase any space between us.

The kiss is perfectly imperfect. Frantic and raw. Unrestrained and unhinged. We're reduced to base desires and my desire demands more.

He positions me the way he needs, then fills me with one glorious thrust, sparking intense waves of pleasure.

Slow and gentle takes a turn as the heat between us explodes into animalistic lust. His hips move in a primal rhythm, thrusting, rocking, and fucking while I hold on for the ride.

He drives his hips harder, thrusting deeper, hitting the one spot inside of me guaranteed to drive me crazy me. Each delicious thrust takes me higher until I can no longer avoid moaning as he takes me to the brink.

I'm so close. So ready. My breath turns to shallow gasps as he fucks me against the shower wall. An intense rush of heat builds within my core. Chase definitely knows how to fuck.

And kiss.

And drive me insane as he holds me on the edge of pleasure.

But even he can't stop the inevitable. My orgasm crests and crashes in a tsunami of pleasure rushing through me. I cry out, saying his name over and over as successive shockwaves of intense sensation flood my senses. He drowns my body in ecstasy, and then he follows me over that precipice, driving hard with his hips until we're both blissfully spent.

He continues to hold me, unburdened by my weight, as his ragged breathing slows.

"Fuck, you're incredible." He nuzzles my neck, pressing his lips against my skin. "All I want is to take you to bed and keep you there forever."

"Sounds like a nice life."

"Nice?" He pulls back, as if offended.

"More than nice." I clench my legs around his waist. "It sounds devilishly divine, but I think the others will wonder what happened to us."

"The others know exactly what's happening, and they're happy to wait."

I don't know what it is, but those words send a new rush of heat flowing through me. I bite my lower lip and thread my fingers through the short hair at his nape.

"Well, if they're content to wait, I can think of a few more things we could do." I release the grip my thighs have on his hips. He lowers me gently to the tiled floor, brows lifted with interest.

I grab the soap and lower myself to my knees. His cock is spent, but not yet done. After a little coaxing with my hands and the slippery soap, I bring it to life again. He returns the favor, washing every nook and crevice and showing me exactly how talented he is with his tongue.

I could happily spend the rest of my life in his arms, but the others are waiting for us.

We rinse off and get out, and I wrap myself in a fluffy towel, feeling revitalized and energized. Chase wraps me in his arms and kisses me again, then whispers in my ear. "I love you."

My heart swells with joy, and I smile, looking into his eyes. "I love you too."

After we finish showering, we get dressed and head back to the great room where Mitzy and the rest of the team wait for us.

THIRTY-TWO

Cara

WHEN CHASE AND I RETURN TO THE GREAT ROOM, EVERYONE IS gathered around the fire: Skye and her medical team, the men of Bravo team, Mitzy and her technician, Jack, and finally Forest and the enigmatic Paul. The moment we step into the room, Mitzy jumps to her feet.

"I've analyzed the chip." Mitzy holds up the small device. "It looks like a microchip but is definitely a tracker. I can say with confidence, this is how Artemus Gonzales tracked your movements. This thing continually sends data to someone."

"You're sure that's how he found me?"

It shouldn't come as a surprise. Nothing shocks me anymore, and it makes sense. It explains the men at the airport, the ones in the desert, the ones at the motel, the ones at the train, and the raid on Forest's estate.

"One hundred percent sure." Mitzy gives a firm nod of her head. "How it was implanted is a mystery for another day. We need to decide what to do with it."

"Can't we destroy it?" All I want is the offensive thing destroyed.

"I thought about that, but we can use this to our advantage." Mitzy tosses the thing in the air and catches it.

"How?" I've never hated anything as much as that tracker. All I want is to pulverize it, or burn it to ash.

"I see where you're going with this." Forest sags back in the overstuffed leather chair, looking pale and exhausted. His shoulders droop and he looks unwell.

"Where?" I tug Chase's sleeve. "What does that mean?"

"We have two options. You look like shit, by the way." Mitzy hands the tracker to Forest. "We use it to track Artemus."

"He won't be the one tracking it." Forest ignores her comment like she never said it. "I'm almost certain this is something he'd hire out. The man's got resources with tons of men willing to die for him and tons of money to throw away." Forest lifts the tracker to the light and peers at it intently. Paul hitches a hip on the arm of the plush leather chair and looks at the chip while Forest holds it to the light.

"What's the second option?" I grasp Chase's arm, perhaps a little tighter than I should.

"While it would be nice to use it to figure out what Artemus is up to," Chase begins, "I agree with Forest. We'd only be tracking whoever he hired. Now that the damn thing isn't in Cara, we can use this opportunity to let her slip away for good."

"Like destroy it so he can't find me?" I don't know if that's what Chase is saying, but I like that plan. Anything that destroys that thing is a good idea in my mind.

"Not destroy." Chase shakes his head. "It's been taking him a day or two to find you, and whoever is tracking you isn't in contact with the men on the ground. If that were the case, you never would've shaken the men at the airport. So, there's a lag of information we can take advantage of. We've got a small window of time to move you." He looks to Mitzy. "If we destroy it, he'll know we found it. But if we send it on a little joy ride... Say, mail it someplace else? He'll follow the tracker, giving Cara and me several days to slip away."

My mind races as I process everything. I barely register the voices of Chase, Forest, and Mitzy as they discuss the tracker.

"Instead of mailing it." Mitzy looks to Brady and the rest of the guys of Bravo team. "What if we give it to one of them? Let them lead Artemus on a wild goose chase?"

"You think that's wise?" Forest tugs at his ear.

"I'll do it," Alec pipes up. His voice radiates confidence. "I've got leave saved and was planning on asking for a few weeks off. I'd love to mess with Artemus."

"We wouldn't ask you to burn leave." Forest shakes his head. "But I like the idea. It'd be fun to fuck with Artemus, and the more of a lead we can give Chase to squirrel Cara away, the safer she'll be."

"Then it's settled?" Chase leaves the question open to the group. "All I need is a way out of here."

"I wouldn't use any of the vehicles out front." Forest shakes his head. "He's got all the license plates and can track them."

"What about the helicopter?" Chase looks toward Skye.

"Again, easy to track its flight plan." Forest makes a dismissive gesture. "With trackers and microchips, we have to assume this organization is far more advanced than we gave them credit for."

"We could always jump back on the train," I offer an option that sounds equal parts crazy and perfect.

"Not a bad idea." Chase tugs me to his side. "You'll be a hobo hopping pro before you know it." He turns to the others. "What does everyone think about that?"

"Put the two of you back on the train?" Mitzy appears to like the idea. "Let Chase decide where to get off and where to hide her. Meanwhile, Alec takes the tracker. That should buy a few days, especially if you keep the tracker on the move."

"Yeah, that's no problem at all." Alec wanders over to the fire and tosses a log on the flames. Paul seems to have abandoned his fire tending duties as he sits protectively next to Forest. "I already planned on a trip to Napa. Do some hiking? Some wine tasting? Head back into BLM land like Chase did for some rock climbing? I can really confuse the hell out of them. I'll stay on the move for a week? Two?" Alec looks to Forest to confirm.

"Two weeks should be good enough," Forest says. "Relocate each day, lead them on a merry chase."

"There's just one thing." Mitzy speaks up again. "We still need to unlock the microchip we found in Cara's grandmother's watch. I'm not burning up whatever her father put on that chip with the wrong password. I still need Cara."

"I don't know if I can figure it out." I furrow my brow, trying to remember.

"I say we wait until morning to move out." Chase gives me a squeeze. "That gives you the rest of the night to work on it with Mitzy. If we don't figure it out, you'll have to try another way." He directs that comment to Mitzy, not me, letting her know his priority is me. "I'm not leaving Cara here for the next wave to attack. Hope that's not stepping too far out of bounds?"

"No, no." Forest holds up a hand. "That's perfectly reasonable. What's the word on the local authorities?"

"Already called in," Brady speaks up. "We completed the ID on the bodies. Chase is right about them being cartel. I gave Sam an update, and he's speaking with the FBI."

"Who's Sam?" I turn and whisper to Chase.

"Sam's in charge of Guardian HRS."

"I thought Forest was in charge?"

"No. Forest and Skye created the Guardians. Sam is the head of operations at Guardian HRS."

"Oh." I have a feeling Guardian HRS is a much bigger organization than I ever imagined.

"Well…" Forest tips his head back and pinches the bridge of his nose. "We all have marching orders. Bravo is dealing with the authorities. Cara, you'll come with me and Mitzy to crack this microchip. Jack, that means you too. Bravo-One, if you're willing to cut Alec loose, I suggest he leaves now. Artemus won't expect Cara to stay here after what happened outside."

Poor Jack is nearly invisible. I didn't notice him in the room. Alec is impossible not to notice. He's like all the Guardians; every woman's wet dream. With his blond hair and blue eyes, he's not my type, but I bet there's a string of broken hearts in his wake.

"Ryker and Tia, get your gear packed. You leave on the chopper in the morning with Skye."

"I'm not leaving until you and I have a talk." There's something about the way Skye speaks to Forest that feels like a whole lot of context is lost in translation. "I want to examine you."

"I'm not spending my night getting poked and prodded by you. This is the last night you have with Chase. Your time is best spent getting reacquainted with your baby brother." He glances up at Paul and something passes between the two men. It's as if the air shifts between them. "Besides, I have other things to do tonight."

Paul clears his throat. "One of those things might turn into getting poked and prodded by Skye. You and I aren't finished with that conversation." He directs his comment to Forest, but Forest holds up a hand.

"Not here. Not now." His deep voice growls in warning, but Paul meets Forest's hard gaze with a stony expression.

"As I was saying…" Forest turns his attention back to the group. "Mitzy, you're with Jack and Cara. Chase, spend time with Skye. Sort through the things the two of you need to sort through. No idea how long it'll be before you can talk again. Until Artemus Gonzales and that prick, Maximus Angelo, are put down for good, you need to disappear. Alec, pack your bag. Brady, handle the cops."

"Understood," Brady answers for everyone.

"Questions?" Forest glances around the room, taking everyone in one by one. Satisfied we all know what we're supposed to do, he looks to Paul and gives a nod; a sort of acquiescence I don't understand.

With that, Paul and Forest are on their feet. They leave the rest of us to split up and complete our assigned tasks. For me, that means trying to get into my father's head and figure out what he could have used to password protect the chip in the watch.

THIRTY-THREE

Chase

CARA AND MITZY HUDDLE AROUND THE MICROCHIP. MITZY HOOKED it up to a screen where a blank password box sits with a flashing cursor.

"Grandma's birthday?" Cara takes a deep breath and types her first guess. She presses enter, but the box flashes an angry red and displays: Incorrect Password: 4 Attempts Remaining.

"Don't worry." Mitzy provides moral support. "He had to have made it easy enough for you to know without question."

"Okay. Easy?" Cara blows out a breath. "The name of our pet? My dad named our cat Hester. It's unique and memorable."

"Hester?" Mitzy gives Cara a look.

"After Hester Prynne?" I jump in, supplying the full name.

"Who's that?" Mitzy pulls out her phone, getting ready for a Google search, but I know the answer.

"Hester Prynne is widely considered the first and most important female protagonist in American literature." I rock back on my heels, perhaps a little too impressed with myself that I know the answer.

"How do you know that?" Mitzy glances down at her phone, confirming by now this is a fact.

"My mother's favorite book was The Scarlet Letter." I wrap my hands behind my back at parade rest. "Stories about strong women are her jam. Props to your father for recommending great American literature to his daughter."

"Thanks." Cara dips her head, deflecting my praise.

"Everyone vote for Hester?" Mitzy looks to me and then to Cara. "We've got four tries left."

"Let's try it." Cara turns to the keyboard with excitement. She types in her next guess.

Again, the same red warning appears.

"My birthdate? My dad's?" Her brow furrows as she leans back in indecision.

Only three more chances remain.

"Don't worry, we'll figure it out." I give Cara a reassuring squeeze on the shoulder.

Cara nods, but there's no denying the frustration in her eyes. She's determined to unlock the chip and find out what her father died trying to protect, but it's clear that the multiple failures with breaking the code is getting to her.

"This is tougher than I thought." Mitzy taps the table. "What kinds of special things might your father have picked? Things he knows will stick with you. It needs to be simple, memorable, and something you'd never forget."

"My grandmother's birthday. His birthday. My mother's? Mine? There are too many variables and we only have three more chances." Frustration fills Cara's face, but she's not giving up.

"What about my grandmother's name and birthdate?" Cara types in her grandmother's name and birthdate as the password. But it doesn't work.

"Too obvious. Your father wouldn't have used that." Mitzy shakes her head.

Cara sighs heavily. "This is impossible."

I step in, trying to help. "What about something from your childhood? A nickname or a favorite toy?"

Cara's eyes light up with realization. "My favorite toy was a stuffed bear named Bobo."

Mitzy types in "Bobo" as the password, but the screen remains locked.

"Damn it." Cara raps her knuckles against her temple in frustration.

"Wait, what about the day your mother died?" I hate bringing up her mother's death, but Mitzy said memorable and simple.

"That could be it." Cara's eyes widen. "But we only have one attempt left. This is impossible."

"Not impossible," Mitzy says. "Your father would've made this easy for you. We're thinking too hard. Tell me more about the watch and its significance to your family. Why is it important?"

"It was my mother's favorite possession, and she told me it would be mine one day. That it's passed down through the generations to remind each daughter that family isn't just blood. It's love, support, and sacrifice."

"That's a beautiful saying." I move to stand behind Cara and place my hands on her shoulders. The muscles of her neck are tense and I gently knead the knots.

"Mmm, that feels good." Cara closes her eyes, enjoying the massage. "My mother said it was to remind us that family is about loving each other, supporting each other, and sacrificing for one another. That we built a foundation on selfless love, unwavering support, mutual respect, and a willingness to sacrifice for one another. She said the secret to life is love, support, and sacrifice." She suddenly sits up and twists to look at Mitzy. "Do you think...?"

"We only have one more chance." Mitzy continues tapping on the table. She curls in her lower lip, unsure.

"Cara, what do you think?" I lighten the massage on her shoulders. "Is that something your father would've thought you'd remember?"

"It's up to Mitzy. We only have the one chance left."

"I say go for it." Mitzy scratches at her pixie-colored hair. "I can always try to salvage what doesn't get wiped."

"You can do that?"

"Maybe?" Mitzy shrugs, then gestures to the keyboard. "Try it."

"Okay." Cara faces the keyboard but pauses.

"What's wrong?" Mitzy leans forward.

"Do I include the commas? Capitalize?"

"This passcode is older technology. Punctuation in passwords weren't allowed and capitalization didn't matter... I hope."

"Okay." Cara interlocks her fingers, stretching, then wiggles them over the keys. She hesitates, but then quickly types in: *LoveSupportSacrifice* and presses enter.

The screen flickers then unlocks, revealing the contents of the chip.

"We did it!" Cara jumps up from the desk and loops her arms around my neck. Lifting on tiptoe, she drags me down for a kiss.

A kiss I don't mind her taking.

"See." Mitzy scoots over into the vacated chair. "Your father didn't want this to be too hard. He knew you'd figure it out." Mitzy beams with a victorious smile.

"Now what?" Cara takes her grandmother's watch and kisses the delicate scrollwork.

"Now, I get to work and do what I do best. Hopefully, there's something here that might help in our fight against Artemus Gonzalez and Maximus Angelo. As for the two of you, you've got a train to catch in the morning. It'll be in the meadow, where Forest and Paul picked you up at 0600hrs. Jack is working on new identification, cash, and credit cards. I suggest you pack what you need and say the goodbyes you need to say." Mitzy looks directly at me when she says that last part.

We all let out a collective sigh of relief, but then Mitzy shoos us out of the room with a wave of her hand as she gets to work. I can't help but feel proud of Cara. She's proven to be resourceful under extreme stress.

"What do you want to do?" Cara grips my hand and hops with excitement.

"I want to celebrate with you, but I feel like I need to talk with Skye before we leave."

"Ah, yes." Cara doesn't bat an eye. "How about I check with Jack about what he has for us? Other than snacks for the road, there's not much to pack, but I'll get it all sorted."

"You sure about that?" I'm hesitant to leave Cara alone.

"Absolutely. You and Skye need a moment to process what you found out."

"We don't *know* anything. The chances of us being related is a million to one."

"Well, I believe in Fate, and I'm gambling on that one in a million chance being true. I mean, can you imagine if it is? If you found your sister after all this time? And you heard what she said. That horrible foster father told her you died. That's why she never looked for you. I don't know what it takes to prove you're related, but I hope it's true."

"Then I definitely need to talk to her." I leave Cara and head in search of Skye.

We haven't had a moment to really talk since we discovered the truth about our family connection. I don't know about her, but I'm struggling with a tremendous amount of guilt. I can only imagine what's going through her mind.

The knowledge we're brother and sister is a shock that was buried by the excitement of the armed men coming after Cara, but I can't deny feeling a connection with Skye.

I meander my way through the winding halls, lost in my thoughts, and find her alone in the study, curled up with a book.

"Hey." I rap softly on the doorframe. "Mind if I come in?"

"Hey." She turns to me and our eyes lock. She unfolds herself from her comfortable position and sits to face me with her feet on the floor.

There's so much I want to say, but I don't know where to start. Silence falls between us. I hover on the threshold while she grounds herself, placing her bare feet on the floor.

There's a heaviness in the air; a nearly insurmountable chasm to cross. I clear my throat and break the silence.

"I'm sorry."

"You're sorry?" She leans back in the chair and folds her legs up to sit crisscrossed. Skye gestures to the chair beside her. "Have a seat. What are you sorry about?"

"My life turned out so much different from yours." I know all about the abuse she and Forest endured at the hands of her foster father. "Yours was…"

"It was what it was, and I've come to terms with what happened."

"But I feel bad."

"Why?"

"I was adopted by loving parents. My mother was gone a lot, but my father was always there. I was loved. You…" There's no way to complete that sentence without getting choked up. Skye endured horrific abuse.

"I found Forest in the darkness and he's an extension of me. I wasn't loved by my foster father, but I am loved deeply by Forest. He is the only family I've ever known, and now my baby brother might be alive?" She leans back and a soft smile brightens her face. "My husband believes in Fate, and I suppose it's time for me to believe as well."

"I just found you, and I have to leave. It's hard leaving, knowing you're…"

"I'm right here, and I'll be right where you need me when things settle down with Cara. She's a wonderful woman, incredibly brave and strong. The two of you are a good match. I'm happy for you."

I nod, feeling grateful for Skye's compassion.

"Thank you, but I can't help feeling guilty about leaving you behind."

"Don't. Focus on protecting Cara and getting out of here alive. That's what's important." Skye stands up and walks over to me, placing a hand on my shoulder. "We're family, no matter what happens. That's all that matters."

"Thank you for everything." Relief rushes through me. Skye may be my older sister. Or maybe it's just coincidence our stories are so similar. Regardless, I can't help the protective instincts rising within me to ease her pain. Instead of taking care of her, Skye's words provide me with the comfort and reassurance that I need in this moment.

"I assume that since you're here, Cara found the password?"

"Yes. And the moment she did, Mitzy kicked us out of the room."

"Classic Mitzy." Skye gestures for me to stand, which I do, then she folds me into a hug. "My little brother." With a laugh, she pulls back, craning her neck to look at me as I'm easily over a foot taller than her. "Go find Cara and celebrate your victory. You deserve it." Skye gives me a small push toward the door.

My sister's been through so much, yet she's still able to remain strong and positive. I take one last look at her before leaving the room, feeling a sense of determination and purpose.

Love, support, and sacrifice.

Those are three incredibly profound words. I love Cara and I'll sacrifice my life to protect her. Cara is starting a new life with nothing. I'll stand by her side, supporting her through whatever comes next.

I can't wait to get Cara out of here and start a new life with her. Together, we can overcome anything.

THIRTY-FOUR

Cara

I STAND IN THE OPEN MEADOW WITH CHASE, THE MAN I LOVE, waiting for the freight train that will take us from this place into a new life.

In the predawn twilight, there's a glow on the horizon to the east. Crisp and refreshing, the cool air feels light and free.

Chase wraps his arm around me, tugging me close. As he does, my heart swells with emotion. I stand on the edge of a precipice, leaving one life behind to begin another. I'm both terrified and exhilarated, but with Chase by my side, I'm ready to face any challenge.

In the distance, the low rumble of a freight train grows louder, reminding me this is both an ending and a beginning. I take in a deep breath, feeling a bit of sadness mixing in with my excitement. I leave behind new friends, new family, and brace myself for the goodbyes that need to be said.

The danger against me isn't gone, but Artemus Gonzales can no longer track me. Alec is out there, sending Artemus's men on a fruitless chase, giving me the time I need to disappear for good.

Chase squeezes my hand, providing me with the support and reassurance I desperately need. When I look up into his warm eyes, we stand in silence, surrounded by the beauty of nature and the promise of a new future.

"I can't believe this is happening." My voice shakes. "I'm really leaving everything behind."

Chase looks down at me, his eyes softening. "Not everything. You have me."

And we have Mitzy, Forest, Paul, and Skye who stand off to the side, giving us a moment of privacy before saying our farewells.

The men of Bravo team said their goodbyes shortly after we woke, and Tia and Ryker stayed behind to load the helicopter that will take Skye home.

Skye steps forward and places her hand on my arm. "We'll keep in touch." She turns to Chase and a smile fills her face. "To think we spent a lifetime apart. That my baby brother is not only alive, but…" She glances down at the way our fingers intertwine. "You're an amazing man, everything I would've hoped for in a brother. I hate that you have to leave, but you've filled the hole in my heart I spent a lifetime pretending wasn't there. I hope you get a chance to meet Ash. I hate that you have to leave, but fate will bring you back to me." She steps toward Chase, arms open for a hug.

My eyes well with tears as the two siblings embrace. After a lifetime of being lost, they found each other only to be separated once again.

Chase grasps Skye and brings her in for a big bear of a hug, then speaks to Forest. "I owe you a tremendous debt. You brought my sister back to me and did so much more." He releases Skye then surprises Forest with a hug as well.

Forest stands as if in shock for a moment, then wraps an arm around Chase. "I'll take care of her." His deep, rumbly voice chokes up.

Skye joins the men, wrapping one arm around Chase and the other around Forest. "I am truly blessed to have not one, but two brothers in my life."

My heart fills with emotion as the three of them embrace.

"Oh, my God. Will the three of you stop? You're making me cry." Mitzy steps forward, her hand on her heart. "Hurry up with the hugs and let me get in there." Mitzy joins Skye, Forest, and Chase, wrapping her arms around them.

Paul and I exchange a look. He shakes his head and I can't help but smile. With a jerk of his chin, we join Mitzy, Forest, Skye, and Chase, turning the group hug into a mix of tears, smiles, and love.

The train sounds again, growing closer. We break apart, and the group hug turns into a series of individual goodbyes.

When Forest hugs me, he holds me in his arms and looks down at me. "You're an incredible woman, and you've been through so much. Your father did some terrible things, but he made amends in the end. That list is the missing link we've been searching for. We finally have a list of buyers to match to so many women sold over the years."

"What are you going to do with it?"

"Free them." Forest's response is immediate and certain. "You're going to save so many lives."

More tears prick at the corners of my eyes. I look up at Forest, my heart heavy with emotion. "I don't know how to thank you. You and the Guardians. You saved my life. Protected me. You gave me hope."

"I won't take credit for that." Forest releases me and gives me a little push toward Chase. "Take care of her, lover boy."

"I will." Chase takes my hand and gives one of his reassuring squeezes that makes my stomach flutter and my heart soar. The train whistle sounds in the distance, and Chase pulls me close, pressing a gentle kiss to my forehead. "It's time."

I take a deep breath and turn to people who were strangers not more than a week ago, yet are family now. Mitzy gives me a hug. Her words of encouragement to keep going fill me with hope.

Paul is the last to say goodbye, but his farewell is just as heartfelt as everyone else's.

"Goodbye." I give a little wave, my voice trembling.

Chase takes my hand, leading me toward the tracks. The train rumbles into view, its headlights illuminating the misty meadow. I'm both filled with apprehension and excitement for what lies ahead.

My heart beats faster as we run with the train as it slows for its journey back down the steep mountains. Chase jumps onto the slowing train without incident. Like before, he reaches down for me, pulling me up and into his arms.

Waving with joy, we say our goodbyes, until Forest, Paul, Mitzy, and Skye are no longer in sight.

As we settle in for the ride, I lean into Chase, feeling his warmth and strength surround me. We promised to keep in touch with Skye and the rest of the Guardians.

I can't wait to reunite with the family that found me. Until then, there will be challenges ahead. I still need to disappear until the Guardians put Artemus Gonzales away for good. I won't be safe until then, but I'm ready for this next chapter in my life.

Especially since Chase will be by my side, taking me into the unknown and the future that awaits us both.

As for what Guardian HRS is going to do with the information in that chip, I have no idea. Except, they will save everyone they can.

THIRTY-FIVE

Paul

DEBRIEF

"ARE YOU SURE YOU'RE UP FOR THIS?" I TURN TO FOREST, concerned he needs rest instead of work.

"I think I can run a meeting, Paul. Seriously, back off. Wrong place, wrong time. I don't answer to you here." His eyes meet mine, flickering with anger, yet beneath his strong exterior lies a flash of vulnerability.

After bidding farewell to Chase and Cara, I stand with him in the great room of our retreat in the mountains, attempting to penetrate the walls he's erected. We've been through this scenario too many times, and I wish I could slap some sense into him.

Tia and Ryker departed early this morning with the rest of Bravo team. The helicopter that took them and the Rufi dropped off Sam and CJ. Leaving Sam, CJ, Mitzy, Skye, and the two of us behind. It's the perfect opportunity to discuss the new intel gained from the microchip Cara unknowingly carried for her father. Forest and I converse in hushed voices, awaiting the others.

"Not saying that you do." I'm very clear on when and where our roles revert to the darker aspects of our lives. I have never crossed that line, using my dominance over him to force his hand outside of that space. "I'm speaking as someone who cares about you, for Christ's sake."

"And I'm telling you to back off. I'm fine. Leave it be."

Only he's far from fine.

Forest is nowhere near fine.

"I'm worried about you." I admit my fears, firmly holding his gaze. "You're trying to hide it, but you're unwell. And it's affecting your ability to lead."

"Fuck off." Forest takes a step away from me, firmly ending our brief conversation. "You're so out of line it's pissing me off."

The first time I laid eyes on Forest Summers, I knew he was extraordinary. He took my breath away and revealed how I, too, could become a better man. After spending so much time together, that feeling still lingers. Forest is my life, my breath, and the beat of my heart. He's the reason I exist today.

In countless ways, Forest saved my life. Is it wrong that I worry? That I want him healthy rather than this... this ghost of his former self?

His piercing ice-blue eyes delve into my soul with an intensity demanding respect, yet reveal profound vulnerability. As the creator of Guardian HRS, Forest dedicates his life to saving those who have been kidnapped, trafficked, or forcibly taken. He pours everything he has into that task, despite the toll it takes on him.

Over the past few months, he appears somewhat less than his best, more fatigued and drained of vitality. While I've repeatedly urged him to take it easy, he remains committed to his life's work, growing increasingly frustrated by my attempts to persuade him to take time off. Similarly, the pleas from Sara, the third member of our throuple, and his sister, Skye, fall upon deaf ears.

Forest isn't listening to those closest to him, making me wonder what he's hiding from us.

The thought of his job potentially destroying him weighs heavily on me. It gnaws at my soul.

Though I love him wholeheartedly and control him within the boundaries of our private space, I have no influence over any other aspect of his life.

Like making a damn doctor's appointment for a checkup.

He's unwell, and he stubbornly refuses to address it. Resigned, I let out a sigh, standing by Forest, just as I have since the day he captivated me with his penetrating gaze. It frustrates me immensely that I can't persuade him to do the one thing I want him to do— take care of himself.

Sam enters the great room accompanied by CJ and Mitzy, followed closely by Skye. I glance at Skye, sharing a look of mutual frustration. She and Sara take turns, just like me, attempting to reason with Forest.

Today, it's my turn.

All of us are concerned about Forest, and neither Sara nor Skye have been successful in getting through to him. I shake my head sharply, conveying to Skye that Forest remains oblivious to what is clear to everyone else. Frustration fills her puffed-out cheeks, mirroring my own.

Once everyone is seated, Forest claps his hands together, commanding attention with his resounding voice. "Alright." His words reverberate through the room, capturing everyone's focus. "We have a substantial amount of work ahead of us." His gaze sweeps across Sam, CJ, Mitzy, and Skye. Forest allows himself a faint smile, surveying the talented individuals who make up his team. "I demand much from each of you, but it's because I believe in you. Together, we will make a difference."

What Forest fails to acknowledge is that he has already made a significant impact, saving numerous lives. Standing by Forest's side fills me with immense pride, both as a member of this extraordinary team and as part of my unique throuple with Sara and Forest.

Sara and I complete Forest, offering distinct forms of support as he carries the weight of his mission to save the world while grappling with his past, present, and personal needs. She embodies light to his darkness, while I stand guard against the darkness that threatens to consume him, as it has done before.

Forest raises a steaming mug of coffee, his hand trembling slightly as he brings it to his lips. With the recent progress made against Maximus Angelo and Artemus Gonzales's human trafficking ring, coupled with the new information Cara provided, he's been pushing himself harder than ever. I dislike the direction this is taking.

"Let's focus on the task at hand." Beads of sweat form on his forehead as he stands in front of the colossal fireplace. If I challenge him, he'll say the sweat is from the fire, but it would be a lie.

Skye shoots me a concerned glance. We both wish he would take better care of himself. Yet, we also understand his unwavering dedication to the mission. With a heavy heart, I settle back and listen to Forest.

"Maximus Angelo and Artemus Gonzales," Forest clears his throat. "They've eluded us, slipping through the cracks of graft and corruption in Nicaragua. However, thanks to our team's efforts, we finally have what we need to bring them down." He turns to face Mitzy. "Tell us about the new information Cara brought to us."

Mitzy folds her legs under her, nearly swallowed by the oversized leather chair. She shoots Forest a pointed look. "By the way, you look awful. You should lie down and take a nap instead of hosting this meeting. None of us are fooled by your act."

"For the love of—" Forest bellows, redirecting his attention to me instead of Mitzy. "Is everyone against me?"

I raise my hands, palms out, and take a step back. While I may be aligned with Sara and Skye, my involvement ends there. He needs to realize that everyone sees through him.

"Oh, geez, don't get your panties in a wad." Mitzy shifts her focus to me, but I shake my head, signaling for her not to drag me into it.

"My panties are not in a wad." Forest grinds his teeth, barely containing his anger.

"Whatever." She bats her eyelashes and rolls her eyes in exasperation, and leaves me out of it. "The microchip—"

"Yes, let's discuss that." Forest interrupts her, and she flips him the bird.

Mitzy is probably the only person in the world who can get away with that.

"I am trying to, but you keep interrupting me."

"Apologies." Forest mutters and takes a seat on the hearth. "Please continue."

"As I was saying…" She pauses, giving Forest the eye, waiting for him to interrupt again. When he doesn't, she continues. "It's exactly what we need to put down Maximus Angelo and Artemus Gonzales for good. With evidence of US buyers being solicited to purchase victims of human trafficking, we have the leverage to initiate an international task force. Unfortunately, Maximus and Artemus are cunning. The moment they realize we possess this information, they'll go into hiding, putting everything at risk." Mitzy addresses her next comment to Forest. "How am I doing?"

"Solid. Peachy." He's in a shitty mood, showing off to those closest to him how much he needs a good swat on the ass or something more creative.

"With Alec taking the tracker for a joyride," Mitzy says, "I hope it buys us some time. If we can keep him on task as long as possible, it'll give my team an opportunity to match the buyers to the women they purchased. Additionally, we need time to establish the international task force to permanently shut down Maximus and Artemus's operations."

She shifts her attention to CJ. "Will it be a problem to keep Alec on this assignment?"

"Naw." CJ rubs at his chin. "Bravo team is on a training rotation as it is. While all this shit is going down, they're providing 24/7 coverage for Carmen and Rosalie at their townhouse in the city."

In this instance, 'the city' refers to San Francisco. Carmen and Rosalie were staying at Guardian HQ under protective watch as Guardian HRS sought to dismantle this particular operation. They recently revolted, insisting on leaving the confines of HQ. Now, Bravo team is providing security at the townhouse they share with two other women, Kaye and Barbi.

"I can spare Alec for a couple of weeks if necessary." CJ massages his strained muscles. "I know he's eager to take some time off."

"He can save his leave." Forest interrupts again. "As long as he keeps that tracker moving, leading Artemus's men on a wild chase,

290 · ELLIE MASTERS & MASTER OF ROMANTIC SUSPENSE

he's on the clock. If he wants time off afterward, he can burn leave then."

"I'm sure he'll appreciate that. He's at your disposal for as long as you need him." CJ leans back, crossing his foot over his knee, settling into his oversized chair.

"Good." Mitzy nods. "Two weeks should suffice. At some point, Artemus will realize the tracker is no longer in Cara. That's when the countdown begins."

"And what's our plan?" Skye, who has remained silent until now, directs her attention to Forest. "Are we going after Artemus and Maximus, or are we going to liberate those women?"

"I suppose that's what we need to decide." Sam, the official leader of Guardian HRS, overseeing all three branches of the organization, takes a sip from his steaming coffee mug. "To rescue as many as possible, we must coordinate our efforts. Once buyers catch wind of their slaves being rescued, they'll either go underground or take more extreme measures."

"They'll dispose of the women." I take a seat on the hearth next to Forest, close but not touching.

"That's what I'm afraid of." Mitzy tugs at her colorful hair. "I don't like it, but I believe our priority should be dismantling Maximus and Artemus's organization. If we destroy that, we can regroup and follow Sam's suggestion. It'll require the collaboration of all our teams. We'll need help." She turns to Sam. "Now would be a good time to reach out to your FBI contacts."

"It can be done." Sam taps his forehead. "That'll definitely take more time than our little problem in Nicaragua."

"So it's settled?" Mitzy looks at Forest. "We take down Maximus and Artemus first, then shift our focus to rescuing the women who have been sold. Are you on board with that?"

"I'm not okay with it. Any day spent as a slave is one day too many."

"Forest..." Skye turns to her brother. "Even a minute is too long, but we can't change their past. They have already been taken, their lives already shattered. I vote for Nicaragua. We take them down and prevent any more lives from being ruined. Afterward, we save as many as we can."

"I know." Forest's shoulders slump. "I just don't like it."

"Then it's settled." Mitzy struggles to extricate herself from the chair. "We'll head back to HQ and do our part while you and Paul stay here."

"I'm coming back with the rest of you." Forest's deep voice lacks its former strength. He's struggling, and won't stay behind while the rest of his team takes action.

"No." Skye springs to her feet. "We're going. You stay here... with Paul. Just the two of you."

Skye and Forest share a troubled past, one that has shaped them both. Skye has managed to break free from her darkness, but Forest continues to struggle. I may not be able to guide him in front of others, but when we're alone... Well, let's just say we both need time alone together.

"I'm going." Forest can be stubborn, bull-headed, and thick-skulled.

"No." I step in, letting him know I'm stepping up and taking charge. "We stay."

When I use that tone of voice, it's as if a switch flips in Forest's mind. He won't argue. He won't resist. But there are limits to what I can do.

"It's settled then." Skye gestures to the others, ushering them out of the great room before Forest can change his mind. "When is the helicopter returning?" She asks Mitzy, who looks up from the tablet she's working on. Mitzy is already engrossed in the information from the chip.

"In five minutes." She responds without looking up.

"Good. I suggest we all head outside." Skye turns to Forest, takes a step toward him, then pauses as he lifts his haggard face to meet her gaze. "If you won't take care of yourself or let me examine you, then you need Paul more than you realize. I don't expect to see you at work for the next few days. Stay here. Be with Paul." While Skye understands the complex bond between me and her brother, she doesn't approve of what we do.

We're too feral, too raw, teetering on the edge of what it means to be safe and sane. However, she knows Forest needs to embrace his darkness. She knows what will happen if I'm not here to travel that path with him.

Forest is a complicated man, and while he relies on me, I alone cannot provide him with everything he desires. For that, Forest needs Sara in addition to me. She's the light to my darkness, and we are the two halves that make Forest whole.

Together, the three of us will save the world—one life at a time. Until then…I have Forest to myself.

∿

The Guardian Hostage Rescue Specialists Saga continues in Rescuing Barbi.

> Dear Reader,
> I hope you enjoyed reading Chase and Cara's story.
> As a treat, I give to you, a sneak peek of Rescuing Barbi: Alec and Barbi's story, and hope you enjoy the thrilling conclusion to Guardian Hostage Rescue Specialists: Bravo Team.
> Before you take that peek, enjoy this Special Bonus Scene and watch the Guardians and Protectors prepare to do what they do best.
> Rescue those who've been taken.
> xoxo
> Ellie Masters

CLICK HERE AND GRAB THE BONUS SCENE TODAY!
elliemasters.com/CarasProtectorBonusScene

Then turn the page for a Sneak Peek of Rescuing Barbi.

THIRTY-SIX

Rescuing Barbi Sneek Peek

CHAPTER 1

Dear Reader,
Don't forget to grab your copy of Rescuing Barbi before
you leave. I hope you enjoy this thrilling conclusion to
Guardian Hostage Rescue Specialists: BRAVO Team.
xoxo
Ellie Masters

~

Grab Rescuing Barbi Now!
elliemasters.com/RescuingBarbi

Ready for a Sneak Peek of Rescuing Barbi?

Graduation Day
Barbi

KAYE AND I TWIRL AROUND CARMEN; OUR GRADUATION GOWNS billow in the breeze blowing off the Bay. It's a chilly San Francisco day, but the sun is burning away the morning fog from the Bay.

A group of co-graduates stand off to the side, shaking bottles of champagne before popping the corks. Fizzy foam shoots into the air and they guzzle what remains in the bottle. We made it through four long years at UCSF and are ready to party.

Carmen stands silently in her cap and gown, watching us celebrate. She should be as happy as we are, but something weighs on her. Kaye and I do our best to lift her spirits.

Today is for celebrating. No frowns allowed.

"We did it." Kaye shouts triumphantly, lifting her arms overhead in celebration.

I pull Kaye close while grabbing onto Carmen's graduation gown. There's no way she's escaping this post-graduation hug.

"Yes, we did." Jubilation fills my voice.

Kaye grabs Carmen's hands, trying to get her to join in the dancing, but Carmen only has eyes for the motorcade parked at the curb.

"What's wrong?" I prop my hands on my hips.

She looks like someone killed her puppy.

"Come on... We have to celebrate." I grab her, spinning her around. "Dance with meee!" I shout over the cheers of all our fellow graduates.

Ignoring Carmen's hesitation, I join Kaye and shout at the top of my lungs. Our fellow graduates hoot and holler as they spill out onto the street heading towards their celebrations with family and friends. Their exhilaration is overpowering—but it doesn't reach Carmen. Everyone's excited.

Everyone except our friend.

Carmen shifts on her feet, looking sheepish. "Ladies, I have to bow out." Her shoulders slump and that frown remains. There's more. Hesitation and apprehension thread through her downturned expression.

"Bow out of graduation night? But we've been planning this

night for months. You can't bow out." Kaye's lower lip pushes out in a pout.

I'm right there with her. After months of planning? How can Carmen possibly back out?

"I've been summoned." Carmen gestures toward the motorcade, as if it explains everything.

But it explains nothing. Carmen's father is some sort of bigwig in Nicaragua. She comes from a wealthy and powerful family, but why would he snatch her up now when he didn't even bother to attend graduation?

Nothing is that time sensitive.

"That's Father flexing his muscles." The sadness in Carmen's voice is a palpable thing.

"Down with the patriarchy!" Kaye and I shout the feminist slogan at the motorcade.

The crowd around us echoes the words, not understanding the context.

Not caring.

Carmen lifts her shoulders to her ears, looking like she desperately wants to disappear. "Ladies, I wish I could stay, but I can't ignore this summons."

"Don't spoil tonight." Kaye takes Carmen's hands in hers. "We've been planning this for ages."

My brows bunch as I scan the motorcade. "He couldn't give you one night." More than Kaye, I read the situation and understand the message. Her father is an asshole.

"Doesn't look like it." She's defeated. "I'm so sorry."

"Don't let him steal your dreams or extinguish your light." I take her hands in mine, lending what support I can. "You're meant for more than marriage and babies." I fold Carmen in a hug, wondering if this is the last time we'll see her.

Everything's changing and I don't like it.

"Don't go." Kaye hugs Carmen next. "We'll make a run for it."

"In four-inch heels?" Carmen's laugh is strained. "Ladies…" She grabs our hands and pulls us in for a group hug. "Promise you'll tell me everything you get up to tonight."

296 • ELLIE MASTERS & MASTER OF ROMANTIC SUSPENSE

"I promise." Kaye wipes away a tear.

"Promise you'll call?" I squeeze her hand. "I don't want to lose touch."

"I promise. We won't."

"I'll keep you to that promise." I wrap her in my arms for a hug ten times tighter than the one before, because I'll probably never see Carmen again.

I'm losing her, and by the end of the summer, I'll lose Kaye as well. Then it'll just be me.

I hate everything about that.

Together, Kaye and I watch Carmen go.

"I can't believe her father did that." I prop my arms over my chest, watching Carmen leave. "He couldn't give her the night? One lousy night?"

"He's such an ass." Kaye stands beside me, equally enraged.

"And a buzz kill for our night." I loop an arm around Kaye's shoulder.

"But we can still have fun." Kaye takes my hand. "Let's run home, ditch the graduation gowns and see who can wear the sluttiest dress tonight."

"Oh, you know I'm going to win."

I've got the best spray on dresses, tits that torment, and the hourglass figure to pull it off. Unlike Carmen, who loves her four-inch heels, I wear flats, which are vastly superior in my mind.

"You on the hunt tonight?" Kaye whips out her phone and gets us a ride.

"Aren't I always?"

"You really should get a man."

"Why? They're needy and I haven't met a man yet who knows how to take care of himself. I'm not saddling myself with that kind of baggage. All I need is a well functioning dick."

"Lord, you and the way you talk about men's dicks. You objectify them."

"It's the best part of them, and the only part I want anything to do with. The whole lovey-dovey relationship thing is draining."

Men complicate life. Turn something easy into something burdensome and exhausting. I don't need a man to make my life complete, but I do need his dick.

A girl's got needs.

"You can't call yourself a feminist, and be offended by men objectifying you, if you turn around and objectify them right back."

"Why not?"

"It's hypocritical. You're doing exactly the same thing that you hate."

"I call it fair play. You know what they say; All's fair in love and war."

"I don't think anyone actually ever said that, and you don't know what you're missing by avoiding healthy relationships. There are plenty of good men in the world."

"Tell me again how uncomplicated your relationship is with your professor?"

"That's not fair." Her smile turns to a frown.

Scott Parker is Kaye's professor. They've been having a sordid affair since the beginning of last semester when she enrolled in his class. I keep telling her he's trouble, but the chick won't listen to me.

"Our ride's here."

"Saved by the bell." I'm not against giving Kaye grief.

Kaye points at our ride-share and drags me to the car.

We hop inside and head to the townhouse we share with Carmen.

Shared.

It's the last year the three of us will live together. After the motorcade whisks Carmen away, I don't know what's going to happen to her. I don't know what's going to happen to me next year. I mean, I know what I'm doing. I'm staying in place, trading undergraduate studies at UCSF for attendance at the prestigious University of San Francisco School of Law.

Kaye is moving inland, to UC Davis, where she'll begin her studies at Davis' highly competitive veterinary school.

Carmen was supposed to return to UCSF in the fall to pursue a graduate degree, but I don't know if that's going to happen now that her father's called her home.

Crazy to think it's been four years. On the one hand, I feel like we've known one another forever. On the other hand, four years feel like I blinked and missed it.

I lucked out when I found Kaye and Carmen as roommates freshman year. Over the past four years, we've become the best of friends, tighter than tight. We call each other sisters by different mothers and misters.

Now, I wonder if I won't be all alone in the townhouse next year? I'm not interested in breaking in new roommates, and the thought of having to do that feels exhausting. I found the best friends a girl can have in Kaye and Carmen.

Now, I'm losing them.

After a quick trip back to the townhouse, Kaye rushes upstairs to get dressed for our night on the town. My bedroom is downstairs and I pick out the sluttiest dress I can find; a slinky green phenomenon that barely covers my ass.

My goal?

Easy, I intend on getting laid.

If guys can go on the prowl and brag about their conquests, then I can go on the hunt and not feel like a slut.

The double standard pisses me off. Kaye may say it's hypocritical, but I say fair's fair.

All I want is satisfying sex. No names. No numbers. No commitments.

No emotional entanglements.

As far as I see it, sex is no different than going to a restaurant to eat. Food fills the basic need to eat. Sex fulfills my basic need to have satisfying orgasms.

And yes, that's plural.

The moment Kaye comes downstairs, I grab my purse and meet her by the front door.

"Dayum! You look hot." Kaye gives me an appreciative once over.

"Do I look fuckable?"

My dress is green, sparkly, skin tight, barely covers my ass, and I wear nothing underneath it. I know what I look like; sexy as hell. With my breasts ready to spill out at any moment, the dress hugs my curves, draws the eyes, and advertises a good time.

"You look hot." Kaye takes a good look. "I don't know how you manage to go the entire night without an embarrassing wardrobe malfunction."

"It takes skill." I give her a cheeky grin. "I'm going for fuckable. Not hot."

"I don't know how you fit into those sprayed on dresses, but you look absolutely stunning."

"But do I look fuck-a-ble?" I ask my question again, enunciating it clearly.

Some people drink to escape their worries. Some do drugs. I do something far safer than either of those. Some might call me a slut, but who are they to judge? Drugs are no-go territory for me, so I lose myself in the arms of a man and the talent of his dick.

Don't judge. I always use protection, and I see my Gyno twice a year. Just in case. It's far safer than getting drunk, doing drugs, or God forbid, getting roofied at a bar.

"Barbi, you look very fuckable." Kaye pulls me from my thoughts.

"Perfect." I give Kaye a once over in her tiny black dress with its thin leather straps looping over her shoulders. "And what does Professor Parker say about his co-ed going out looking like that?"

"He knows I'm chaperoning your ass. Besides, I'm headed over to his place afterwards."

"For a little roll in the hay?" I arch my brow suggestively, then cock my head. "The leather's a nice addition? Are the two of you doing the Fifty Shades thing?"

"Something like that." Her cheeks blush.

"Lucky girl." I mumble under my breath, but Kaye catches me.

"Huh?"

"Nothing."

I try to brush it off, but the truth is, I'd love a little bit of Fifty Shades action myself. Hell, more than a little. I'd like it a lot.

Problem is, I've never found a guy—a man—with enough balls to dominate my ass. My personality is too strong, and they all pale in the face of it.

Not to mention, it's not safe with strangers, and I'm all about being safe.

I have my fantasies though, and get my fix in books. It is what it is and I'm happy to settle for that.

I check myself in the hall mirror one last time before we head out. Unlike Kaye, who wears her hair up, I keep mine down to give a guy something to hold onto while he's pumping away inside of me. I like it rough. I like it dirty. I like it wild and crazy. The crazier and more animalistic, the better. The hair pulling thing is the closest I'm ever getting to the fifty shades stuff.

I touch up my lipstick and give the girls a plumping up until I'm happy with my cleavage. This dress may be sprayed on, but it's stretchy; good for hiking up my ass and good for hiking down over my breasts. It's also, surprisingly, good at staying in place. Despite Kaye's comment, this dress doesn't have wardrobe malfunctions. My curves keep everything in place.

"Ride's here." Kaye glances at her phone when it dings, announcing the arrival of our ride. "You ready?"

"Ready as ever."

We head outside and climb into the ride-share.

When we arrive at the club, Kaye takes my hand and leads me up the steps. We're young, hot, and give the bouncers a little wave as we waltz right into the hopping club, bypassing the line..

On the hunt, I'm looking for a man who doesn't care if we never swap numbers or names. I've got an itch to scratch and that comes from a sexy man with a magic dick.

Immediately upon entering, the chaos of the nightclub overloads my senses. Music blares through the speakers. People dance energetically to the pulsing beat. Their laughter and conversations echo off the walls. It's a good crowd, filled with attractive men.

Plenty of options.

There are people everywhere, all somewhere along the spectrum of sober, blissfully drunk, and unapologetically high. I can't help but smile. It'll be good hunting tonight.

I follow Kaye to the bar, weaving my way through the crowd. We find a spot to sit and take in the scene. Kaye orders for us while I scan the crowd.

Neon lights pulse with the beat of the music filling the club, vibrating through our bodies. People dance wildly all around us, most on the dance floor, but plenty crowd around the various seating areas sprinkled around the club.

Anticipation fills me as I draw the stares of men.

It's hunting season.

And that's when I feel it.

Eyes on me. Not the hungry stares of the multitude of hopefuls working up the nerve to approach me.

No, these are different.

I scan the crowd and find a man staring at me from across the room. He doesn't flinch, or turn away, when he catches me looking at him.

His bold gaze travels over my body, lingering on my tits, then drops down to the hem of my dress. He takes his time, then slowly reverses the appreciative path before he meets my gaze. A lazy smile curves his lips and he holds my gaze far longer than a moment before turning away.

I stare after him, trying to catch another look, but he disappears into the crowd as if completely disinterested in me.

"Who was that?" Kaye hands me a bottle of water.

"Don't know." I twist off the cap and take a sip, letting the cool water slide down my throat.

Ever mindful of those who think to take advantage and spike my drink, I twist the cap back on after each and every sip.

"Was he hot?" Curious Kaye may have her professor, but she lives vicariously through my many conquests.

"He's dangerous." I give her a reassuring smile, and tell myself to move on from the stranger.

I don't do dangerous.

"You say the weirdest things." Kaye grabs my hand and pulls me out onto the dance floor. "Come on, let's dance." We down the last of our drinks and head to the dance floor.

We dance, laughing as we join the other dancers on the floor. I scan the room, trying to find that mysterious man and come up empty.

Bummer.

The music is fast and upbeat. We dance like it's our last night on earth. I bump and grind suggestively with a few hopefuls, but none of them hold my interest.

When the song ends, Kaye and I wander back to the bar. I don't see the man, but he's still here. I feel his eyes on me.

He's a predator, that one. Not the psycho-killer kind of predator. There's something about him. Something that makes me want to know more.

And while I don't see him, I feel him watching me. He wants me.

Well, I'm happy to play his game.

RESCUING BARBI IS THE SEVENTH BOOK IN THE EXHILARATING NEW BRAVO TEAM series. It's an angsty, steamy, romantic suspense chock-full of edge-of-your-seat action, exciting adventure, and all the protective hero yummy goodness you can handle.

It's hot, H-O-T... HOT!

If you're looking for *Heart-Stopping, Pulse-Pounding, Can't-Stop-Reading Romantic Suspense* filled with all of your Swoon-worthy, Passionate and Protective Ex-Military Heroes, and you CRAVE an unputdownable, read-all-night romantic suspense that sweeps you off your feet then you need to read RESCUING BARBI!

Get Your Copy Now. Click HERE to begin reading!

elliemasters.com/RescuingBarbi

Grab your copy of the thrilling conclusion to the Guardian Hostage Rescue Specialists: BRAVO Team and let the Guardian Hostage Rescue Specialists restore your belief in modern day heroes.

Please consider leaving a review

I HOPE YOU ENJOYED THIS BOOK AS MUCH AS I ENJOYED WRITING IT. If you like this book, please leave a review. I love reviews. I love reading your reviews, and they help other readers decide if this book is worth their time and money. I hope you think it is and decide to share this story with others. A sentence is all it takes. Thank you in advance!

ELLZ BELLZ

ELLIE'S FACEBOOK READER GROUP

If you are interested in joining the ELLZ BELLZ, Ellie's Facebook reader group, we'd love to have you.

Join Ellie's ELLZ BELLZ.
The ELLZ BELLZ Facebook Reader Group

Sign up for Ellie's Newsletter.
Elliemasters.com/newslettersignup

Also by Ellie Masters

The LIGHTER SIDE

Ellie Masters is the lighter side of the Jet & Ellie Masters writing duo! You
will find Contemporary Romance, Military Romance, Romantic Suspense,
Billionaire Romance, and Rock Star Romance in Ellie's Works.

YOU CAN FIND ELLIE'S BOOKS HERE:

ELLIEMASTERS.COM/BOOKS

Military Romance

Guardian Hostage Rescue Specialists

Rescuing Melissa

(Get a FREE copy of Rescuing Melissa

when you join Ellie's Newsletter)

Alpha Team

Rescuing Zoe

Rescuing Moira

Rescuing Eve

Rescuing Lily

Rescuing Jinx

Rescuing Maria

Bravo Team

Rescuing Angie

Rescuing Isabelle

Rescuing Carmen

Rescuing Rosalie

Rescuing Kaye

Cara's Protector

Rescuing Barbi

Military Romance

Guardian Personal Protection Specialists

Sybil's Protector

Lyra's Protector

The One I Want Series

(Small Town, Military Heroes)

By Jet & Ellie Masters

EACH BOOK IN THIS SERIES CAN BE READ AS A STANDALONE AND IS ABOUT A DIFFERENT COUPLE WITH AN HEA.

Saving Abby

Saving Ariel

Saving Brie

Saving Cate

Saving Dani

Saving Jen

Rockstar Romance

The Angel Fire Rock Romance Series

EACH BOOK IN THIS SERIES CAN BE READ AS A STANDALONE AND IS ABOUT A DIFFERENT COUPLE WITH AN HEA. IT IS RECOMMENDED THEY ARE READ IN ORDER.

Ashes to New (prequel)

Heart's Insanity (book 1)

Heart's Desire (book 2)

Heart's Collide (book 3)

Hearts Divided (book 4)

Hearts Entwined (book5)

Forest's FALL (book 6)

Hearts The Last Beat (book7)

Contemporary Romance

Firestorm

Cocky Captain

Billionaire Romance

Billionaire Boys Club

Hawke

Richard

Brody

~AND~

Science Fiction

Ellie Masters writing as L.A. Warren

Vendel Rising: a Science Fiction Serialized Novel

About the Author

Ellie Masters is a USA Today Bestselling author and Amazon Top 15 Author who writes Angsty, Steamy, Heart-Stopping, Pulse-Pounding, Can't-Stop-Reading Romantic Suspense. In addition, she's a wife, military mom, doctor, and retired Colonel. She writes romantic suspense filled with all your sexy, swoon-worthy alpha men. Her writing will tug at your heartstrings and leave your heart racing.

Born in the South, raised under the Hawaiian sun, Ellie has traveled the globe while in service to her country. The love of her life, her amazing husband, is her number one fan and biggest supporter. And yes! He's read every word she's written.

She has lived all over the United States—east, west, north, south and central—but grew up under the Hawaiian sun. She's also been privileged to have lived overseas, experiencing other cultures and making lifelong friends. Now, Ellie is proud to call herself a Southern transplant, learning to say y'all and "bless her heart" with the best of them. She lives with her beloved husband, two children who refuse to flee the nest, and four fur-babies; three cats who rule the household, and a dog who wants nothing other than for the cats to be his best friends. The cats have a different opinion regarding this matter.

Ellie's favorite way to spend an evening is curled up on a couch, laptop in place, watching a fire, drinking a good wine, and bringing forth all the characters from her mind to the page and hopefully into the hearts of her readers.

Connect with Ellie Masters

Website:
elliemasters.com
Amazon Author Page:
elliemasters.com/amazon
Facebook:
elliemasters.com/Facebook
Goodreads:
elliemasters.com/Goodreads
Instagram:
elliemasters.com/Instagram

Final Thoughts

I hope you enjoyed this book as much as I enjoyed writing it. If you enjoyed reading this story, please consider leaving a review on Amazon and Goodreads, and please let other people know. A sentence is all it takes. Friend recommendations are the strongest catalyst for readers' purchase decisions! And I'd love to be able to continue bringing the characters and stories from My-Mind-to-the-Page.

Second, call or e-mail a friend and tell them about this book. If you really want them to read it, gift it to them. If you prefer digital friends, please use the "Recommend" feature of Goodreads to spread the word.

Or visit my blog https://elliemasters.com, where you can find out more about my writing process and personal life.

Come visit The EDGE: Dark Discussions where we'll have a chance to talk about my works, their creation, and maybe what the future has in store for my writing.

Facebook Reader Group: Ellz Bellz

Thank you so much for your support!

Love,

Ellie

Dedication

This book is dedicated to you, my reader. Thank you for spending a few hours of your time with me. I wouldn't be able to write without you to cheer me on. Your wonderful words, your support, and your willingness to join me on this journey is a gift beyond measure.

Whether this is the first book of mine you've read, or if you've been with me since the very beginning, thank you for believing in me as I bring these characters 'from my mind to the page and into your hearts.'

Love,
Ellie

THE END

Made in the USA
Monee, IL
18 June 2023

36115677R10194